DUDLEY PUBLIC LIBRARIES

The loan of this book may be renewed if not required by other readers, by contacting the library from which it was borrowed.

D1350710

000003023544

IT'S MARRIAGE OR RUIN

Liz Tyner

MIX
Paper from
responsible sources
FSC
www.fsc.org
FSC C007454

This book is produced from independently certified FSC™ paper
to ensure responsible forest management.

For more information visit www.harpercollins.co.uk/green.

Printed and bound in Spain
by CPI, Barcelona

MILLS & BOON

First Published in Great Britain 2019
by Mills & Boon, an imprint of HarperCollins*Publishers*
1 London Bridge Street, London, SE1 9GF

© 2019 Elizabeth Tyner

ISBN: 978-0-263-26937-6

Dedicated to Tianne and Anna

Chapter One

Emilie Catesby could not be dancing at the wrong moment.

She stood in her very best dress, with her very best demeanour, which she quickly changed to her very best frown should any man try to catch her eye.

Finally her mother departed for the ladies' retiring room and Emilie saw her chance. She'd not been fetching those lemonades for her mother purely out of daughterly devotion.

Lightly clasping the side of her skirt, so she could lift the hem enough to move quickly, Emilie made her way across the ballroom floor, one destination fixed in her mind. The pianoforte music and violins faded into silence; all her concentration was on her task.

Her mother didn't want anyone to be reminded of Emilie's fascination with art, but Emilie *had* to examine the portrait of Lady Avondale.

The likeness rested on an easel, to the opposite side of the musicians, its unveiling the excuse for the soirée.

Then she stopped, gazing at the life-sized replica of the Marchioness, the scent of the dried oils still lingering.

Emilie folded her arms behind her back and examined the brushstrokes. The blending of colours. Lady Avondale's interlaced fingers were almost hidden by fabric and her aunt had painted them by blending skin tones with the hues of the dress. They gave more the appearance than the reality. As Emilie browsed from the outside of the portrait to the centre, she realised the painting became more detailed. An observer's attention was being directed by the artist. Emilie was entranced. Such mastery.

The features were well defined. Wrinkles were hinted at on the subject, but were softened. This was not Lady Avondale upon serious scrutiny, but the woman a loved one might observe. A true likeness seen through devotion.

The painting had captured the spirit. It said more than colours on canvas. It spoke of vivacity.

Emilie sighed.

Her aunt was beyond great. She was not only an artist, she was a master of the brush.

'A good painting.' A deep baritone voice

resonated in her ear, coming from behind her shoulder.

Emilie didn't turn, still gazing. 'Magnificent.'

'You've been staring at it and, while it is beautiful, I cannot but realise that you are used to seeing more loveliness in the mirror each morning.'

'Mmm…' What nonsense. This was true splendour. Captured for—well, eternity. A legacy. The woman's visage would remain in the family's midst for ever. Alive. A child generations in the future would view the image and feel they knew this woman.

'The hands…' Emilie said. 'I had no idea you could paint them that way.'

The voice sounded closer, as he peered over her shoulder. 'I had not noticed them before.'

'That is the purpose.' Emilie unclasped her arms and held her fingers near the frame as if she could cup the face on the canvas. 'And the skin tones…'

'If you say so.'

Oh, the picture truly was a work of brilliance. Emilie blinked back tears, both of awe for her aunt's talent and sadness that she herself had not perfected her own skills. She had wasted so many hours on fripperies when she could have been improving.

'Might I share a waltz with you?' the voice asked, so softly she could barely hear.

'Have we been introduced?' Emilie gazed at the tints of the painting of the Marchioness, still unable to take her gaze away from it, tears almost blinding her now. It would not do at all for someone to notice her sniffling over a painting. Her mother would be enraged.

'We have.' The words were clipped.

'Of course. I recall now,' she said. Her mother had insisted she meet so many people that she'd not remembered most of them. 'Certainly.'

'A waltz…'

'That would be enchanting.'

Thankfully, he moved away and she used her glove to wipe the moisture from her face.

Her mother returned, standing by Emilie, then taking her arm to guide her away from the likeness. 'You picked the right moment to study the painting—when the Marchioness's eldest son was viewing it. For once, your fascination with daubs of pigments did you well.

'Avondale's son,' her mother continued, leading her closer to the musicians. 'I overheard the Marquess of Avondale's eldest son ask you to waltz. The eldest,' she repeated. 'The Earl of Grayson.'

Emilie realised she'd agreed to a dance. She'd not been paying attention to anything but the portrait in front of her. She glanced at her mother and put sincerity into her words. 'I'm so very thrilled.'

Her mother frowned. She whispered in Emilie's ear as the music for a reel started, 'You were not paying any attention, were you? You were staring at the canvas. Lord Grayson and his brother, Mr Westbrook, are matrimonial prizes—at least, on the surface. Their cousin, Mr Previn, as well, but he's not here tonight.'

'But you said they were all rakes,' Emilie responded, remembering the quick whisper of warning her mother had given earlier.

'I know.' Her mother's scowl speared Emilie as she spoke. 'But you can't be too choosy. You've waited a little late for that.'

Emilie didn't argue. She knew that was the true reason her mother had brought her to London. Her mother had married out of the peerage, for love, and had raised her children away from society. Then she had decided that, while love was nice enough, love and a title would be much better.

Actually, the one person Emilie truly wanted to spend time with, her aunt, was surrounded by well-wishers. Her aunt laughed, the sound reverberating in the room, causing others to chuckle along.

Emilie sighed. There was so little difference

in their ages, yet her aunt had succeeded, where Emilie had not.

Emilie's deepest dream—the dream which made her spirit live—was to create art which mattered to people. Portrayals which people noticed. She wanted to leave a legacy. James Gillray was gone and still people kept his caricatures of the Prince Regent.

Her mother snorted, ever so delicately, and Emilie knew she'd best give her mother full attention.

'Do not get your expectations up, Emilie. Avondale's son is likely to be considering you for a dalliance, nothing sincere. But by dancing with him, the other men in society will notice you. This is indeed beneficial to your marriage prospects.' Her mother looked at her, then in the direction the man had taken. 'He's speaking to his brother now. Perhaps both of them will dance with you tonight.'

Emilie tilted her head so that her mother might not study her too closely and notice the remaining tears. 'Very beneficial. Yes, Mama.'

She compared the two brothers, talking, with drinks in their hands. They were too far above her in every way. She would say one reached almost to the doorframe and the other was taller still. Well, she was tall enough herself. She would not oversize them. The tallest one grinned at her. The other one reminded her of someone she couldn't place. It was as if she'd seen him in a painting before, yet she was certain she would have remembered a portrait with that image in it.

She bit the inside of her lip, concentrating.

The more serious one took a drink from the glass in his hand. His frown changed and she assumed he'd glanced her way, but she wasn't sure. A tiny crease showed on one side of his mouth. He seemed to be paying attention to his brother, but the tickle inside her told her she'd been viewed—pleasantly. Not as a country miss overstepping her bounds, or as a woman in search of a marriage, but as a person who might be interesting.

Both men were completely comfortable at the soirée, speaking as if they were alone. She wondered what brothers could find to talk about. But everyone in the room seemed to have plenty of things to discuss with their friends, or to be enjoying the spontaneity of the gathering. Even the other young woman whose mother inserted her directly into the line of marriageable men appeared at ease.

Marriage wasn't in Emilie's future. She knew that. She pretended to be on a husband search because bringing down the wrath of her mother never ended well. Paints could be tossed away. Brushes broken.

But she rarely had a chance to study features on men near her age and the serious brother was familiar. 'Do you mind if I stand near the Marquess of Avondale's sons so I will be ready when the waltz begins?'

'That is a questionable plan, Emilie. You must not talk much, and remember to say pleasantries. You've not demonstrated that as a ready quality.' Her mother paused. 'But we'll make the best of it.'

'Which is Lord Grayson and which is Mr Westbrook?' Emilie asked, realising she didn't know which brother was the eldest.

'Nature was fair. The younger son, Mr Westbrook, inherited Avondale's handsome face and immense charm. Lord Grayson inherited the title,' her mother told her.

Then Lady Catesby contemplated Emilie and whispered. 'But don't remind anyone of our connection to Beatrice. Your aunt Beatrice was a late-in-life baby and our parents doted on her far too much. Father was busy training Wilson to take over the ducal estates and Mother spoiled Beatrice. She married for the wrong reasons and ended up on the worst of terms with her first husband. The worst.'

'I've heard of her attacking a carriage.'

'Shush,' her mother whispered. 'Fortunately, that husband died and she married someone who calms her. Mostly. But she has excellent conversational skills when she wishes and that has advanced her somewhat. Could hold a conversation with a teacup and kettle at the same time. Probably has done so and doesn't care at all how she embarrasses us.'

'She is my favourite aunt.'

'I know. I've kept you apart from her for your own good. You have the same leanings as her. It is so obvious. I would not have let you attend tonight had I not known how many marriageable males would be here and received your promise of good behaviour.'

Marcus watched Miss Catesby. He could remember her from many years before, but he was fairly certain she didn't recollect him.

The soirée was a crush—the largest one this Season. Sometimes his mother did get her feathers in a swirl and decide to show everyone that she was the Marchioness of Avondale. She stood, talking with Miss Catesby's mother.

Miss Catesby had wandered again into his line of vision. He regretted asking her for a waltz. He'd spoken with her to help him recall where he'd seen her before. It wasn't until after she spoke that he'd remembered she was the hoyden at the wedding.

If he'd known she was going to keep her atten-

tion on the portrait when he'd spoken to her for
the dance, he'd not have requested her to partner
him. His brother had watched the interchange,
and found it amusing.

She moved closer, and he and his brother,
Nathaniel, greeted her.

'You are radiant tonight,' Marcus said, taking
her gloved hand to bring it to his lips for a kiss.
The glove smelled of springtime roses.

'Thank you.' Emilie turned to his brother. 'I'm
so looking forward to our dance.'

Marcus's eyes narrowed and he studied her.

Nathaniel tensed, straightened a bit, but then
gave a bow and took her glove to raise it almost
to his lips and brush a kiss in the air above it,
fighting a grin. He didn't release her glove as
he should. 'I would indeed love to partner you,
Miss Amelia.'

Marcus waited for Emilie to correct the mis-
pronunciation of her name, but she didn't. Nor
had she, it was obvious, taken notice when Marcus had been the one to ask her to dance.

'It is my good fortune that you accepted. My
immense good fortune,' Nathaniel continued.

He finally released her fingers. 'But can you
imagine the dilemma that this presents for me?
While I asked you to dance, my brother asked
Miss Geraldine the same question and she mistook him for me.' He put a hand over his heart.

'Happens repeatedly. They are thinking of me when he appears and, well, I suppose it is a purposeful game they play to try to get closer to me. So, I really should waltz with Miss Geraldine as she has been expecting it. You alone can make this faux pas fade into nothingness, Miss Amelia. Please do me the great honour of saving the evening and my brother's deep embarrassment, and move to the floor with him.' His lids lowered. 'Of course, I would be happy to partner you before the night is over.'

Marcus stared at his brother's grin and the confused regard of Miss Catesby, whom he now rather disliked.

Her eyes opened wide.

'It would indeed be fortunate if you saved me grave embarrassment, Miss Catesby.' Marcus shot a glance at his brother before giving her a bow.

'Oh, how awkward for you.' She turned to him in sympathy. 'Of course I will partner you.'

'If you will pardon me, I must fetch Miss Geraldine,' Nathaniel said, moving away.

Marcus nodded to Emilie. Her heart-shaped face and delicate lips were beyond ordinary. He regarded her enthusiasm. She could sparkle with radiance when she inspected splatters of colour…or his brother, Nathaniel, or even a particularly good lemon, he recalled.

The music started and he held out his hand for hers.

She moved into his arms and the waltz began. Marcus planned this to be his last tête-à-tête ever with Miss Catesby.

She stared at his cravat and he looked over her, noting that she did feel rather perfect in his arms.

'This must be awkward for you. But I assume it's the curse of the younger brother,' she said.

'I have a younger sister, who is married and in Staffordshire. She is a treasure. And I would have to agree with your assessment that it can feel a curse to *have* a younger brother,' Marcus said.

'There is one younger male than you in your family?'

'Yes. He is dancing with Miss Geraldine now.'

She gasped. He felt it. 'Oh, I thought him the eldest.'

'He just looks older. It's all the dancing he does. It wears on him.'

'Then it really must chagrin you,' she spoke as he swirled her around, 'when people confuse the two of you.'

'They don't often.'

'And you are a wonderful conversationalist,' she added. 'I dare say you could carry on a conversation with…a…a teapot?' She frowned. 'That did not come out exactly right, did it?'

'Perhaps you should have said *anyone.*'

She shrugged. 'I'm not very good at speaking with people. It's I who lack conversational skills.'

'Perhaps you could practise.'

'I prefer to speak through my canvas. I know nothing of the subjects that other people talk about.'

'The trick is to listen and encourage them to speak more.'

'A brilliant theory.' She paused. 'And what interests do you have?'

He firmed his lips, set his jaw, then gazed at her. 'Beautiful women. Fine refreshments.' He gave a slight twist to his lips. 'A night of dancing.'

She raised one eyebrow. 'You have your conversational skills honed.'

'I practise.'

'And what interests do you truly have?'

'I gamble, on occasion. Small amounts. Drink. Small amounts again. And then, of course, I prefer an occasional soirée, but not masquerades. I know the object is to pretend to be someone else, but it's too frivolous for me.'

Her mouth opened, then her lips turned up. 'I saw a reproduction of *Dressing for a Masquerade* once and the event looked exciting.'

Marcus took a moment before speaking. 'I've witnessed that particular portrayal of Thomas Rowlandson's and I would advise strongly that you take caution when you see anything with his name on it. He doesn't consider that a woman might view what he creates.'

'I live for drawings and oils and charcoals. And sometimes the life that is reproduced is not always polite.'

'Miss Catesby, that doesn't mean that it shouldn't be. The world doesn't begin and end at the end of a paintbrush, and artists should only create to educate.'

'Well…' she moved within the waltz and the distance between them lessened '…the world doesn't revolve around gambling, women and drink for me.' She beheld him through her lashes. 'Please allow me my vice.'

'I would prefer to credit you with only virtues.'

She laughed. 'Yet you prefer me to presume only vices for you.'

'Where you are concerned, that is probably for the best.' He'd so wanted to dislike her, but when she laughed, the sound resonated inside him and made him want to hear it again. 'And accurate.'

'Shame on you, Lord Grayson. If I may be so straightforward, you have a dashing profile.'

He bowed in acknowledgement of the compliment.

'What did you think of Lady Avondale's portrait?' she asked. 'I know you said it is good, but…'

He glanced down. 'I should like to view a likeness of you.'

She gasped with pleasure. 'That is so kind of you. Are you fascinated at all by art?'

He blinked. 'No. I don't see colours the same as other people. I can't tell the difference between most of them.'

She closed her eyes for a moment. 'I am so sorry you have missed out on the beauty of hues.' She shook her head. 'I will try not to be bothersome to you, Lord Grayson. I feel for you. I could not live without the colours of my paints.'

'I am sorry I have missed out on the beauty as well.'

When the music ended, they stopped, but didn't immediately separate. He imagined her in a portrait. On his wall. To gaze at. He swallowed. His conversational skills had evaporated.

'Would you like a stroll in the gardens?' he asked.

She studied him. 'You don't like art?'

He firmed his lips. 'Not usually.'

'Oh…' She peered beyond his shoulder. 'If

you will pardon me, your brother is beckoning me.'

Neither spoke as they went in opposite directions.

Emilie walked away from the couples, feeling she'd just stumbled, instead of dancing. And she was certain she'd not missed the steps.

Mr Westbrook strolled her way and she asked him if he liked watercolours, and he regaled her with a day his father had hosted the caricaturist Gillray, years before, and Mr Westbrook continued on, discussing prints he'd seen, and agreed that he, too, dabbled with paints. The talk of tints and hues should have been more interesting. But it wasn't really.

Then he led her into the swarm of dancing people and she beamed in all the right places and feigned all the fascination she could and hid her relief as the music ended.

When she reached her mother at the refreshment table, she peeked at Lord Grayson. He was observing Lady Elliot and her two daughters.

Then, another man approached the group. The man glared at Grayson, which was wise of him, and offered his arm to the younger Miss Elliot. She accepted the invitation and they sauntered away.

Then Grayson turned, an indulgent smile on

his lips. He gave Emilie the barest glance before he turned to the elder daughter, spoke and she tucked her hand under his arm and let him lead her to the Roger de Coverly.

Emilie tapped with her fingertips against the side of her lemonade glass, watching Lord Grayson with Miss Elliot—the woman dancing was obviously revelling in the experience of being so close to him.

Grayson spoke to his partner when they met. He moved as if he had wings on his boots. The woman floated along, too.

He gazed at the woman as if he'd never had such a captivating audience.

When he changed position, Emilie knew he'd perceived she was observing him.

He spoke again to the woman and indicated the doorway.

That wasn't appropriate. He would likely take that woman to the gardens as he had suggested to Emilie. True, the garden had many guests conversing in it, but a later meeting could be planned.

That unrepentant rake. That scoundrel. He was aware she watched.

Well, if he wished her to be aware, then she would give him a taste of his own medicine. Emilie turned to her mother.

'Did you notice how Lady Elliot appears pained?'

Her mother's brows furrowed and she inspected Lady Elliot, her grey hair swirled at the edges of a feathered band. 'No,' her mother said at Emilie's side. 'I perceive nothing out of the ordinary about her.'

'I should ask her to take a turn around the gardens,' Emilie said. 'For her—for my health. If I say it is for my health, that might make her feel better and not make her ashamed of her weakness.'

'That is so unlike you.'

'It is the society, Mama. It makes me feel… um, not like an artist so much, but more like a…' She paused, listening to the nonsense she spouted, but it had truth in it. 'I feel…womanly.'

Her mother groaned. 'If I had known that getting you to a gathering such as this would change you, I would have made sure to have done it years ago.'

All her mother would have had to do was guarantee some interesting artists would be there and Emilie would have jumped at the chance.

She meandered to the mother of the woman Lord Grayson had danced with. She was engrossed in conversation with a dowager. Chaperonage fell to the wayside when a mother's daughter was close to a potential peer and a longed-for son-in-law.

'Lady Elliot,' she whispered, touching the woman's arm and interrupting the discussion. 'Could you please join me in the gardens? I may have had more wine than I should have. I had two glasses, but perhaps more.'

The woman raised her eyebrows. 'The wine is delicious, but a lady must always pace herself.'

Emilie touched her gloved hand to her forehead. 'I agree. But sometimes a faster pace gets the better of me.'

The older woman patted her hand, spoke briefly to her companions and took Emilie's arm as they strolled to the cooler air.

Emilie saw the darkest edge and aimed for it, leaving the strains of music behind.

'If you'd stay with me for a moment longer...' She kept Lady Elliot at her side. 'I am feeling better, but...'

'Dear...' Lady Elliot patted Emilie's glove '...do be careful of the drink. It doesn't always improve a woman's complexion. A little does add a rosy glow, but take a lot and the headache isn't worth it. You'll be ghastly the following day.'

'Well,' Emilie admitted, brushing away a wisp of hair that had loosened from her bun, 'now and then, I do forget about my appearance.'

'You must never do that.' Lady Elliot sputtered. 'A woman's decorum and fashion should always be of utmost importance in her mind. My Cecilia Ann has been schooled in that. Proper manners and a good wardrobe can take a woman far.'

Emilie frowned. She wouldn't make it far then.

They found a bench in the darkness. 'It is a lovely evening,' Lady Elliot said, 'except for Mrs Hodges's dress. The colours would favour Mr Hodges better.'

'Um…' Emilie said, imagining a painting of Mr Hodges. 'It would not work with his complexion. He would fade away into nothing.'

They discussed the varieties of colour in the ballroom, then feminine laughter and one rich baritone interrupted their chat. The laughter and the baritone were obviously moving towards Emilie and Lady Elliot.

The woman beside Emilie stilled.

Lord Grayson and his dancing partner were nearly directly in front of them when the two standing saw the two sitting. Even the air stopped.

The young woman spoke, voice high. 'Mother?'

Lady Elliot moved to her feet. She took her daughter's arm. 'You promised the next reel to Sir Calvin.' She took her daughter's arm. 'Cecilia. Inside. Right now. Immediately. I cannot fathom how you got confused. That is inexcusable manners.'

Lady Elliot didn't slow as she twirled her daughter around and moved towards the lighted house—forgetting all about Emilie.

Chapter Two

Lord Grayson remained perfectly still for several moments before he moved. He rearranged the hem of his sleeve and his eyes fell over Emilie, making the air she swallowed fill her with a fresh warmth. 'We meet again.'

'You knew I was out here,' she said.

'Whether I did or not, it doesn't matter.'

Even in the darkness, Emilie could imagine him plainly. Nature had sculpted a visage which could have inspired Michelangelo to do better work.

Her hand wanted to caress, to run over the planes of his cheek so she could experience him with the feeling of touch as well as sight.

Inwardly, she berated her traitorous thoughts. She pulled herself from the momentary stupor, blaming it on her fascination with form.

How unfair that someone such as Lord Grayson, a man who said he liked frivolities, would have such a pleasing appearance. Her mother had been so wrong about which of Avondale's sons had been graced with handsomeness.

The humour on his lips faded. 'Miss Catesby, you are an accident waiting to happen.'

She tossed the words out. 'Accidents do happen and I am not the cause of any of them.'

'You cause things to happen on purpose.'

'Occasionally.'

He reached out, taking her hand, and she moved, letting him pull her to her feet.

'When you are near, Miss Catesby, I suspect they happen more than usual.' He touched her waist, gently connecting with her garment and pouring sensation into her.

'I would not claim that.' She forced her voice to be firm and tried to examine him closely in the darkness—an error. Something pushed her heartbeats faster.

'We have seen each other before,' he said. 'Years ago.'

'I don't…' She searched her memories. 'Are you certain?' she asked.

She heard the leaves whispering to each other as they rustled in the darkness.

He didn't answer with his voice. But his expression told her. 'I remembered where earlier. But it has been many years. I didn't recognise you at first.'

Emilie paused.

'I should go inside.' The words didn't sound like her own. 'I wouldn't want either of our reputations harmed.'

'Miss Catesby.' His free hand closed over her gloved fingers and before she knew what he intended, he lifted her fingertips as if to kiss them. The scent of his shaving soap teased her. She'd never come across a soap like that, but she wasn't sure if it was the soap that made him smell so good, or if it was the man himself.

'If my reputation were to be harmed, I would be pleased if you were the one to do it.'

She felt disappointment when he dropped her hand instead of kissing it.

He moved closer and she realised he still held her waist, rotating his fingertips against the covered corset which felt thicker than any mattress, yet the warmth of his hand penetrated the garment. His mouth moved closer to her own and he held her still, keeping her so steady she couldn't have moved away. She presumed him about to kiss her, but instead, he spoke.

'Miss Catesby. Stay away from my brother. He would ruin you.'

She touched the light wool of his waistcoat, letting her fingers flatten against him. Leaves rustled again as the wind touched them. The breeze strengthened, and the air tingled her cheeks. 'I would say it's not your concern.'

'Miss Catesby. You're an innocent.' His fingers pressed into the fabric at her waist and he moved back a whisper.

She trailed her fingers up the waistcoat, touching the cravat, the edge of his jaw, the curve of his lips. She could have been touching a Michelangelo when she felt his face. This was something she'd never imagined before. Her heart pounded from the merest touch of his skin.

To feel a true masterpiece overwhelmed her. She dropped her hand and clenched it, keeping it at her side. She could hardly wait to capture in paint a masculine jawline. One with a hint of darkness in it. In shadows. Such a challenge. To put this image on canvas. A man in the shadows. Darkened features. She could never call it *The Dark Angel*. Her mother would destroy it. She would call it *A Saint In Repose*.

She could not calm her heartbeats, but inspiration came at the strangest moments, and one should relish them, hold them close, hug them to one's heart.

But she could not touch him again. He was the forbidden fruit. The crevasse that could swallow the as-yet-unmade creations that were inside her and turn her into nothingness.

'Art is my passion.'

His mouth parted. 'You could have more than one passion, perhaps.'

'I do. Oils, then watercolours.'

'Oils?' he spoke, moving so close, and somehow he'd turned the word into something else. Something intimate.

Her scrutiny never left him and her hand escaped again. She had to study him. She retraced his jawline. The linen cravat. The rougher wool. She stopped where she started, trapped in some trance that he had spun around her.

Her love of shape and form and inspiration travelled from her fingertips to deep inside her.

He stepped away and her fingers followed, lingering at his waistcoat.

'No.' His voice roughened.

'Your brother would not refuse my touch.'

'No.' The word destroyed the magic. 'I am telling you no for both of us.'

He touched the hand at his chest, took her fingers, kissed above the glove and released her. 'And you must stay away from him.'

'Really, Lord Grayson?'

'Yes.' He brushed a touch across her cheek and she swayed towards him.

She whispered, 'I know what I'm doing.'

'You are creating an accident and it is your choice.' Grayson took her shoulders and moved inches from her, hinting at things both darker and softer. 'Do you prefer my brother?'

She didn't speak.

He whispered at her ear, his voice becoming even richer. Fingertips touched her chin. 'He is wrong for you.'

She turned away, pulling from his grasp.

He increased the distance between them, using his voice to make a barrier, but a barrier that could be moved. 'Say it, Miss Catesby. Say whether you prefer me over my brother.'

'Why should it matter? I hardly know him.' She examined Lord Grayson again. 'I know even less of you.'

'I feel I have known you for ever.' He paused. 'Please call me Marcus.'

'This is the first occasion we've met. Truly.' Yet he stirred something deep inside her. She wanted to tell him the energy he inspired within her. How fortunate she'd been to have the opportunity to approach him and to feel the sensations. She gave him her greatest compliment. 'You would make a lovely portrait.'

In that second, he retreated, turning the night cold.

His head tilted back and, even in the dim light, she could tell he scrutinised something in the distance. He flexed his jaw. 'I hope you enjoy the soirée.'

'And you as well, Marcus.'

She couldn't force herself to leave him, but he turned and moved back to the light.

She took her glove from her hand and touched her lips. Marcus. So much better than Michelangelo's *David*. David was almost a child. Marcus was a man.

Unable to move inside, she waited in the darkness, listening to the muted music and the laughter. Her aunt had a book with an engraving of the sculptor's *Moses*. Marcus was not bearded or old, but she imagined him as a likeness of that sculpture. Oh, the arms. They were magnificent in the engraving.

She touched her chin, retracing the movement of his hand. She must stay away from Marcus.

To create was one thing. To love that moment was glorious. But to be swallowed inside one piece of passion could destroy the creator.

Look what Michelangelo had done to Moses's head. No matter what the protuberances truly were, they hinted at a darker side of inspiration. The face warned her. The same man who had sculpted David had created Moses. Moses, with the glare, the judgemental regard and the condemnation within him.

Marcus condemned her. His voice, his movement and his face did.

Then she paused. He condemned her. When

he was not staring at her as if she were the only woman in the world.

But she wasn't a woman. She was an artist. And she'd been born to be alone and to create.

Then she thought of Marcus. But what if she must experience deep feelings in order to reflect them in her paintings? What if she must have a tortured soul in order to paint with depth…?

Or perhaps she had heard that somewhere and it was nonsense. Perhaps she just needed a roof for her studio, an imagination and paints.

Yes, she decided, thinking back to her struggles with paints.

Art provides all the torture an artist requires.

She would ask her aunt if that were true. She could imagine Beatrice's laughter.

For now, she wanted to observe Marcus.

She preferred Marcus as a subject. She preferred him to speak with. She preferred him far above Mr Westbrook. But Westbrook was the safer of the two. He thought her name Amelia and she had no desire to correct him.

Marcus watched her as his brother twirled Emilie around the room warmed by all the people moving about. Their second encounter of the night, but neither one a waltz.

Nathaniel appeared entranced with Emilie,

but then Nathaniel was taken with every woman he spoke to. It did him well.

The violins stopped and the musicians raised their bows with a flourish. The talk surrounding Marcus faded into nothingness while he watched his brother and Emilie. Never before had he been jealous of his younger brother, but Nate was looking at Emilie so.

Marcus had no reason to be envious. None at all. In fact, he'd felt guilt for being the eldest and the one who would inherit the title.

He enjoyed verbally jousting with his brother. He loved Nate. Loved him, but if his brother did not stop making eyes at Emilie, Marcus would take him aside after the evening ended and throttle him.

Emilie was not another conquest. She was a country girl and not used to the soirées and light talk his brother excelled at.

Both Nathaniel and Emilie went their separate ways without hesitation. Marcus exhaled. Perhaps they were both wiser than he.

He went to his mother's portrait now that the guests were beginning to leave and stared at it. It was a fine painting, but no different from any of the many others in the family gallery, except it was of his mother.

'Lord Grayson.' Instantly he recognised Emilie's voice. He turned to her and saw that her mother was behind her.

'It is an amazing picture,' Emilie said.

'True.' In those seconds he meant it. His mother liked the painting. Everyone said it portrayed her well. And anything that could bring such raptness to Emilie fascinated him.

'You do appreciate some art?' she asked.

'Occasionally.' When it appeared before him as Emilie did.

'Most everyone does, even if they don't know it. Usually if they don't like paintings or sculpture, it is because they haven't seen the right work. Something that stirs them.'

He took in the tendrils of her hair that trickled from her bun. He didn't have to have a portrait painted of Emilie for her to remain in his mind. 'I agree.' His voice barely reached his ears.

Emilie was about to leave when she stopped and looked for her mother. Her mother stared at her as if Emilie had said something rude. Confusion filled her. She'd spoken nicely with Marcus.

Surely it was not so terrible to have a conversation with a rake.

Emilie gave Marcus a peek from under her lashes, surprised that he still watched her. He almost smiled, turned and went on his way.

Her mother's lips tightened and her fingers

clasped Emilie's arm. 'Come along, Emilie Marie. The carriage is waiting.'

Her mother marched ahead.

The carriage ride would not be a smooth one and she had been on her best behaviour. Well, except for fetching her mother so many lemonades. And eavesdropping, but she'd not been detected. And the moments in the garden.

Emilie hid her sigh. She was not tailored for society.

They reached the carriage and her mother didn't speak. Emilie was certain it wasn't a good thing that her mother was so quiet.

Settling on to the squabs, Emilie prepared for a recital of her errors to be repeated, but her mother remained silent.

The carriage rumbled along, returning her mother and Emilie to her aunt Beatrice's home.

'Goodness, Emilie, Avondale's heir was speaking to you at his mother's portrait and you brushed him away as if he were of no consequence. You have no skills in courtship.'

Emilie sighed inwardly and then her mind wandered to Marcus, but she forced herself to concentrate on his brother.

Mr Westbrook had good qualities. They were hard to identify, but lurked under the surface, she was sure.

At the soirée, she'd wandered by a group of

men talking and couldn't avoid overhearing their conversation. A gruff voice said if a man were to be lost in the desert, it would be good to be lost with Mr Westbrook because he would find the quickest path to the nearest woman and could do so without a smudge on his boots.

Then another man claimed Westbrook's sense of direction was sad because he could never locate a path back to the same woman twice. The other men had laughed. And one claimed Westbrook had his compass in the same place as all men carried one.

'Emilie.' Her mother snapped out the word, pulling Emilie's concentration back into the carriage. 'I must talk privately with you. That is why your father and sisters remained at home and we have been visiting London.'

Emilie frowned, but she hid it before she turned to her mother, waiting. She'd known that her father had stayed home because her mother could be forceful about pushing Emilie into marriage and he preferred to stay out of the discussion.

These motherly speeches always went on overly long and it was best to pretend interest.

Her mother raised her chin. 'It is not so horrible to want a family. Children. Sons…' she raised a brow when she observed Emilie '…or daughters who marry.'

'I've not found anyone who suits me.'

Her mother pulled her wrap closer and gripped her fan.

Emilie toed her slippers into the floor of the carriage, and let her stocking feet wiggle free while she rested her toes on the footwear.

'Search about and uncover someone who suits.' Her mother paused before raising her voice. 'And put your slippers back on.'

Emilie dared not meet her mother's eyes and she pushed her feet back inside the shoes. Even her feet had to do as they were told.

'Your father,' the older woman continued, 'and I are distressed at your stubbornness where men are concerned. It is not just your prospects you're scuttling—you are not doing your younger sisters any favours either,' she grumbled. 'You are twenty-five. Twenty-five. You should have married years ago.'

'Oh,' Emilie mumbled and felt her lip tremble. She had so hoped to have her artistic talent noticed earlier. She must try harder. Elisabeth Vigée Le Brun had achieved fame with her portraits, but her father had encouraged her from such a young age.

Emilie sighed. She should have been as dedicated, but, no, she had spent her youth learning nonsensical matters. Watercolours had hardly interested her at all until she discovered oils and then everything had burst into fulfilment for her. Even the watercolours became worthwhile.

Emilie studied the dark outlines of the passing shops, wondering how a night-time drawing of them would be best accomplished.

All she needed was watercolours, or oils and canvas. To paint was her greatest joy. To hide away somewhere with a brush and palette would be the best excitement of all.

No one understood.

When she irritated her sisters enough, they avoided her, which gave her a chance to sketch and enjoy her work.

'You even discourage your sisters' prospects.'

'Mother, if a young man of worthiness approached any of my sisters, I would do all I could to encourage a courtship.' Emilie crossed her arms. Her sisters were green girls. They couldn't imagine the truth of men and needed her guidance.

'You cannot fault me because no man among the *ton* is worthy of them.' Emilie straightened her shoulders. 'Except for timid Bertram Reynolds and Marthe ignores him.'

'Dear.' The seat creaked when her mother turned to Emilie. Her mother's voice gave Emilie no option for refusal. 'You must let them decide whether the man is worthy or not. Or me or your father. You are not to keep distressing their beaus. Don't demand perfection in their suitors. At this point, we may consider a man of medium worthiness if he is willing for a match. You certainly should do the same. We do not aspire to be relegated to less-than-medium worthiness because the others have been scorned.'

'A man of value would not let a few words of truth dispatch him,' Emilie muttered.

'I would not want my daughters to obtain a match with a man whose main quality is persistence.'

Emilie felt the sharp rap of a fan against her fingers. Never a good sign when the fan came out.

Her mother continued, voice rising. 'Timid beaus can have many desirable attributes. Your father—' she pointed the fan at Emilie '—was so timid, I near had to—' She stopped, waved her hand and turned to the window. 'Never mind. I had no trouble with your father's reserved behaviour.'

Emilie knew her mother and father cared too much for the state of marriage and too little about the state of men. They were happy. They didn't observe the disastrous lives among them.

'Mother, you must forget about a wedding for me. I shall never marry. I shall paint.'

'Emilie Marie—you are not destined to paint. You are destined to have children. You are destined to maintain a household and serve your husband.' She pressed her teeth into the words. 'Forget your fanciful nonsense. No more paints will be purchased. I have told your father and he agrees with me. This trip is to locate a suitor for you. If there is no agreeable man, then I will acknowledge your spinsterhood. However, I will not accept the scent of turpentine in my home any more. The rooms reek of it. You will not be dabbling in oils there, indoors or out.'

Emilie fell back against the seat, fingers closed tightly. 'I must,' she said.

'No.' Her mother turned to stare out of the window. 'You will have to content yourself with pencils, and stitchery and gentle pursuits. There are people in the world, Emilie, besides artists. And it is time you found that out and put away that folly. This discussion is over.'

In bed that night, Emilie kept envisaging the colours on a palette. The joy of her hands as they mixed the colours. The scent of turpentine.

She loved the scent of turpentine, no matter how unpleasant. It spoke of creation and love. She could not live without turpentine, aquamarine or burnt sienna.

She sniffed. She sighed. Perhaps she was cursed.

She would marry. She would discover a husband who would not notice if the money he'd allotted for clothing and jewellery was spent on the finer things, like easels or pigments.

Catching a senseless male could not be difficult and she hadn't noticed any unwilling to be led by a woman hinting at delights.

Marriage would quiet all those titters her sisters made as they claimed Emilie was more suited to kiss her paintbrush than a husband.

If she married, it would no longer matter how small her waist was or if she got a drop of burnt sienna—a drop so small as to be invisible—on the rug. A man surely wouldn't notice if she received a briar scratch on her cheek from searching for perfect berries to examine their hues. Her mother had wanted to flog her—and goodness, the scratch faded away, but the drawing of the berries had been enlightening.

Once she got the ring on her finger, she wouldn't care what he did or where he went. Her goal was to be abandoned to her own ways. She knew she would have to survive kisses, but she would tolerate them, and knew she would have to do other things a wife should do, but she didn't foresee *that* would take for ever. She would make sure it didn't.

Then she would devote herself to watercolours and oils.

She must choose carefully.

The trick was in locating a man who didn't have the inclination to control his property. One who might leave his belongings lying about, so to speak, so his possessions could do as they were inclined.

She would try hard to keep from overwhelming a nursery with children, but a little one would be dear to hold.

Actually, she would be pleased to have several children, she realised. Le Brun reportedly had created the most beautiful self-portrait of herself with her daughter. It was said that the portrait reflected the love between the two of them.

That would be a wonderful opportunity.

Marriage could work, assuming it was not taken too seriously.

Her husband must have money to buy all the paints she needed and an appearance to work well in oils.

And handsome men didn't dig beyond the surface. They had wandering attentions and admired beauty. After he had acquired her, an attractive man would tire of his wife. His eyes would flicker to the other women who fluttered near.

She surmised the considerate thing to do would be to make certain he was a man who didn't mind that he'd married a woman who had little use for him. If the things she'd overheard were true, it would be simple to locate such a man.

She didn't want a suitor who had a heart—she might break it. She didn't want a suitor who might have motivations deeper than a bird flitting from one spot to the next.

She examined her hand and decided a wedding ring would fit. Yes, she decided, she would accept a proposal. Now she had to decide on the date and the husband.

A very unsuitable husband would be perfect.

Chapter Three

'Mama, Lady Cramson's ball was divine last night and I am so anticipating Avondale's birthday celebration.' Emilie practised the words a dutiful daughter and a soon-to-be wife would speak. She was running out of occasions to get a proposal.

'You're attending? Of your own will? Another one? Are you considering marriage?' She slanted her head back, studying Emilie.

'Mother.' She inhaled deeply. 'I'm not intending to stay on the shelf. A betrothal might suit me better than I realised.' She would get those paints back if it killed her. She had survived so far because she had been using her aunt's paints in the night-time hours while her mother slept. And the lamplight was disastrous.

Oils, however, those had to be mixed and she could not manage to get them by her mother when they returned home. Her mother was wise to Emilie's ways.

She grabbed Emilie by the shoulders and positioned them eye to eye. 'You are not trying to trick me?'

'I really should be married before the leaves turn their autumn shades.'

'Emilie.' Her mother frowned. 'Perhaps you should go to Bath. The men of London society know you.'

'They do.' Emilie held her posture straight. 'But they're forgetful.'

Her mother dropped her hands and turned to the candle on the table. She moved it away from the book, closer to a vase. 'I have already written to your father about taking you to Bath in the autumn because the men there will be more unlikely to have heard tales of your awkward ways.'

The words ran down Emilie's spine like cold waste water from rinsing her brushes.

Emilie squeezed her hands into fists. 'You don't anticipate a man will see me as attractive?'

'Not the true you, Emilie. You must be giddy and flutter your eyes and act more ladylike. You must act demure.'

'Of course, Mama. I love my new dress.' She batted her eyes, then turned away.

Emilie heard the clatter and turned back. Her

mother was picking up the vase she'd knocked over. Fresh-cut roses lay on the table.

'Not like that, Emilie.' Her mother's voice was soft. 'You startled me.'

'I am trying.' Emilie briefly pressed her palm against her jaw and let her hand fall to her side as she examined her feet. 'I have worn out a pair of slippers dancing, I'm sure.'

Her mother turned to arrange the flowers in the vase. 'Be aware, Emilie. Keep your mouth shut. Tuck your chin under. Do *not* discuss anything to do with sculpture. Keep your corset tight. Let him talk, while you admire his every word.'

'I'll do what I can,' Emilie spoke softly and forced her chin high when she departed the room. How was one expected to learn how to bat one's eyelashes? she wondered, shaking her head.

She retired to her room, shut the door and, still holding the knob, stared at the new dress.

The gown was lying on the bed.

Walking forward, Emilie ran a delicate touch over the aquamarine silk enhanced by a second layer of even finer material flowing over it like a cloak of clear-spun sugar. She'd never owned a dress so feminine. So delicate. Exactly unlike her and exactly what she needed.

After she married, she could use it to wipe

her brushes with if she wanted. Well, perhaps not. She touched the silk again and pulled it to her. This was another woman's masterpiece and she would guard it carefully and be thankful to have it.

She held it closer to the window and repeated her needs to herself. *Handsome to inspire creativity. Money to make sure he could live in town while she painted in the country. Someone who would forget all about her.*

A quick rap sounded on the door and it opened. Aunt Beatrice sauntered in, her emerald bracelet sliding on her wrist. 'I'm curious about the new clothing your mother has bought for you.' Her eyes widened when she saw the dress. 'It reminds me of one I used to have. Please don't spill oils on it.'

'I won't.'

'Your mother has been asking me to talk some sense into you.' She rolled her eyes. 'That's a first. She must really be desperate to get you married if she's asking for my help.'

Emilie shuddered. 'You know how she is about seeing me well placed.'

'Yes. I do. She is nothing like me. She is exactly like your grandfather. A man I cannot even bring to mind except he smelled like camphor and cloves, and who has been described much like they fitted him well.'

'Mother speaks of him as if he floats above the clouds.'

'I'm sure he did, Emilie. But we are mortals. Except we paint. Which puts us in a world of our own. But a romance could add some depth to your images.' The mirror caught Beatrice's attention and she took both her hands and poked at her hair. Then took out a few pins and managed to secure her hair.

'Is that true? That romance could add depth to the watercolours?'

'I told your mother I would say that. And it could be true. But you have to marry someone who is right for you, or you'll be breaking your own brushes. I had the worst of luck until I met Andrew.' Her aunt gave a dismissive toss of her words. 'If not for the naked picture I finished of him, I doubt we would have made it to the altar.'

'The wrong husband could be intimidating. He could destroy my dream, just as Mother is doing.'

'You know that inheritance powder? Arsenic? You could always poison him later if it doesn't work out.' Beatrice gave Emilie a wink and laughed. 'You know I am jesting.' She twitched her shoulders. 'My first husband—may he…stay wherever he went—had more problems than I could create and, trust me, I could cause plenty. But I had lots of instances to indulge in creativity after he abandoned me. Even more after he died. And Andrew loves my work.'

'I've heard he can be dismayed by it.'

'Yes—' Beatrice's head nodded in agreement '—but he loves it—from a distance. I keep myself between him and it and we get along wonderfully.'

'I understand,' Emilie said. 'I don't know what to do. I have a plan, but it's flawed.'

'A flawed plan?' Beatrice tapped her earlobe. 'Well, if you have a notion it's wrong, then based on my experience I would say it is certainly a mistake.'

'Or I could return home.'

'You can stay at your parents' home and dabble in your paints. You will be avoided, perhaps, but you'll be all but forgotten.' She had a bubble of laughter under her next words. 'You can perfect an evil cackle and everyone will be afraid of you. You'll be a sinister, spinster painter.'

Apparently, her aunt did not know that her paints were now forbidden. Emilie made a decision. A flawed plan was better than no plan and to do nothing was unthinkable.

She pressed her lips together, pushed her uncertainty out of her mind and said, 'I have a plan with Mr Westbrook. Avondale's younger son.'

'Oh, no, no, no. Not him.' Beatrice shuddered. 'He's a rake to the core. He won't propose.'

Emilie turned back to lift the dress and hold it to her shoulders. 'If I were to be caught in a compromising position…'

Beatrice stood, her gaze on the dress. 'Then you would be ruined and compromised and likely unmarried.'

'True.' Emilie put the dress on to the bed, pulling it straight so it would not wrinkle. 'I am not matrimony minded, except as a last resort. There are few men in the world like your Andrew who appreciate a woman of substance.'

'To let you in on a confidence…' Beatrice spoke softly and stretched her arms wide '…he doesn't really relish my work. He adores me.'

Emilie put her hand to her neck. 'Truly. And you are happy?'

'Of course…and I'm painting better than ever. Not as much. But still, better than ever.'

Emilie bit the inside of her lip. Usually she trusted her aunt, but she didn't believe Beatrice's skills were better now because of Andrew. Truly, it was talent.

Except for Beatrice's Andrew, Emilie now realised a husband could treat art like a rival, and wouldn't accept it any better than her mother did. Beatrice had admitted she was working less and she'd not grasped that her skills improved with practice, and she had spent years and years perfecting her talent before finding Andrew.

'I have to convince my mother that a wedding will never happen.' Emilie stared at the silk and straightened a puffed sleeve. 'Once she forgets that, she'll leave me alone.'

Beatrice clucked her tongue. 'You really should consider wedded bliss, Emilie, to a man who can afford good staff. Those large portraits get heavy.'

'I have, but I cannot decide between whether it is better for me to be married or to be ruined.' She took her aunt's hands and, even with Beatrice in heels, Emilie rose above the other woman. 'Please help me, Aunt Beatrice. And if Mr Westbrook is such a rake, he would survive a compromising position and be elevated by it. I, on the other hand, would be disgraced.'

Beatrice frowned. 'I would not be a party to this, but I know how much the oils mean to you. Plus, Mr Westbrook will never marry at this point. He's living it up too much. You'd best forget marriage if you're thinking of the second son.'

'True. And I shouldn't be forbidden the love of my life, art, and Mr Westbrook won't be trapped into a marriage with a woman who can hardly tolerate him.'

'Make sure you do not let your mother near any of that inheritance powder after this. She is going to be very, very angry with me.'

* * *

Emilie would hardly have counted the Marquess of Avondale's birthday celebration a celebration. Avondale had disappeared early into the event. A duchess and her friends were taking turns at the pianoforte in the next room, playing verses of different songs, adding occasional bursts of laughter. Marcus had played several songs earlier, singing along. His voice had floated through the air. She'd heard the ladies ask him to play more, but he'd begged off.

Her aunt Beatrice had disappeared, chatting with someone.

Most of the men had congregated in the library and were playing a wagering game of cards, calling out to each other as if they were all brothers. Emilie did not know who was Horsey, Al, Bottles, Dupes or Doughy, but she was certain that Terry was Lord Terrance, and of course, Nathaniel was Mr Westbrook. She couldn't imagine calling him Nathaniel, which surprised her as she had no trouble conceiving Lord Grayson as Marcus.

Mr Westbrook had showered attention on her when she arrived, but the men had finally called him into the card game, leaving her with the older women.

Lady Avondale sat with her friends and a servant stood by to bring them refreshments or attend to whatever they required. Emilie's mother was perched on the outer edge, leaning in, and on her very best behaviour. And Emilie settled at the edge of that, her back straight and the rest of her as hidden as possible.

When they departed London, she would not miss society as much as her mother would.

'Miss Catesby.' Marcus's voice moved over her like a song.

She turned, surprised he'd entered the room. 'Lord Grayson.'

'Her Grace asked that I might fetch you to sing with us.'

She glanced at her mother and her mother beamed. Emilie knew that if Marcus had asked her to plummet from the edge of the earth, her mother would have said nothing to disrupt Lady Avondale's conversation.

Emilie rose and walked with him. As they neared the pianoforte, the Duchess asked Emilie if she would like to play a tune with them. Emilie declined. 'I fear I'm not musical.'

'Neither am I,' the Duchess said, shaking her head. She wrinkled her nose. 'I try to surround myself with people who are talented, so I don't have to play, and it makes everyone else happy. And trust me, everyone prefers me to listen.'

Her friends chuckled and she suggested a tune

to one of the ladies and the conversation swirled in a different direction.

Marcus stayed at her elbow.

'You're accomplished at the piano,' she told him, recalling the tune he'd played when she'd been in the other room.

He acknowledged her words with a lift of his brows. 'My father insisted I learn. It was an easy way to make him happy.'

Emilie realised she felt a pocket of silence blanketing her and Marcus, yet she didn't want to move closer into the circle of women. She would dearly have loved to have asked him a question. Any question. Just to hear his voice again. But the silence between them continued beneath the music.

A woman played a quick, rousing tune, then glanced in their direction. 'Your favourite song, Grayson.'

Everyone laughed, including Marcus, but Emilie didn't get the joke—and she realised she wasn't sure that she liked the sound of his name the way the other woman said it.

'I fitted words to the music.' Marcus tilted close to Emilie so their conversation didn't interrupt the others as they moved on to something else.

'They recall it.' And she'd been envious of the rapport they'd all shared.

'It's an easy melody to play with.' He moved his left hand as if playing the piano. 'Good tempo.'

She forced her gaze away from his fingers. Emilie realised she didn't have to ask him to pose if she planned to reproduce his hands. That small movement, the fluttering of his fingers, imagining them over piano keys, would stay in her mind, locked there.

Her shoulder touched his. She didn't know which of them had moved.

'Bravo.' He spoke to the woman at the piano when her song ended and Emilie's shoulder chilled when he moved away.

The other ladies concurred that the last musical piece had been stellar.

He touched her elbow as the next song began. 'You'll want to peruse the family's art collection,' he said, gently moving her to the room where her mother sat.

Lady Avondale took a platter of biscuits from the servant and was holding it to the ladies nearest her.

'I would like to show Miss Catesby where you have placed your portrait,' he spoke to his mother, 'If neither you nor her mother objects.'

Lady Avondale's lips turned down, deprecating, as she shooed him away. 'Oh, please. Do not make the child suffer so.'

Emilie's mother's head jerked to assess Marcus and then Emilie's eyes. Her jaw clenched, but she relented. 'Of course, if it is fine with Lady Avondale.'

'Do have some more biscuits, everyone.' Lady Avondale commanded attention again. 'The cook adds beetroot juice to these, which gives them a nice colour, and the dried berries add something. We jest that they are goat food because of the oats, but they are tasty.'

While his mother served, Marcus moved to an adjoining door and opened it wide. He ushered Emilie inside.

The room was little more than a sitting room attached to the main one and as she entered, Emilie checked her surroundings. Instead of a portrait of the Lady Avondale, she viewed a life-sized rendition of the Lord Avondale. The other portraits, some little more than miniatures, were scattered here and there about the room. No true design to it—the portrait of the Lady Avondale had been added last and not in an appropriate place beside her husband, or their family portrait, but in a conspicuously inappropriate place to the side and closer to the floor.

Emilie gasped, rushing to it. 'It should be in a place of honour.' She waved her hand to the bigger picture of Lord Avondale. 'By him.'

'She is happy to have the portrait where it is.

She claims she doesn't particularly care to view herself when she is in here, but her children.' He looked at the painting. 'That is what she says.'

Emilie moved to the wall and began to scrutinise the larger likeness of Lord Avondale. When she finished with her viewing of the largest image, she turned, appraising Marcus, as he relaxed against the door jamb, half in the room, half out, lost in his musings.

She returned to her perusal of the collection.

'Miss Catesby.' Marcus's voice jolted her, even though the words were quietly said. She returned to the world at her elbow.

Marcus watched her, smiling.

'Yes?' She stumbled over the word.

'Your mother is telling the Marchioness she's leaving and she's asking for you. You've been in here nearly half an hour.'

Emilie collected herself. 'It is the brushstrokes. I have to study them. And the colours. Most of the artists are talented beyond belief.'

Marcus's gaze turned wistful. 'I would agree that you adore their skills.'

Their eyes locked. He understood.

'It's true.'

His shoulders lifted briefly, in both acknowledgement of her words and somehow telling her again that she loved her craftwork.

'I can't help myself.' She extended her hands, palms upraised.

'Sometimes beauty does that to us,' he said.

'Like with music, to you.'

He shook his head. 'No. Not music. I learned because I was taught well. I did it to please my father. I have a gift for it and it is a pleasant way to pass a morning or a way to amuse friends. A tool.' He flicked his words away with a smile. 'Much like a teapot.'

'Or a paintbrush,' she added.

'Is that truly all you comprehend to be worthwhile?' he asked.

'Frequently, it is. I want to stay in my room with a portfolio. I keep getting pushed out to gatherings.' She checked back over her shoulder at the portraits again. 'I must appreciate the social events, as they enable me to experience rooms such as this. A grander thought might be if I was shut away in a tower, much like a princess, but I wouldn't want to be rescued. I would need my portfolios.' She paused. 'I would need new subjects to examine and gardens so that I might have the best light, but it would be a haven.'

'Pardon?' He bent closer. 'Did you say heaven?'

'No.' She laughed. 'A haven. I surmise you are right about heaven, also.'

'That sounds plain, coming from the Duke of Kinsale's niece.'

'My days are plain when I am not in London,' she said. 'My grandfather was pleased when my mother fell in love with a cleric and made my uncle promise that he would provide a parish for Father always. Father is so very quiet. He prefers his role of a cleric and gets on well with the parish, but not so easily with Mother's family. You can tell he is uncomfortable. Sometimes I'm the same way. Preferring solitude.'

'You've seemed to revel in the last soirée.'

'I had planned to have a delightful evening, no matter how much effort it took.' She glimpsed him from beneath her lashes. 'Why should I not enjoy myself? You can enjoy art without seeing the true colours and I can hear music when there is none.'

She lifted her skirt enough to swirl around. 'When I'm in the presence of landscapes that I enjoy, I can hear the symphonies in my head. The colours create music.'

She swept through the door and away from him, moving into the next room, pretending she was an actress making her stage entrance.

The men had joined the women and Mr Westbrook was telling her mother some outlandish tale judging by the laughter in the room.

Then Mr Westbrook saw her and observed

his brother following behind. Immediately his attention switched back to her mother.

'Lady Catesby, have you seen our ancestral portraits?' Mr Westbrook asked. 'You must before you leave. My brother can tell you who they are much better than I. He's aware of distant cousins that have faded from my memory.' He dipped his head to the Marchioness. 'Mother has an impressive family history of her own.'

Lady Avondale laughed away the compliment.

'I would like to explore the gallery,' Emilie's mother answered, surprising Emilie with the sudden interest.

Marcus waved a hand for her to precede him and her mother went ahead.

The Lady Avondale ushered out the other guests who'd been leaving, and Emilie stayed alone with Mr Westbrook.

'I would relish being in your presence again. Please tell me you won't be leaving town soon,' Mr Westbrook said.

'I'm uncertain.'

He took her hand and she did not pull away.

'Please let me know if we might meet again some day. I would be at your disposal. To take you on a carriage ride…' he said. 'To assist you in any way that I might…'

Emilie heard the interest in his voice. 'Are you certain?'

'Very much so. To have a woman like you in our midst is a grand thing.'

'I paint,' she said.

'So do I.'

'I know you mentioned that you dabbled in it.'

'Yes. After my lessons ended, I've spent a few stretches of time with a canvas. Father wanted Marcus to focus on music and languages and the more boring aspects of learning, and I was the second son. I liked charcoals and oils, so Father indulged me. My mother has one of my paintings on the wall. I signed it simply Westbrook.'

'I saw it. It's good. Skilful.' A fine showing, but not exceptional. Especially adept if he didn't practise. He had natural skills. She realised he had signed his family name and it hadn't occurred to her that he was the one who'd painted it.

He bowed in acknowledgement of her words. 'Marcus doesn't let me scatter around my attempts at landscapes in his residence, but I have a few tucked away there. Of course, I would be pleased to dig out a few for you to critique, privately. If Marcus knew of your presence, he would be so angered. Propriety and all.'

'That is thoughtful of you.'

'We artists should support each other.'

She pondered her choices. Mr Westbrook seemed willing to ruin her. Considerate of him.

She pushed aside her awareness that she really didn't care for him. He would certainly make her option of choosing marriage or choosing to be ruined easier. Marriage to him would distress her so.

Her mother and Marcus returned to the room and she slipped her hand from Mr Westbrook's and increased her distance from him. Her mother's view wavered, uncertain about whether to be upset Westbrook had taken her hand, or to scold Emilie for pulling away.

But if she were to guess, by the glare in his eyes, Marcus's teeth were near to breaking.

Emilie turned, following her mother's exit to the carriage.

Marcus wasn't given to sweetness as his brother was. But Marcus would be so much better for a portrait.

How he had not married gave her cause to guess the women of the town were smart to avoid a rascal, or had no wits about them that they wouldn't try to entrance someone so superb.

She doubted she was up to the task of having Mr Westbrook for a husband. She figured if one got used to having ravening hawks about one, but at bay, one could become complacent. And the sly hawk could wait patiently, relaxing, paying scant attention, until the guard was lowered, pounce on the little weasel, gulp and be done with it.

Such a shame that Mr Westbrook would be the better man for her husband. He did paint, of course. She had noticed the buttons on Westbrook's coat and knew they were mother-of-pearl and had a nice stone in each centre. Marcus's buttons were unremarkable. She knew he, as the elder, could have had as nice a coat as Westbrook had. Perhaps Marcus wasn't inclined to spare the coin, or perhaps he didn't care about fashion as much.

Scrutinising them from memory, she could see why she'd mistaken Mr Westbrook for the eldest. His tailor spared no expense and Marcus wore muted tones and few frills.

But he didn't need embellishments.

She could hardly stand how her stomach turned over when she saw him. That could disrupt her. She must keep him a safe distance from her.

She feared if she lingered in his arms, she might become a shadow of herself. A woman who hid inside herself, waiting for Marcus to notice her again. She couldn't become vulnerable to him. He was just a man.

Emilie couldn't risk corruption from someone like him. Her life had to revolve around her aspirations. Some day, she would enter a gallery and her work would grace the wall, or her landscapes would be purchased as a legacy to hand down to grandchildren. If it meant scrawling a signature across the bottom, and perhaps even letting Mr Westbrook claim credit, she didn't care. She wanted her impressions to live and be noticed. Only by being exhibited would anyone other than her family have access to them.

She could easily paint and display, or sell them as Mr Westbrook's work, although she envisioned herself better than him. Having to sign his name to her creations—actually, she wasn't sure if she could do that.

But no one would dare ignore a painting done by an earl's son. She could pull off the ruse, but she wasn't sure she wanted to. And she wasn't sure she wanted to be in any sort of a compromising position with Westbrook either.

Marcus, on the other hand. She might like to see him more. Purely in the interest of inspiration. But, she would have to content herself with engravings of Michelangelo's work, although she wasn't sure if Marcus was more of a David or a Moses.

Marcus was flesh and blood. Distracting. And he could not see the colours that made her landscapes come alive. He would never know the true appearance of a scene. He'd never comprehend her passion.

Chapter Four

Marcus had watched his brother at the birth-day celebration and noticed Nathaniel could not keep from observing Emilie. He could read the ideas in his brother's mind as clearly as if they were spoken. He wanted to shove Nathaniel into the wall.

With a brief goodbye, he set out on foot, leaving the carriage for his brother.

He strode to Lady Semple's address, letting the exertion calm him.

The butler let him in.

She sat in her chair by the fireplace and didn't burn coal, but had a few twigs which wafted a warm comforting scent into the room.

'So many young beauties in London, yet you have time for a moment with me.' Her turban had a fringe of white hair escaping from it.

'Youth has its allure, but there is much beauty

to be found in the mature appearance as well.'
He bowed to her.

Her visage reminded him of a sage and the
sharpness of her wit and her astute observa-
tions drew him to her. For that reason, he always spoke with Lady Semple when he saw her
and he always found her conversation enlightening. Sometimes too enlightening, as she could
speak about anything without a stammer or a
blush, and she made him uneasy if she got carried away.

'But I fear one must search harder for beauty
in the older countenance.' She reached to adjust her turban and her hair moved in such a
way he wondered if the locks were connected
to the wrap.

'Not with you, Lady Semple.'

'I do not have to search for your flattery,
which is always appreciated and shared with
my friends.' She batted away the words. 'Will
you be joining us again this Thursday for cards?'

'Lady Semple, that is first in my calendar.'
He moved closer.

She got to her feet, and put a hand to the small
of her back. 'Weather is changing. I'd best move
or soon I won't be able to.'

She appraised him. 'So what brings you here?
All flattery aside, as I know that you are deeply

devoted to me, particularly when I am losing funds to you in a game of cards.'

'You know my brother, Nathaniel. The one who refused to let you win the money back.'

'Without spectacles, I can scarce tell you apart from a distance.' She stopped him, reaching out. She tucked away a piece of his neckcloth which had escaped his waistcoat. 'But, I doubt I've spoken to Mr Westbrook in years.'

'Occasionally people mistake me for my brother and he for me. If I am in the act of doing something well, I correct them.' They moved into an alcove. 'If I am not so sure of my actions, I thank them for their greeting. He said he is the same.'

'I am sure you must always correct them.'

'Of course.' He smiled, putting innocence into his words and following them with an exaggerated leer. Her laugh would have fitted a tavern woman.

'And what of Miss Emilie Catesby? Are you well acquainted with her family?' He kept his voice bland, but her reaction told him she read the direction of his reasoning.

'Miss Catesby. I've heard her mentioned.' She straightened the turban, again moving the silver fringe. 'You've not asked me in the past if I know of any female. You tend to know much more about the young women of the *ton* than I do.'

'I suspect she has been brought to London to find out if any of the men might suit her as a husband.'

'That is what I've heard also. I've also been told she's had no beau because it would limit her time at a canvas. Her mother has brought her to search among the rakes of the *ton* for a suitable husband. A shame. With the exception of yourself, many men in this town might blind her to their follies so they could make an offer for her. I know from experience *that* can happen.'

'Do you predict I might not be able to do that?' he asked, smiling.

'I assumed you had no follies to blind her to.' She touched her ear.

'I would hope not.'

'I am sure.' She paused. 'How well do you know her?'

'Hardly at all. She's got some connection to Wilson, the Duke of Kinsale—and the Duchess has seen that Miss Catesby has many events to attend. Perhaps in search of a romance.'

'Sad to have a parent pushing offspring to do such a thing. Your father is still pressing you to marry, isn't he?'

Marcus remained silent.

She laughed. 'Do not let him give you that old rubbish about dying without holding a grandchild. He will likely outlive us all. By many years.' She smiled. 'Remember, *whom the gods love dies young.*' Her lids dropped. 'Please pass that information along to him from me. He is so forgetful. The type who might forget a secret betrothal.'

'You and I both know he has never truly forgotten it.'

Elbows tucked at her side, she shrugged. 'Good. But we both ended up the better for it. Except…'

Except his mother. 'She is not thrilled with him. Perhaps, they share a bond that is between them. They occasionally share a few civil words. Much more recently than they have in many years.'

'I do feel better for your telling me that. He didn't treat either her or me fairly.'

'Mother has also mentioned a grandchild and how she feels inferior to the others who natter on and on about the accomplishments of their cherubs.'

Lady Semple sighed. 'That is a first, isn't it?'

'Yes. But the volume of my parents' discussions hasn't lessened. It's best if they communicate by message or letter. Mother has her discreet lady's maid read Father's letters aloud and the woman omits irritating references. It is the best for everyone and Father doesn't know.'

'If it works for them.'

'Once the lady's maid read three pages, gave her an awkward cough and said, *He judges you are in good health*. Then Mother pointed to the fire and the maid tossed the letter in.'

Marcus had reasoned that moving out of the family home would distance himself from two things: the rows his parents had on the rare occasions they spoke and the opinions of his father. Nathaniel hadn't even asked Marcus if he could move in, just followed with his belongings a few days later. Now their father showed up on a whim, questioning them about their pursuits and chiding them on their responsibilities.

'And now your mother has joined in?'

'Yes.'

'Your father does like to get his way. Like his sons.'

'I would agree. We are more alike than I aspire to be.'

'Many of the women here have tried to catch your eye, have they not?' Lady Semple asked.

'I cannot say for certain.' He clasped his hands behind his back.

'I can,' she insisted, 'as I have watched on the occasions you have graced us with your presence. At least, I think it was you,' she teased. 'Perhaps they were searching for Mr Westbrook.'

'Well, if the women have tried to catch my attention, then you must assume they were hunting for me and not my brother.' The earlier irritation returned to him.

Emilie hadn't pretended to mistake him for Nathaniel. She really had.

Lady Semple clasped his arm.

'Don't marry to spite your father or to please your mother.'

'It would seem a simple task.'

'Your father forsook love to please your grandparents. That turned out wonderfully for your father, to a point, and the best for me, but he's fortunate your mother hasn't smothered him in his sleep.'

'They tend to sleep in different residences.'

'Ever stuck your hand in the fire to see how hot it is?' the older woman asked, eyebrows arched.

'If a woman is on the way to nuptials above all else, what difference would one rake over another make?' he asked.

'This could be interesting.' Lady Semple chortled. 'I will watch to see what happens. Would you invite me to see such a thing? That is the only way I would believe it.'

'I will keep your words in mind. But I don't know that my mother would appreciate it.'

'I don't know,' she said. 'We've spoken.'

'You have?' he asked.

'After I was out of mourning for my husband,

she approached me and told me that I had been indeed fortunate to have had the love of two husbands, one mine and one hers. She asked how I did it.'

Marcus didn't speak. He couldn't.

'I told her. The truth.'

'What?'

'It is the enigma many women have and they don't know it. They believe it is brains. Or beauty. But really it is *joie de vivre*.' She held her hand close to her throat, as if pulling her spirit from her body. 'A sense of fun.'

Marcus watched her.

'Yes.' Suddenly her age fell away and she cavorted as if on gilded slippers. 'When I am about in London, have you ever seen me act any way but as if I am at a soirée? A soirée of grand proportions. That the world is a game and I have the winning hand.'

'It's true.' He recalled the first day he had seen Emilie and the way that she—even though they were both young and he was twice her size— had called herself a highwayman.

Then, today, Nathaniel had found time for a private conversation with her. But he was certain Nathaniel saw her as a conquest, nothing more.

'I hope you would like to see me close to a spirited woman like Miss Catesby, not Nathaniel. I admit I have not always done as I should, but he often gives the notion he would prefer to never do as he should.'

'You must mend your ways for me to encourage a romance.'

'A flawed concept, but entertaining.'

'You men do like your entertainments.'

'Agreed.'

He scrutinised her expression and thought of the lively and forthright conversations they'd had and he didn't think he could be wrong in his assessment of her. Although he didn't always admire her choices, he admired her discretion.

She snorted, making her hair flutter. 'Don't forget to join us for cards. I love having a man of your age visiting me.' She raised her brows. 'Please be dishevelled as you leave.'

'Only if you agree to have a chaperon.'

She let her eyes drift heavenwards. 'Josephina, Millie and Meg will be there. That will give us enough to complete the table.'

'Plan on it.'

He departed, ruminating on the misery a union could bring and the knowledge that he couldn't put it off indefinitely.

His father had claimed matrimony to be much like thrusting oneself on to a blade, but the bloodletting was very necessary for the peerage.

If one must be impaled, Emilie would not be as bad as others. However, he was not so sure

Emilie wouldn't choose Nathaniel over him. But, still, his attention kept following her.

He strongly doubted Emilie could ever ignore a man's indiscretions.

No, he suspected Emilie would react much as his mother had. Fire and brimstone.

Now he could not shut the memory of Emilie dancing from his mind.

She had swirled across the floor.

He forgot her elegance for a moment and could see the image of her creamy breasts above the bodice of her gown and realised instantly he must put his mind elsewhere.

Chapter Five

Well past midday, Marcus awoke when Robert cleared his throat in the room.

He waved his valet away.

'Your father is here. I have told him that you have been out and about earlier taking nosegays to the debutantes of the *ton*,' Robert said. 'And, that you returned to your room to change as you had got a smudge on your cravat which smelled of a marriageable innocent's perfume.'

'Father has arrived?' Marcus thrust the pillow at Robert, who caught it easily.

'Yes. And I fear he suspects I have misinformed him of your habits. He practically called me a liar…' Robert dropped the pillow on to a chair '…which, of course, is often the case.' He indicated the trousers and shirt he'd laid out for Marcus and added a waistcoat and cravat near the mirror.

'I will see him,' Marcus groaned, pushing

himself from the bed. He donned the shirt and trousers.

Before he was completely ready, Robert had the brush to his hair. 'Can I not trim your locks a small amount?' Robert grumbled. 'Your father complains of it, as if I have nothing better to do than hold scissors. He makes certain to do so loud enough that I hear.'

'I will tell him that I was searching for a bride and he'll be mollified.'

Robert stared at Marcus.

'He might be right,' Marcus continued. 'I should not be so skittish about being wed. Perhaps if one does not forcefully throw oneself against the blade, but does so only a bit, one can recover to continue with living.'

'Are you daft?' The valet dropped the brush and took a cravat and began to unroll the linen. 'I thought I'd raised you better than that.'

Marcus felt the tugs as Robert put the cravat in place. 'I might do my duty and make my father less angry with me.'

Robert snorted. 'The day I see you marry—I cannot even imagine such a thing. Besides, we have no room for a woman's nonsense.'

Marcus scowled. 'A bachelor's household has been fine, but now perhaps it's time to change.'

'Whatever you wish. Whatever you wish. And I wish for you to make a wise decision.

You know, like the winter you skated on that iced-over pond. Now that was a wise decision— making sure that when the ice cracked you would only go into the water up to your knees.' The valet raised his chin, put his eyes to half- mast and opened the door for Marcus to leave. 'Your feet thawed out quickly and I'm sure you hardly felt the cold.'

Marcus ignored Robert, grabbed the waistcoat and strode to see his father, making sure he was in control of himself before he opened the door.

His father sat at Marcus's desk, holding his arms extended so he could read the papers he'd pulled from the drawer.

'You and Nathaniel were at the birthday cel- ebration yesterday.' His father squinted at the page in front of him. Then he put the missive down and tapped his fingers against the wood. 'You spoke briefly to many young ladies and only gave much attention to an Emilie Catesby.'

'Yes.' Marcus finished doing up his buttons and pulled the chair near the doorway closer to the centre of the room, turned it so that he was facing the back and sat astride. He crossed his arms across the back. The light from the win- dow behind his father shone in and the window dressing was open wide so that the contrast of the brightness into the dark room made it hard to discern his father's expression.

'Am I to imagine you have listened to my counsel?'

'Of course,' Marcus answered. 'I always listen to you.'

'Because I give you no choice.' His father lifted the lid on a carved box, checking what was inside. 'Where are the cigars Robert always has hidden away?'

Marcus pointed to the book on the desk. His father tipped up the cover of the false book, finding the cigars. 'Have you selected a bride to offer for?' He put one in his pocket and picked up a letter from the table.

'No.' Marcus frowned. 'Last night, I gave serious thought to what you said. I can't make the wrong selection.'

His father read as he talked. 'That I can imagine, as I have been stating the same thing for years now. And don't worry about the permanence of the union, that's not a finite promise. The children, you will keep them for ever. Choose a good mother for your heirs. They'll thank you.'

Marcus considered the silver in the other man's hair and the set of his jaw. He had been told that he stood exactly like his father. But he knew he didn't have the same chip on his tooth that his father had—but then he had not been caught by a jealous husband. He'd never once kept company with a married woman.

'While I do respect your view,' Marcus continued, arms still resting on the chair back, 'I must reflect on my own and will choose someone not distasteful.'

'You have selected many mares for our stables,' his father insisted. 'This is no different. Pick some well-bred stock, acquire it and nature will take care of the rest.' He threw down the letter after glancing at the script.

'I do not like the implication that I am only needed to sire a grandson for you.' Marcus bit the words out. Nor did he like his father reading his correspondence.

'Then we will let your brother do so,' his father stated. 'I am getting tired of waiting.'

'Father, my son would surpass his in inheritance anyway. Do not rush him.' He certainly didn't want his brother pushed towards Emilie. 'I realised the value of your words recently. Give me some leeway to view the options before you start grumbling anew.'

The older man selected another missive, then let the paper flutter to the table. 'You say you take into account my words, yet you didn't parade about with more than a few women when your mother's likeness was unveiled. I keep listening for tales of you with one of the peer's daughters, yet I hear nothing. It's as if you are putting on a charade to make your mother and me keep silent.'

'I'm not.' Marcus kept his words calm. Blast, his father had been asking questions of someone about his son because he hadn't been at the unveiling. 'But I remained near the fence and tried to discern bloodlines.'

'Pick good breed stock,' his father repeated, rising and glaring at him, 'although the lineage is important, it's still no guarantee of siring the most agreeable offspring. Your mother and I both are from well-bred families.'

'Thank you, Father. While I deeply love Mother, I am so pleased to have inherited your traits.'

'You are welcome, my son.' He moved closer, planting a soft kick at the leg of Marcus's chair. 'I am pleased to hear that you are considering my words. I don't want to grow old without the comfort of a grandson.' At the door, he said, 'And I especially don't want you to grow old without the discomfort of a son.'

'Thank you, again, Father.'

'And those whiskers.' His father appraised Marcus. He raised his voice so that it might carry outside the room. 'Robert needs to get a better shaving kit for you. And the hair. Sad no one ever taught him to trim it properly.'

As his father departed, Marcus touched his chin and swore softly.

Then Robert entered. 'I do thank you for leaving the door open, sir. I would have hated to miss your father's encouragement.'

'I feel it is easier for you that way.' Marcus gripped the top of the chair, before he relaxed his elbows.

'You are like my own…nephew,' Robert admitted. 'Not that it is anything to be proud of.'

'Not that I am proud of it.' Marcus crossed his arms on the back of the chair, rested his chin on them, while his thumb was pressed against his cheek. 'But if a man were to have an uncle underfoot, one like you would do.'

Robert hastened to the desk and studied the top.

'And he rifled your papers, didn't he?'

'Yes.'

'He should respect your privacy.'

'As you do?'

'Of course.'

'And?'

Robert picked up one of the papers and also stretched his arms out, squinting.

Marcus reached out and ripped the paper from the valet's hands before tossing it on to the table. 'I should have a wife. And if she could annoy

Father, it might reduce some of the pain of marriage.'

Robert clasped both hands over his ears. 'I cannot trust what I'm hearing.' Robert coughed, gulping. 'I must have a lie down to absorb this tragedy.' He pulled the door shut with a soft click.

He realised Robert had not mentioned bringing breakfast to him. The man could be counted on for many things. Finding the best brandy. The best cigars. But his skills as a valet were lacking and he surmised that was a fact Robert prided himself on.

He'd been Marcus's second tutor, then he'd guided Marcus to Oxford and been the only person to write regularly. The only person to ever visit.

When he became of age to have a valet, Marcus had talked Robert into leaving his post, and changing his profession. Robert had driven a hard bargain.

He was certain that Robert would be happy to see him married to such a woman as Emilie, who would hardly care for anything else but the canvas in front of her. Their duties would not intersect so both could continue as they had before. Oh, Emilie might add a nursery, of course, but Robert would avoid that as if it were diseased.

He realised Lady Semple was right about Emilie. She had a passion for something. Just not him.

If Marcus married, Robert could continue on as always. Emilie would be lost in her own world and Marcus could uncover something that drew him to do more than merely exist.

Boredom had lingered inside him so long that it had taken up residence and had grown dusty.

He would have satisfied his duty to the peerage and would have a chance to learn if anything could cure the utter uselessness inside him.

Emilie.

He wanted to see her again. The woman who found purpose with the most simple task of swirling colours on canvas and had no need at all for the diversions of London.

She saw the hues he could not see.

Emilie pretended interest in the book she held and her mother stitched along beside Beatrice, who drew a picture of Emilie.

Emilie grasped why she preferred art over anything else. Her father had warned her that most men weren't trustworthy. In fact, he had said all men were corrupt at heart, but her mother had disagreed, pointed to her father and begun a litany of his virtues.

Marriage would lead her to a union with

someone who liked to talk as if they were important while they drank, smoked and played cards. They liked impure women for diversions. They liked pleasant meals and quiet wives and quiet children.

She knew they could be easily led into temptation, but she was not too sure how to present temptation properly.

Mr Westbrook would be a perfect husband to leave her alone, but she doubted she could choose to marry him. With him, she would have to settle for being ruined.

His brother, however. Dancing with Marcus had felt like floating on a cloud. When he had whispered to her, she had noticed the faint smell of cigars on him. They had smelled better than turpentine and she had always hated cigar smoke. She must try not to notice so much, but she could not help herself.

Too bad that he was not as flighty as Westbrook. But even if he were it would not matter. Marcus was not to be easily snared into the parson's trap. She was certain. He would never trust her as Westbrook would. He understood her better.

While he was at the soirée, he'd stayed near the men, watching, talking and giving the impression he was above all that nonsense. If he had an interest in marriage, he had only to speak to one of the green girls at the party and look deeply into her eyes. She might be dazed, the good kind, and would go along with him.

His face appeared in her mind.

Marcus even took his frivolities seriously, she guessed. She was sure if he were lost in the desert, he could find his way to a woman as fast as Westbrook could. But Marcus would not dash headfirst after her. He might review the situation and change his mind after he saw her.

He liked Lady Semple, and had spoken with the older woman at the dance as if they were friends. That woman was rumoured to have spent her youth on the edge of immorality. Without her wealth, doubtful her fancies would be ignored so easily.

Yet Lady Semple certainly knew a lot of things about seducing men, if half the stories were true about the widow.

She'd once heard Lady Semple had bought the house she lived in because the secluded area made it easy for a visitor to enter and leave her unnoticed by neighbours. From the gossips' words, she had no question Lady Semple was suspected of having male visitors for inappropriate dalliances.

Emilie inhaled, letting the air linger in her lungs. Lady Semple had been married and, from what Emilie's mother had said, the marriage had not improved her at all. Emilie nibbled the inside of her lip. A woman did not always need improvement. She needed an avocation. A husband would work for that.

Emilie intended to get the ring on her finger and make sure the band gave her more freedom instead of less.

True, a woman became a husband's property upon marriage. But she knew ownership could be tenuous.

She'd even seen how a woman who wasn't happy with being a possession could take matters into her own hands. Her mother's cousin Tilly had never let marriage slow her down. Her husband lived two streets north of Tilly, but she let him visit on occasion. She simply made plans to be elsewhere during his return so she would not distress him and she never complained about him.

Even though she didn't like Tilly, her cousin had a good notion of how a marriage should proceed.

Interrupting Emilie's thoughts, her aunt and mother devised an outing to the shops and Emilie elected to stay behind.

At the desk, she touched the pen, lifted the paper and sat down to compose.

Her hand trembled over the note as she wrote. She forced herself to make the large W of Mr

Westbrook's name. Surely he would know better than to let her meet him alone in his residence. At midnight.

She wished she'd written Lord Grayson on the page, but she couldn't. Marcus would never fall for something so foolish. Even his brother should not be so daft.

She stared at the words, and lit the wax, then tilted the candle to let the wax pool on to the paper. Taking the seal her father had had made for her, she daubed it to wet it, then dipped the metal into the wax. She'd sealed her fate, either way.

She would be married or ruined, and she would capture the world on canvas.

She picked up another piece of paper dipped the quill into the ink and shook the nib above the bottle opening, releasing a drip.

A spouse of a peer might be permitted a certain type of freedom and particularly freedom in her pursuits.

She drew the pen closer. As a wife who dabbled in paints, the future would no longer be a problem. People wouldn't fight her about her hobbies any more. She would be alone and allowed her freedom.

She wouldn't embarrass him by openly pursuing her talents.

Signing a different name to her artwork might be for the best.

She could imagine the whispers. Eventually, most of society would be aware of her identity, but if they felt they were privy to the secret, it wouldn't hurt anyone's standing.

She had already sold two paintings that she'd signed—not Emilie, but *Emile*.

She scratched the pen across the paper, completing her message. And if she was ruined, well, no one would push her to a suitor.

Then she tapped her fingernails on to another blank page, staring at the white and imagining Marcus's hands breaking the seal and holding the paper open. Dipping the pen again, she wrote a second note and addressed it. They both said the same thing. One addressed to Lord Grayson and one to Mr Westbrook. She didn't know which to send.

She took the letter to Marcus and held it for a moment. Marcus. She really couldn't comprehend what went on in his mind. She held the missive over the candle for the sealing wax, letting the paper flutter before she pushed it into the flame.

She dropped the last embers on to the wet cloth she'd used for preparing the seal.

Marcus had said his brother would ruin her. Not marry her.

Perhaps he was wrong. Perhaps he was right.

She suspected Marcus knew his brother better than she did.

Her heart thudded in her stomach and she accepted the fatal flaw in her plan. Westbrook was a rake. He likely wouldn't marry her.

No one of any regard would court her if her reputation was so damaged.

Her mother would be furious for a while, but would agree that Emilie was to remain a spinster. She might even send Emilie away. But once Emilie's future was locked into place, her mother couldn't use Emilie's dream as a bargaining tool.

Emilie's heart still beat and her problem was solved, but the weight of what she was about to do didn't make her tread lighter when she reached for the pull to summon a servant.

Mr Westbrook. She would send the letter to Westbrook asking to meet him in the late hours at his address.

She would creep out into the night alone and find her way to marriage or to ruin.

Chapter Six

Marcus could hardly taste the food on his plate. He stabbed at it more than ate it. Something about that Catesby woman remained in his mind.

Robert waltzed into the room, humming and swirling the silver salver he held in his hands as if it were a dancing partner. 'A messenger has brought a letter. Not for you.'

Robert examined the missive, flicking it open at the sides, studying it before dropping it. 'Possibly it's from a young lady, which is odd as your brother hardly visits with ladies who might take efforts with written correspondence.'

He stopped near Marcus and bowed, holding out the salver on his palm. 'If it is held to the light, the surname appears to start with C.'

Marcus snapped back his comment telling Robert to leave. He saw the swirling W on the paper. He dropped his fork and snatched the paper from the tray.

Robert gasped. He held the tray at his side. 'Is that your brother's? Is he not with you? Sadly, I have erred again.' His voice dripped chagrin. 'I *just* remembered he is on his way to see a woman he is fond of—perhaps they are planning to discuss *The Iliad*. Or having a go at an *Odyssey*. Who knows?' He infused innocence into his words. 'My sincere error.'

Marcus broke the seal and turned so Robert could not see the words. Marcus held the paper in his hand, the paper crumbling under his clench. 'You are to be disciplined, Robert. An extra half-day off whenever is convenient as punishment for the error of your ways.'

Robert groaned. 'I shall contemplate heartily my mistaken delivery. I have so disgraced myself that I may voluntarily increase the length of the punishment.'

Marcus clamped his jaw, read the missive to the end and his fingers tightened more with each word he saw. 'Bring me a lit candle. Now.'

Robert did as directed.

Marcus held the candle over his plate and let the letter burn and fall into the dinnerware.

One speck of paper still glowed hot on his plate.

'Get me some paper and ink. Nathaniel will accept her invitation.'

Robert rotated. 'The note should have cleared your head of any serious notion about her.'

'Wait,' Marcus said, stopping the movement. 'I need you by the rear door well before midnight. Show the guest into the main sitting room.'

Robert's mouth opened so wide his teeth were hidden. 'Sir, I do not aspire to see your life take a downward turn.'

Marcus answered, 'Prepare for a woman to be sent on her way with a good talking to and an explanation of how foolish she is.'

'You must consider your actions. Don't expect to explain to a woman she is foolish and escape easily.'

'You saved my life once, Robert. And I will never forget it. But it's mine. I shall proceed.'

Slowly, Robert blinked twice.

'You can have a room in my dwelling, with no work and the same pay.' Marcus gripped the table. 'It is what I promised you to get you here and the promise stands. But you will not direct my path.'

Robert held his chin high. 'To me, you are the son I did not sire. If I determine fault with your actions, I have myself to blame.' He dipped his head and his voice became husky. 'I blame myself a lot.'

'Whatever you have to do, whoever you have to send, make certain Nathaniel is not to return until well after one in the morning. Get in touch with his carriage driver and see that it happens, should Nate plan to reappear. The carriage should get lost, the horses should bolt into the countryside or the carriage men can use whatever methods to distract him that's needed. See that it is done and done subtly.' He frowned at Robert. 'And he is not to be bruised or damaged in anyway.'

'It is unlikely he will return so early should he be doing what he is doing where I predict he will be doing it.'

'Make certain.'

Marcus touched the ashes, blackening his fingers as he brushed the darkness from his plate.

That night, Marcus sat on the sofa, arms crossed, waiting for Emilie. He would tell her, without taking care of his words, that she was courting disaster. Totally insensible. Lacking the least awareness of her reputation and a hoyden. A reckless woman with no concern for how her actions could affect others.

At one in the morning, he wished he'd not burned the paper so he could reassure himself of the assignation time. But some people were always late.

At two, he began pacing. He could hope the woman had come to her senses and that she hadn't been attacked by a cutpurse out in the night. He wanted to send a carriage out.

That infernal woman. Lady Semple had not warned him how that spirit of *joie de vivre* could wear on the person watching it.

Marcus was still awake when Nathaniel returned early in the morning, complaining of the foolish errors of the staff that had got him lost and the carriage had been stuck and he could not understand how the carriage had got stuck in such a small puddle, and the men had refused— the staff had *refused*—to let him sully himself by helping get the carriage from the puddle or over the tiny rocks in front of it.

Nathaniel's anger was in full swing. He wanted Robert sacked as there had been an unfortunate incident with a spot of manure on his boot and the man had acted as if he were treated abominably to lower himself to Nate's footwear, as if Marcus's boots had the only manure in the world worth scraping away.

Marcus half-listened and knew his valet most likely was being informed of the night's events by the groom.

Nathaniel grumbled on, then muttered as he stalked away, still unaware of the true reason for the mishaps.

Robert entered the room. 'The maid is cleaning your brother's boot as he has not been able to afford a valet of quality as you have.'

Marcus reached up, touching the hair at his collar. 'I need this trimmed,' he said.

'Whatever for? I have heard rumours of women running their fingers through your locks and telling you how it does not matter at all that you are in line to inherit a large estate and have a title as well—that they love you for the scoundrel you are. The jewels and riches you could provide for them are so incidental.'

'They see beyond that. They also know that I have a valet and he livens up the household.'

Robert flicked his lashes. 'It is my eyes. Women cannot resist such lovely blue eyes.' He put a hand on Marcus's shoulder. 'Do not despair that you have not been graced so.'

'I will have a haircut,' he said. 'I will put all this nonsense behind me.'

'I'll collect the water.'

Marcus walked to his dressing table and took off his waistcoat, cravat and shirt.

Robert returned. He took care of the clothing as Marcus sat.

Marcus's jaw ached. It had been doing that entirely too much over the past twelve hours. He forced himself to unclench his teeth.

'Not too much off,' Marcus said, waving a hand towards his hair.

Robert groaned, flapping a towel, snapping it Marcus's direction. 'Get over her. She sent a post to your brother and she is not for you.'

'I have never been attached to Miss Catesby. I have no need to get over her.'

'Remember, she wrote your brother a letter.' Robert put the towel over Marcus's shoulders. 'She has no designs on your virtue—only on the name Westbrook.'

'But she didn't show up.'

'Not a good sign. She cannot plan a rendez-vous properly.'

'I can.' Marcus's jaw popped. 'I can sign my brother's name as well as my own. We will see what happens when Nathaniel requests Miss Catesby's presence at Hatchards. In the bright of day. And you are not the person you profess to be if you cannot locate where she is staying and also a way to get this delivered discreetly to her this morning.'

Robert gave a slight shrug. 'Of course.'

Marcus took pen to paper after the haircut.

He begged her apologies and sincerely hoped he had done nothing to offend her. He also mentioned that he had a very important question regarding a book of engravings he was hoping to purchase at Hatchards. He told her the hour he would be selecting it. Could she please, he begged, be of assistance?

He signed Nathaniel's name with a flourish, then threw the pen across the room.

Chapter Seven

Emilie pulled another book into her hand, well aware that her mother refused to let her near any tome at Hatchards that had anything to do with the old masters, so she had concocted the idea of buying a novel as a present for her sisters.

Her mother gasped. Instantly, Emilie glimpsed Marcus entering the shop and searched behind him.

Marcus greeted Emilie's mother.

'What a shock seeing you here,' her mother said, giving a narrow-browed glance at Emilie. 'A total surprise to both of…us.'

'Lord Grayson?' Emilie asked, peering at the window. 'Is your brother with you?'

He shook his head. 'He was called away on urgent business today. A flower he wanted to pick or some such thing.'

'Oh,' she said, shrugging. 'It is just as well.'

'Miss Catesby.' Marcus picked up the first

book he saw, the fingers of his right hand running along the closed pages. 'I'm searching for a volume for my dear brother. Might you help me choose one?'

Emilie demurred. 'I must ask first to see if the task is acceptable with my mother.'

'I will be right here, watching,' her mother's words rushed out. Then the older woman caught herself and held her head straight. Her words slowed. 'Of course, you may consider all the volumes, as long as there are no improper engravings. I *detest* improper engravings.'

Marcus turned to Emilie, his view no longer in her mother's line of vision.

Emilie touched gloved fingertips to her cheeks. 'I could never do such a thing.' With her mother present.

'I am completely in agreement with your views on that, Miss Catesby.' He spoke softly. She read his thoughts. They were in agreement.

'Might we go and choose from the most wholesome selections, Miss Catesby?' He pointed the book in his hand towards the art section.

'Indeed,' she said.

Unsurprisingly, her mother followed them, remaining within earshot behind Marcus.

Marcus put his choice on the shelf and selected another book, thumbed through it and put it back with the others, his arm moving closer to Emilie's side. Then, his tongue pressing against his cheek, he viewed a third volume. 'My brother would like this book.'

'Perhaps you should purchase it for him.'

'Perish the thought.' He shoved the book back on to the shelf. 'I assume he would like it because the engravings are large and the words are few.'

'That is not a kind thing to say about your own brother.'

He remained close, their shoulders brushing. 'Sometimes I don't cherish him as much as others. Like last night.'

She immediately studied the book in front of her. 'This has excellent reproductions.'

He glanced over her shoulder. 'The words are too long for Nate.'

'You are not being kind.'

'I wasn't kind to him last night. I sent him on an errand.'

She pulled another book from the shelf. 'Why did you send him on an errand?'

'It's best to keep him busy. You never know what kind of trouble he might get into on his own.' He scrutinised the cover of the one she held. 'And he had such bad fortune. The carriage became stuck in the mud.'

She scrutinised him. 'Truly stuck?'

'Sadly, yes.'

'You can't blame yourself. After all, you couldn't have known the vehicle would be mired. Particularly with not a lot of rain recently.'

'I would never, in a million years, have guessed such a thing.' He paused. 'First time such a thing has happened in my lifetime with our carriage.'

'Did you wait on him?' she asked. 'To arrive at your address?'

'More or less. I waited. I was concerned. I mean, to be about on such a dark night. That did not make sense to me.' He hefted a heavier tome close and flipped it to the middle pages. 'What if he had been waylaid by a cutpurse, or a highwayman?'

'I am touched that you are so concerned about your brother, but I am sure he can take care of himself.'

'Miss Catesby, spare me. You never know what can happen on the dark streets at night.' He snapped the book shut.

'Perhaps he planned to take someone with him.'

'I would certainly hope so.'

Her eyes widened. 'That is mindful of you. And I forgive you for the unkind things you said about your brother's preference for short words.'

'Don't forgive me. Please. No need. It's true.'

Again, he tucked his tongue against his inner cheek for a half-second. 'And, my poor, misguided, brother is also very forgetful.'

'Well, he cannot help that.'

'He could. In theory, he could remember the short words. Like *I will. I do. I don't.* But I'm absolutely sure he will not.' He turned from the books and directly towards her.

Her mother stared at Marcus's back.

'I had a lovely night,' Emilie said. 'I spent many hours with my mother and my aunt. We shared many stories.' She squinted to see her mother beyond him. 'Did we not, Mama?'

Her mother didn't answer, just examined Emilie's face.

Emilie turned straight into his gaze. She could see the faint hint of blue under his eyes, the dark lashes with a wisp of curl at the end, and the deep brown below them.

'I'm glad you didn't have to wait on an errant brother.' His voice softened. 'In fact, I cannot imagine you easily waiting on someone.'

Her mother humphed in accord.

Emilie swivelled to her. 'It's very true. And has been almost an abomination to my family. My lack of patience, for which I am very sorrowful.' Then she turned to Marcus. 'And for you to oversee a brother is very thoughtful. I'm sure he appreciates it.'

Marcus looked closely at her. 'Nathaniel? My brother, Nathaniel? We love—another short word—each other devotedly and would fight anyone other than ourselves who dared to stab us in the back.'

She shrugged away the words.

Marcus considered the book in her hands. 'You don't seem particularly picky. Not picky at all.'

She examined the volume. 'I'm very much so. Excessively so if you ask anyone who knows me. This is a good selection. Still, it will spend a lot of long periods on the shelf. Where I will place it when not in use.'

'A purchase to last a lifetime, I would presume. Would it be one you would hold close to you for years upon years?'

'Heavens, no. A few months would be the utmost of use I could get from it. Then I will put it away until I skim through it at intervals when needed.' She turned a page. 'My attention would probably be fleeting. That's why it is so particularly good for me. It would improve my creations, not distract me from them.'

'Pick a book, you two, and let us each be on our way,' her mother grumbled.

'I have chosen mine,' Marcus said, raising his chin. He tapped the book he still held. 'I have decided.' His chin jutted out. 'And I challenge you to pick the best and prove to yourself that your skill means more to you than a book does.'

'The best?' She waited, ignoring the sounds of the other patrons.

'Yes. The best book for you. Why settle for anything else? Pick a story that you can read tonight.'

'Tonight? You suggest I should read tonight?'

'Well, you didn't read much last night.'

'No. I didn't.'

'If you had planned to read last night, then you should plan the same again tonight. In the same place, at the same time.'

Her mother marched around Marcus and seized the tome in Emilie's hands.

'Lord Grayson,' Lady Catesby said, and tapped the book against her palm. 'My daughter will be with me and her aunt tonight until they creep away to pretend to read, then I'm sure they'll talk *ad infinitum* about shades of sunsets and Emilie will arise in the morning with a smudge of colour on her cheek that she received from *reading*.'

Marcus stared at Emilie and it was as if he could see beyond her into the indecision and the woman and into the little girl she'd once been and all the moments in between, except he could see no moments that she spent with the paints.

He could see the woman she could become.

The true masterpiece. The princess he would have given a kiss to freely if he had but known the possibilities of them.

The hiss of her mother shoving the book on to the shelf broke their gaze.

'We are leaving now and we are leaving London tomorrow, Lord Grayson, so we must bid you farewell. Really, farewell.' Lady Catesby's shoulders rose and she scowled at both of them.

'Miss Catesby, this is your last chance,' Marcus said, lifting the volume in his hand.

Her mother angled her chin at Marcus. 'I am sure there will be many, many good books in the world for my Emilie Marie. Books that she might read in the light of day. With a chaperon present.' She grabbed Emilie by the arm and rushed her out of the shop.

Chapter Eight

Marcus felt like a virgin. One to be used for sacrificial purposes. But he could still cancel their plans. And likely Emilie would not show up, or likely she would. Either way, he lost the gamble.

He sighed. That was not the way to wager with a future. You should never stack the cards so that it would be impossible to win.

Lady Semple had agreed to hold her card game at his residence and he could send Emilie packing and tell Lady Semple not to proceed as directed.

The women were happily making wagers in the main sitting room on the floor above and he'd noticed a heightened sense of laughter in the room. The women likely didn't have faith in Lady Semple's excuse of rotting carcases of volumes of rats killed by arsenic and trapped in the walls of her house, particularly as they had been meeting there for years and he doubted they'd seen as much as a paw print.

Normally, such a change in plans would not have led them to Marcus's bachelor dwelling. And when they arrived, as Marcus had requested, the ladies had fluttered like flies detecting a stench, to Nathaniel, which had removed him quickly.

Now the clock ticked and Marcus waited.

But he couldn't postpone Emilie's visit. He could not stop himself.

Robert leaned on the billiards table, ankles crossed, and stared at him. 'I will be at the door to answer it for you, even if I cast up my accounts along the way and fall to the rug pained beyond belief, and have to claw myself forward, fingertips bloodied from the efforts. I will do as you ask.'

'Go now. Before I help you obtain those bloodied fingertips. Take Miss Catesby's bonnet when she arrives and her cloak, but don't put them away as she may change her mind and leave. And if she does not leave, ask the ladies upstairs if they might have heard an intruder. Lady Semple will take over.'

'I feel ill.' Robert lightly fisted his hand to inspect his nails.

'And if Miss Catesby leaves, you are to see her quietly and safely to her address, and perhaps warn her about the debauchery of the males in this household and every other male's residence in London.'

'I would die of old age before I finished that conversation,' Robert grumbled, departing.

In the dim light, Marcus turned away from the door and lowered his shoulders, hands on the billiards table.

Minutes crawled by, much like they had the night before.

A creak alerted him that he wasn't alone and a soft whisper caused him to spin in her direction.

'Marcus?' The delicate tone of her word unfurled desire deep within him.

The valet showed Emilie in and then he retreated, leaving them alone.

'The light is dim in here. Do you have a brighter lamp—or several?' she asked.

'What were you planning last night, Emilie?'

'I surmised that if I and Mr Westbrook were to be caught in an embrace, and if the entire staff were awoken, and you were told, the event would be spread throughout London. The word would then get about to your father and that could lead to a marriage. You know. Compromise him.'

'Before he spoke the vows, he would have forgotten them. He likely wouldn't have agreed anyway.'

'I realised that. I also debated whether being

ruined would be beneficial to me. But I could not do it.'

'What about…a proposal from someone you've bewitched so that your non-existent flaws appear invisible?'

'I have no time or patience to find that man, nor your confidence it would work easily. I must get my paints back. My mother has taken them and refuses to release them to me.'

'Rather drastic of her.'

'Yes.' She turned, her focus past Marcus's shoulder. 'I do have a reputation to protect,' she said. 'Of a hoyden. Of a rebellious painter. Of a spinster. I yearn to make my mark on the world. And having a man forced to marry me would certainly embellish the reputation.'

'You have thought ahead.'

'Not far.'

'I would agree.'

'I would like the world to accept that a man could be carried away by passion for me.' She put her palms together. 'I know it is farfetched.'

'Less farfetched than a man who might not be carried away by passion at the sight of you.'

His voice caused more vibrations inside her than any thunder that had ever shaken her, and added a swirl of warmth she'd never experienced before.

'I did not believe you to be so kind.'

'How could I not? Seeing all those books earlier in the day gave me a new appreciation for art and the people who pursue it. This discussion intrigues me.'

He bowed. 'It would be an honour for me to compromise you, Miss Catesby.'

She shifted, recognising only the opportunity of never again having the feeling of needing another person to accept her. No man would, and she'd be freed from the marriage mart. 'That is indeed sympathetic of you to say, but would you be willing for the world to know?'

'I have a reputation as well. It would certainly fit with my plans. Besides, my father is rather urging me much like your mother is impelling you. He's threatening to get a solicitor to break my grandfather's will and delay the funds I receive annually. Father had the impression that I would marry if I bought a town house. A conversation in which I concurred, but I did not set an end date.'

He negotiated around the billiards table, decreasing the distance between them. 'And there is the worst threat of all. If I do not marry soon, he is saying that he will move in with me.'

She raised her hand so that the side of her glove brushed his chest. 'I understand.'

'Yes, he wants the big wedding breakfast with the banns being read and the proper details all being put in place. And he'd rather presumed I'd marry a daughter of one of London's peers.'

'Well, my uncle is a duke. But I have lived outside London and I don't do well in society.'

He touched the small of her back, pressing her nearer. 'That's close enough.'

'A wedding wouldn't suit me. I'm afraid a husband will not respect my necessities after we marry. To be ruined is perhaps the safest course.'

He remained silent.

She warmed as if he held her in a close embrace.

'Will tonight work for you…to be compromised?' he asked.

She didn't acquiesce or disagree, hardly believing Marcus was willing to grant her such a favour.

His fingers trickled down her back as he increased the distance between them, stopping an arm's length away. 'I worried about you last night.'

The softness in his eyes penetrated her and silenced the world. 'You know where I am now.'

He kept his voice low, the rumbles of it caressing her from the inside out. 'Jump off the cliff and fall into my arms, and see where it will take us.'

'What if you get more than you bargained for and less than you hope for?'

'You have raised the stakes. That always makes the gamble more enticing.' His smile could have been straight from the wickedest man in London. 'I've never gambled in a high-risk game, until I met you.'

'I've never wagered with funds,' she said, glimpsing at him from beneath her lashes. 'But I've already lost what is near and dear to me— the purpose I have. The true reason for living.'

'That is a lot to lose.'

'Should we have more light in the room?'

He shook his head. 'We can see well enough to know what we're doing.' He unbuttoned his waistcoat, starting from the bottom and working his way to the top.

She didn't speak, but her contemplation didn't leave his hands.

Then he slipped the waistcoat away.

He touched the cravat and slid the length of the linen from the knot, and tossed it to the table. He grasped at his shirt and pulled the hem from his trousers, letting it dangle at his hips. His shirt collar fell open and so did her mouth.

He paused.

'In the interest of my lack of experience,' she whispered, 'might, for a second, you continue?'

He didn't move. He really did not want to be naked when Lady Semple barged in.

She raised her brows, questioning him again.

'The shirt? Only the shirt. It's a lot to ask. And I will tell no one.'

She bit her lip. 'I understand if it is an inconvenience for you to take off your shirt in front of me. I didn't mean any disrespect. But I may never, ever get a chance like this again. I'm fairly certain I won't.'

He reached up and grabbed his shirt by the tails and pulled it over his head.

She squeaked as he put the shirt aside.

She had fisted her hands and pumped them upwards, gloves covering the length of her arms, and she laughed to the heavens.

'Oh, my word. Michelangelo got Moses's shoulders right.' She fanned herself. 'It was not imagination. It was accuracy. You are a cross between David and Moses, with the best parts of each.'

He moved closer and saw tears forming.

She sniffed. 'Thank you. You may put your shirt back on. And again, thank you. Some day I will find a way to get a plaster cast of shoulders like yours.'

Instantly, he slipped his shirt back on.

'You may leave,' he said. 'Or stay and face the consequences. I'd prefer you to remain.'

She pressed her lips together and marched closer.

'I am here to be compromised, without benefit of marriage. It's marriage or ruin, for me. Just ruin me and we will always be…well, we will be much friendlier than we have been in the past. You do have an exceptionally nice build.'

'If that happened, and you were to leave, your family would not let you stay in London. I'd never see you again.'

'It's not that I want you to actually ruin…ruin me—' Emilie cleared her throat. 'I require the appearance of it. You will refuse to marry me. I will be disgraced. I will be happy. No one will ever ask me to wed. And you will have your reputation as a careless scoundrel enhanced.' She sighed. 'I don't imagine you would like being married to me. And it might prevent your father from pushing you, if he sees how close you came to making a mistake with me as a future partner. Bringing an artist—a female one—into the family might cause consternation. It does with my relatives.'

He had been so right about Emilie and so wrong. His soul collapsed from the weight of a thousand flickers of light joining together to slam him to the cold ground. She didn't want him for his title or his money, but would have happily accepted a plaster cast of his shoulders.

'That is unacceptable. Not the proposal for me. I need a wife. I thought we had decided at Hatchards that you needed a book to keep at hand—when not shoved into the shelf gathering dust.'

'But me?' She lowered her voice. 'Marcus. I have just studied a man's chest and asked for the room to be brightened first. I am not a future countess. I am an artist and it is closer to a courtesan than a countess.'

'Leave or marriage. Those are my terms.'

'I don't understand.'

'I will explain it.' He contemplated her and moved his gaze across her lips.

He moved forward. 'Might I give you one small kiss?'

'Most certainly. I would be crushed if you did not.' She touched her glove above the row of lace that edged the top of her bodice, her fingertips nestling near her neck.

Marcus closed the distance between them without feeling his own movement. He took her glove as if to bring it to his lips for a kiss, but instead, he moved, as if in a waltz, and slowly twirled her in a half-pirouette, turning her away from him, and stopped her with the back of her head at his chin. His hand held hers, resting below her collarbone.

She swept her left hand up and rested it beside his clasp.

The delicate hint of soap and the warmth of Emilie surrounded him. He savoured the feel of her back against him. Their hands so close above her breasts. His arms around her.

He slid his hand down the length of her arm and stopped at her elbow, his fingers resting at the edge of doeskin and lingering on her. He slid the glove away and tossed it to the table, aware of the soft sound as it landed on the wood.

The warmth of her against him ignited his senses, hardening him.

For a moment his arm rested over her, holding her closer, and his touch lingered on her hand, before releasing it, and she rested her palm at her side.

'One kiss,' he whispered, his breath moving the tendrils that had escaped. 'One small kiss.'

Then with the barest movement, he brought his lips close to her neck and inhaled the bouquet of her, letting his lips touch her as he exhaled, and he gave a tender kiss to her skin, tasting beauty, and he lifted his mouth away, but remained so close that his cheek caressed hers and he could scent her rosewater perfume.

Her skin reminded him of passion and pushed her femininity into the deepest recesses of his being. His knees weakened, but it didn't matter. He didn't need them to stand. With her in his arms, he could keep aloft merely from the hint of her hair brushing him.

Then he used his opposite hand to slowly remove her other glove and he tossed it to the table.

'Perhaps marriage is a solution,' he said and his hands slid to the small of her waist, holding the fabric, but not feeling any cloth at all.

She felt delicious.

He no longer needed anything if he could keep her in his arms.

She rested in his hands and he held her against him, his skin responding with a heat that didn't burn, but urged.

Marcus edged back, forcing as much control as he could manage. At least he could still command his voice. 'Emilie,' he whispered. 'Perhaps we should reassess. A proper courtship. The usual route.'

'In the light of day, a courtship will not happen,' she whispered. 'My father is a cleric. He will whisk me out of London if he realises I am in contact with you because he will say that you're Avondale's eldest son and far above me. He has gout or he would have brought me to London himself. He insisted Mother watch me close.'

She pleaded with him, 'You do not understand my life at all. I must have the daylight and this is the night. My father will disapprove.'

'Then… You need to be dishevelled.'

He reached for her hair with one hand and took out a pin, flicking it to the floor, and then another, and with utmost delicacy, he slipped his fingers between a silken strand and wove it free, placing it along her neck, fanning the hair into even more tendrils and caressing the skin beneath.

He led her to the far side of the table, then lifted her by the waist so that she sat on top of it. He moved closer, bending, his lips near hers, hands still holding her.

'Pardon me,' he whispered. 'It will be more convincing this way.' He moved the fabric of her skirt up, stopping when the fabric reached her knees. He put his cheek against hers.

She gripped the muscles of his upper arms and her mind ceased working. The thin shirt was no barrier. The flood of sensations halted everything but the raging feelings caused by their contact.

He tasted her lips and dipped his tongue inside, tasting and savouring, because he couldn't help himself and then he pulled back slightly and rested his forehead on her shoulder, his eyes tightly closed. She should not taste sweeter than any confection—warm as the sunshine on a summer's day and yet with the freshness of raindrops cooling the skies. But she did.

'Marcus,' she whispered into his ear. 'This is enchanting.'

'It's hell,' he said, bumping his head against her shoulder. 'There is no other description I know.'

'You must refuse to marry me when the chaperon enters,' she said.

'You must not count on that. I could not do such a thing to anyone discovered in such a way as we will be. Miss Catesby, we are going to regret this.'

She ran her fingers through his hair. 'Not all of it.'

'No. Not all of it.' He caressed her closer. 'This is insanity,' he whispered, 'and you are fully aware of it.'

'I know,' she said. She wound her arms around his neck. She whispered, 'You find me desirable, after all. I would never have guessed.' She hugged him close and he ran his fingers up the buttons of her dress, feeling the woman beneath, and his fingers twisted over the top button, flicking it open before he could stop himself.

The door opened. Inwardly he pronounced them married and he pulled her protectively into his arms. He kissed his bride's hair.

'Emilie.' He heard the feminine voice and turned. But it wasn't Lady Semple, but Lady Beatrice. So much for the careful plans he'd made.

'My innocent Emilie,' Beatrice stated again, increasing the drama in her voice. 'I have failed you.'

The woman continued as if she could see a grand audience. She raised her chin high and orated, 'And, when I tell her father, sir, you will be aware that you must ask him for her hand in marriage.'

He still didn't speak.

'I am sorry,' Emilie whispered. 'But we have been discovered.'

He didn't speak, but gazed at Emilie.

'Mr Westbrook. Are you prepared to do the right thing?' Beatrice shouted at him.

Marcus swore to himself. He cleared his throat and turned slightly, staring at the woman.

'Mr Westbrook. You will be searching out her father in the morning, asking for Emilie's hand in marriage.'

He didn't speak. Patiently waiting. He didn't favour his brother that much. The woman needed to open her eyes. He moved away, discreetly whisking Emilie's skirt in place.

Soon he might have to introduce himself. He should have carried a calling card.

Marcus coughed, trying to pull her attention to him. Blast it, Robert wandered in behind her, with one of those drunken grins he'd so perfected.

Then Beatrice paused and he heard the door open wider.

'Emilie,' she commanded. 'Come with me now. And you, Mr Westbrook, will have to explain this to her father.'

Emilie sniffed. 'This is Lord Grayson.'

Beatrice stared. 'It's Mr Westbrook.'

'No,' Emilie whispered. 'I mentioned Mr Westbrook yesterday. When I told you of the change of date, I forgot to tell you of the change in persons.'

Lady Semple moved into view and elbowed her way to Lady Beatrice. She handed the woman a lamp, gave her a push and Lady Beatrice tumbled inside, holding the light aloft.

'It is Lord Grayson.' Lady Semple spoke from behind.

Puzzlement was in Lady Beatrice's voice. 'Are you sure? They are hard to distinguish.'

Emilie put one hand on the table and turned a sideways squint at Lady Beatrice. 'Lord Grayson.'

He heard more feminine murmurs from beyond the door. 'Yes. It is Lord Grayson.'

She turned to Lady Beatrice. 'But you can forget all about the wedding. I am compromised. Ruined. Finished in society.'

Emilie put her fingertips to her forehead,

raised her chin and recited, 'I shall die alone. A spinster.'

'Not a chance,' Lady Beatrice said. 'You're going to be married.'

Marcus reached out, snagged Emilie by the waist and propped her on her feet. 'I have the special licence under the lamp. A stableman will collect the cleric. He has been alerted to await a visit.'

Lady Beatrice clasped both hands together at her breast. 'Emilie, he is so organised.'

'I am to be compromised, not organised,' Emilie hissed to Lady Beatrice. 'We discussed it. You are betraying me.'

'I do not remember any discussion at all,' Lady Beatrice said, lips firming after she spoke. 'And I am so fortunate I happened to see you leave and so very unfortunate that I could not stop you.' She mimicked Emilie's earlier downcast air. 'Lord Grayson is the one to reap the rewards in marriage to you.'

'I will be unmarried all of my days. That's for the best.'

'Not so quick, Emilie. My dear, you have managed to catch the eye of one of the most confirmed bachelors I have ever come across. And, forgive me…' Lady Beatrice cornered Emilie '…he is not without pleasant features— and has an inheritance due him. You could do worse and I could not see how anyone could do better.'

Then she turned and waved an arm in a grand gesture, saying to Lady Semple, 'Can you please bring the lamp closer? Lord Grayson has his shirt on inside out. Does that convince everyone here that virtuous Emilie has been compromised and is to be married?'

Lady Semple's friends murmured in harmony.

'You are a traitor.' Emilie faced Lady Beatrice. 'I am not to be given to the highest bidder.'

'No, my dear,' Lady Beatrice said. 'You are going to the bidder you captured. You should not have changed affections so easily,' she scolded. She turned to glare at him. 'You are positive you are not Mr Westbrook?'

'I am not Nathaniel.'

Blast it. Nate was taller than him. And even in the shadows it should be apparent they were not the same.

'One man will have Emilie and I will be that man.' He closed the distance between Emilie and himself. 'We are betrothed.'

'You don't understand.' She shifted away from him. 'I need to be alone to paint. A wife is not what suits me. I'm an artist. Nothing will come before that.'

Like a sea parting in front of him and giving him the choice to stand for ever and risk drowning under the waves, he paused and considered his words. Considered what he would be agreeing to in order to have her as a partner for life. 'I give you my word, you will not be prevented from painting.'

The light reflected the softening of her features as she absorbed his words. 'Paint? Truly?'

A blink gave her the assurance of his promise.

'I suppose…' her words started slowly '…that I am to be married.' Shoulders arched, she touched her palms together. 'Quickly. As I have missed my landscapes so.'

She skimmed the room, observing the other women who'd moved in and made a cluster around them. She repositioned herself at his side. 'It is as if the statues in Italy inspired his form. Is he not the most pleasing man?'

Marcus heard approval from every woman in the room.

'Oh, heavens, no,' a masculine voice inserted, sauntering in from the hallway. Nathaniel. 'I'm an inch taller than him and it was all put to good use.'

Nathaniel bowed to Emilie. 'So, my Amelia has a new sweetheart.'

Marcus stared at his brother. 'We are deeply in love.'

'Ah, deeply.' Nathaniel patted a hand at his heart. Tears glistened, but not tears of sadness.

'I feel I should be the one angry.' He sniffed, and the corners of his mouth proved he wasn't crying. 'As you have stolen my sweeting right from under my nose. I knew something was going on, I could not figure out what you were up to. I returned to find out.'

'Whose name is on the special licence?' Beatrice asked.

'Not mine.' Nathaniel raised both hands briefly, palms out. Then ambled over to the paperwork, picked up the licence, read it and looked around. 'Who is Emilie Marie Catesby?'

Marcus took one stride and snapped the paper out of his brother's hand. 'No one you know.' Then he peered at Emilie while speaking to Nathaniel. 'I'd like to introduce you to the future Lady Grayson.'

'Is this not the event of the Season?' one of Lady Semple's friends concluded. 'And such a coincidence he had the licence prepared.' She laughed. 'And we were invited.'

'They are deeply devoted to each other,' Lady Semple said. 'And have secretly been meeting for years. Years.'

Marcus's head swivelled to her.

'Well.' Lady Beatrice's bracelet jangled as she spoke. 'All those nights she stayed with me, many, many nights, I strongly suspect Lord

Grayson was collecting her by the back entrance.'

'So romantic,' one of the ladies said. 'I foresee a long and happy marriage.'

Emilie agreed. 'As do I. With much painting as Lord Grayson appreciates my art.'

'Of course,' Marcus said, supposing he appreciated it as much as any man did who could not see the colours of it and found it tedious.

Chapter Nine

She stole a glimpse at him and noticed the line of his forehead. He had a perfect profile. His nose sloped gently. His nostrils were not prominent. The chin was proportioned well. Even his earlobes would be good to sketch.

She stared at his earlobe. Memorising. Such perfection. She wondered if the other ear matched as perfectly as it must. Even if it didn't, she could always draw him from this side.

She studied Marcus's skin—gauging the hue variations. She could see the faint touch of paleness where he had shaved, mixed with the dark hint of stubble beneath the skin. The crease at the side of his mouth that hadn't been there in the night. That would not do. He must not ruin his appearance.

He turned to her and destroyed the evenness of his features. His eyes narrowed.

She realised everyone was silent. Even the cleric.

She faced the cleric. His eyebrows were raised and he examined her as if he awaited something. He said slowly, 'Do you take this man…?'

'Of course,' she insisted, loudly. 'Of course I do.'

How could anyone who'd ever studied Marcus's features ask such a question?

The cleric let out a sigh and continued. He spoke much too rapidly. And, she noticed a bead of sweat on his brow. The poor man was taking this much too gravely.

She did hope he would hurry. She'd been awake until encountering Marcus, then everyone had had to gather—except her father who couldn't travel quickly enough to be there for the wedding, but she hoped he would arrive for the breakfast.

She'd never been awake until dawn, but Marcus had insisted they wait on Avondale and he'd claimed his father would take his time arriving. He'd been correct.

Her mother was dazed.

Beatrice had sketched a caricature of Emilie, her mother and Marcus before the wedding and everyone had their arms folded across their chests.

Marcus's mother had sent a note declining to

attend, saying she must scurry to provide the best wedding breakfast possible and would welcome the new couple.

Once Marcus's father had arrived, there had been few greetings as Marcus had put everyone in their places and told the cleric to begin.

Marcus was organised. After they'd met at Hatchards, he'd known he wanted to ask her to marry him and he'd immediately left for the special licence.

Marcus heard not a stir. He felt the tension of the moment had invaded the room when Emilie was asked if she would take him for her husband.

When she had not answered the question, he had been certain she was going to reject the marriage. She was going to announce to one and all that she was going to live alone the rest of her days.

He had turned to her, expecting a demon in a woman's dress, and instead she had been intently staring at him, lips parted. A dazed look on her face. Then she had viewed the poor cleric as if he were addled to question whether she planned to marry.

Chairs and feet shuffled behind him, along with gentle snores from one of Lady Semple's friends. Several guests sighed and he might have done the same.

All he wished for in that instant was a bottle of wine, laughing lips and gentle arms to hold him and he felt that he had taken all those from himself, except the wine. And that was what he wanted least, but even now that would be welcome.

The floor of the sitting room should have opened and swallowed him. Or, the wine he had taken before she arrived would have put him into a deep sleep. But the biggest occurrence, he supposed, to nudge him into matrimony, was when Emilie had once suggested they duel at dawn.

The clock struck six as the cleric pronounced them married.

One of Lady Semple's friends sniffled. 'So lovely,' he heard her say. 'And I helped bring them together.'

Nathaniel began waving the group to the door. 'Let us be on our way and everyone is invited to the breakfast. Eleven? Mother is arranging it now and sending for friends and relatives far and wide. Assuming the world is still here, we'll meet then.'

Everyone went their separate ways, then Nathaniel returned. 'Mother insists my help is needed and Father is rushing to make sure he gets the wedding breakfast of his dreams. You've placed a strain on him, big brother, but we Westbrooks are up to the task. Farewell to you both. I'm going to help Mother now. I'll fetch my clothing later so I can stay with Mother after the wedding so the two of you may get better acquainted.'

He thumped his brow with the heel of his palm. 'Blast it, I forgot. I forgot you two have been meeting secretly for years right under my nose in this house and all over London and it very much escaped me.' He chortled, leaving them alone.

'It's the two of us now, Emilie, for the rest of our lives.' Marcus stood in front of her.

'Us?' She rubbed one side of her neck, then the other. Then her shoulders wavered. 'Us? Just us?' She turned away, but kept her gaze on him. 'You make that sound like a rather seriously long period.'

He put both hands out to hold her steady. 'I fear it will be. I hope it will be.'

'Us and art.'

Marcus remained silent.

'But you have no trouble with my painting?'

'None whatsoever.' He thrust away the unspoken concerns that flared inside him.

Her chest expanded as she inhaled. Tendrils of hair hung loose. 'Marcus, you are the best husband I could ever aspire to. But, I wonder if you can be happy?'

He touched a kiss on her forehead. 'I fear only one of us can be at a time.'

'I'm not very good at taking turns,' she said.

'Neither am I.'

'I'm not worried about it. You are the absolute most perfect husband for me, Marcus. I know that. So far, I have found marriage to be all I expected.' Emilie wriggled as if trying to squirm out from her uncomfortable dress.

'It would not take much for it to be all I expected.'

Then he moved his hands to her and held her face as he put his mouth against hers and dipped his tongue inside and tasted her. One would imagine only words of love from those lips.

She softened.

He held himself back from her and used one finger to trace her nose and the outline of her lips, and used the feeling to calm his own stormy emotions. 'Emilie. What have we done?'

Her eyes were wide, her mouth still open from his kiss.

'We simply married. It's not as if I intend to cause you grief, Marcus. I plan to be a perfect spouse.' She paused. 'Especially as you are of the same mind that my painting must come first. I'll get moved into your residence and direct which things I need to be moved here.'

She patted her hands together. 'I plan to be as organised as you are, Marcus.'

Emilie tried to control the fear that kept wanting to creep in and tell her that she had done a foolish thing.

In fact, Marcus was a near-perfect man. He understood her need to paint and that it would always come first, and he didn't seem to mind at all.

She realised they were alone and he was her husband and there were certain liberties she should grant him, but he had a gift for removing gloves and a remarkably good form. 'I could never have married anyone if he were not as eye-catching as you are.'

'I appreciate your honesty.' His tone didn't match his words.

'You must not frown so.' She reached up to smooth the lines he'd made beside his eyes. That would not do in a portrait, nevertheless, it could on Marcus. She doubted anyone could render an unpleasing likeness of him.

He rested his forehead against hers, his hands gently at her waist as he pulled her softly against him and his palms moved slowly against her back, caressing, moulding her.

'Soon, I must do some shopping.'

'What must you purchase?' he whispered.

'A new portfolio. Or several.' She sighed into his shoulder. 'I filled one to the edges, and I still have the family book and the sketchbook. Mother will not let me have such a simple purchase.'

He felt her fingertips at his sides and a tiny pull as she tugged at his waist. 'Marcus. I must draw subjects several times before I absorb them. And I thought to get a new portfolio for the flowers of summer.'

'Is that all you think of, Emilie?'

'Marcus, you cannot know how much I ache for my work.'

He took a finger and traced the outline of her lower lip, watching the contrast of his skin against hers. The fullness of her lips entranced him. 'It must feel so lonely inside. Not to have what you need most.'

'Incredibly.' She turned. 'My mother burned one portfolio and would not even let me purchase a new sketchbook. I'm sure you understand. It is like wanting the taste of a confection and you can see it, and it's right in front of you, but you cannot taste it.'

He pushed the words out of his mouth. 'I have no idea what that would be like.'

'Well, I must get my clothing some time today, meet you for the wedding breakfast, then I plan afterwards to buy new supplies.' She yawned.

'Do you mind if I rest on your sofa for a few moments? I've never been awake this long into the morning.'

'We don't have a guest room. There isn't a bedroom unused at present. You may use my bed.'

She hesitated and he saw the realisation blast into her of what they had done. She resembled a man who'd just been shown the noose he would be wearing.

He studied her and increased the distance between them, reassuring her with the separation.

'I'll take Nathaniel's room for now. Fetch what you need.'

She stilled except for a flutter of her bodice as her chest rose. 'When I am shopping for the books, would you like for me to select any materials for you?'

'I have no talent for it. The colours would not work out as needed.'

'It's a blessing few are truly graced with. That would be far too much to aspire to in one man.'

She moved to the sofa, but didn't sit. The wedding night concerned her, but if everyone else managed, she would, too. It was a shame she could not wear gloves in bed because Marcus had a masterful method of removing them.

She imagined a drawing of her gloves draped

over the arm of a chair. Or perhaps…dare she do it? In Marcus's hand.

That would be so decadent. So indecent. So perfect.

Touching where the pulse beat in her neck, she examined Marcus.

'I can request my mother send the things I need to me. I'm not sleepy after all.'

'You can use the carriage and get the purchases tomorrow. All you need. Or you can send a maid for them,' he said. 'But we shall be at my father's for the breakfast.'

'I must thank you again. You have made me complete. I will never again have to worry about anyone coming between me and my talent.' Her sisters would be so envious. And her mother would be preening more than any peahen. 'My parents will be so happy not to concern themselves about me any more and that I have a place of my own to establish and display my endeavours.'

'And you will be happiest of all.'

He moved even further from her reach, a determined look to his profile. 'You have exactly what you searched for.'

He assessed her and she steadied herself by grasping the sofa. She'd never been examined so thoroughly and it wasn't as if he were judging her, but trying to see into her soul.

'I'll provide for you. But never expect me to understand the hues and colours. Long ago, I discovered that I can't comprehend pigments the same as some.' Once more he assessed her. 'I've accepted it. Or will.'

Chapter Ten

As the others began to move to the wedding breakfast tables, Marcus saw Avondale speaking with Mr Catesby. Her father leaned on a cane and everyone chatted pleasantly, although the cleric appeared to be apologising and Avondale's smile didn't fully reach his lips.

His mother had told him that she'd been afraid Emilie might not bear up well under the joy of the day and, from the lines at his mother's mouth, she wasn't bearing up well either.

Nathaniel appeared beside Marcus, sympathetic, and he slapped his brother on the back. 'What a momentous day. For the two of you. Much like any other for me, except… I did attend a joyous occasion earlier and I have the opportunity to welcome a new sister, whom I hear from all quarters you have been courting right in front of me. You cannot imagine the number of times I've let it slip I was in on the secret.'

'Watch your words,' Marcus said.

'I welcome my dear sister into the family. She is after my own heart as well.'

'He keeps it under the cupboard in the kitchen,' Marcus said to Emilie. 'So it will not get damaged.'

'Farewell and, to both of you, my best wishes,' Nathaniel said and ambled away.

Marcus met her gaze and he saw past the innocence to something different beyond. Lady Semple had said Emilie hadn't ever had a beau or ever involved her heart with a suitor.

He'd once concluded himself desperately in love with a lively actress, only to lose interest when she performed in a play as a sorceress. Then he realised he could not trust his heart. But now he suspected that he had been unwise to trust his intellect as well, as Emilie was less suited to marriage than anyone he knew.

He didn't know what he truly felt about Emilie, but marrying her should straighten out his thoughts on that. At the moment he wasn't sure he liked her very much, but she'd always been a sparkle of brightness when other women had been the same shades of drab.

But now he needed to protect her and when he saw the way her lips turned up, he realised he would be protecting both of them. Him, from her. And her, from herself.

Marcus noticed his father, features immobile, watching them. He'd only grumbled a greeting to them at the wedding and been the first to leave.

His father should officially welcome her into the family. Particularly with the many relatives and guests present.

He took her hand, tucked it around his arm. 'Emilie, last night was your turn to be happy. Today, it is mine.'

'I will try to assist,' she said.

When she glanced at him, the tiredness he saw softened his heart. This could not have been easy for her. And to be forced into a mould she didn't fit would feel disastrous. Being in a mould that fit wasn't always grand.

'I'll do my best to convince everyone I will be the perfect woman for you. I owe you that, Marcus, and I will rise to the task.'

'I appreciate that.'

'Lead the way.' She squared her shoulders like Boudicca of old, then exaggerated a wilt of demureness. 'I will follow and make you proud.'

'Then let us meet my father together. He's watching us. Avondale does not like to be overlooked and you will have a difficult time meeting his standards. I suggest you imagine yourself a Lady Macbeth.'

'I liked that play.' She touched his arm, then wove her hand in, connecting them, and sending an awareness of her into him. 'Lead me to him. I am certain Lady Macbeth is an easy role to play.' Then she patted his arm with her other hand, bringing them even closer. 'But I shall be your fair Juliet.'

He could imagine her in that role, too, but if he remembered correctly, it didn't end well for either of the lovers.

'Let us search out our own path.'

'I've met your father before,' she said, one eyebrow lifting, 'and I have heard tales of him. I know what kind of woman he would seek in a daughter-in-law. A society sovereign. I doubt I can ever win him over.'

'Try. If you discover a method that works, let me in on it.'

They walked closer to his father and the brows turned downward.

'Father, you've met my Emilie, haven't you?' Marcus gave a nod to Emilie and faced the frost flowing from Avondale without a flinch.

His father's smile appeared briefly only to be replaced by an opposite turn of the lips. 'The lovely lady with whom you will be establishing a family.' The words sounded forced, which didn't surprise Marcus. His father could have easily faked acceptance of Emilie, but it suited him better to exude coldness.

Emilie gave him a greeting, then added, 'I'm

so honoured to be a part of your esteemed family. It was beyond even the greatest expectation I could ever have to catch the notice of someone such as Marcus.'

His glare relaxed, but his chin was at the top of the flagpole and hardly likely to ever be lowered.

'You do not have to worry about me making him unhappy,' she said. 'I yearn for him to have the absolute greatest happiness. I would say we will have a traditional marriage. I…' she touched a hand to her heart '…will of course stay in the background, alone, while Lord Grayson goes about conversing at his clubs. I would not want to irritate him.'

His father opened his mouth and squinted. 'The noise of the guests is so loud—I didn't hear you.'

She moved closer and Marcus heard nothing else but her next words. 'I would hope not to irritate Lord Grayson—' She leant closer still, intent on her speech.

His father's lips tightened. 'I think you should discount that as a possibility. I have given up on that with all my three children and my wife. You should know that Westbrooks, either by birth or marriage, are easily irritated.'

She waved his words away with a gloved hand. 'I am aware that Lord Grayson must have his role. He is of the peerage. Marriage will not be a surprise to me. I would not tie my husband to my corset, or expect him to anticipate my every whim. I am an artist.'

His father blinked, the usual way he had of dealing with an errant servant. 'I am hoping we will be so blessed as to have a grandson soon. The sooner the better.' Marcus's father studied Emilie, then raised a brow. 'I am under the impression it is a possibility.'

She started to speak, then briefly looked at Marcus before beaming at his father. 'I have contemplated that. Motherhood is a noble endeavour. I would like to have one child soon, perhaps another one to follow along shortly behind.' She inclined in his direction. 'Are there, perhaps, twins in your family? I'm not sure I'm up to that, but it would be a magnificent accomplishment.'

Turning to Marcus, she said, 'Wouldn't that be glorious? Two cherubs to start with. And if they are boys, we will be certain that your father is a strong influence in their lives. I want them to grow up as you are.'

His father's eyes narrowed again.

She lowered her voice, speaking to Avondale. 'We will, of course, want the firstborn son to be named after you, but not so close in name as to get you both confused. Perhaps you and Marcus can come up with some suitable names and

I could leave that to the two of you. A lovely surprise for me. Wouldn't that be grand?' She shrugged slightly. 'I would not mind a daughter, you understand. But I strongly believe, with my disposition, sons would be the best fit.'

'You would let Marcus and me choose the name of the firstborn?'

She blinked and he wondered if she even knew she did that almost exactly as his father had. 'I would suppose so. After all, I am sure you had something to do with naming Marcus and Nathaniel, and their names do them proud.'

He grumbled.

'And what is your mother's name?' she asked.

'Cleone.'

She contemplated him. 'Would that be a suitable name for any daughters Marcus and I might have?'

'Perhaps not.'

'I will not give it any more contemplation then. It is rather putting the cart before the horse as I much anticipate sons.'

She glanced over Avondale's shoulder. 'Now I must speak with my mother. She's thrilled at having Marcus in her family and I do want to hear the many praises she is going to heap upon your family's lineage.'

Marcus and his father remained silent as she departed, then the Duke of Kinsale captured

Avondale's attention and the two engaged in comparisons over who was most pleased concerning the event.

Across the garden, Emilie and her mother spoke, heads close together. Cannon fire might have interrupted their attention, but he doubted it.

Emilie crossed her arms in such a way her breasts swelled upwards, while she spoke with her mother. True ladies of the *ton* did not cross their arms in public, but Emilie would do things her own way. He felt like loosening his cravat, nabbing Emilie's arm and making a run for it. The night had been long. No groom should have to endure a wedding breakfast.

Nathaniel appeared at Marcus's side again, this time with a glass filled to the brim.

They both watched Emilie.

'She is a puzzle, lost in her own games and her fascinations,' Nathaniel muttered. 'I do not envy you. Or understand you. I give you my best wishes, however, on your future.'

'Thank you.' Marcus reached to take the glass from his brother's hand.

'I've shared so many humorous anecdotes with everyone regarding your courtship that I amazed myself.' Nathaniel scrutinised his drink. 'You two are thoroughly over the moon for each other, in case you were wondering.'

'Give me a few days alone while I sort out the situation.'

'Situation?' Nathaniel sipped his wine. 'That sounds accidental. But I swear I remember the past year listening night after night when you quoted innumerable verses to her name.'

'Yes. I was eloquent.'

Nathaniel sobered. 'I had no idea it was truly you she was after. As she partnered me the other night, I could have sworn I was in her mind for an encounter.' He watched Emilie. 'I told her a ridiculous story and she laughed, and no one laughs at that jest who isn't foxed. I imagine she was attempting to make you jealous.'

Marcus's teeth locked. She'd cosied up to Nate. He'd known it. But it didn't matter. That was over. Done. Nate didn't even know she'd selected him. And Marcus would lock it out of his mind and forget all about it.

'I concede defeat.' Nathaniel held his own glass up to Marcus's. Glasses clinked.

Nathaniel lowered his voice confidentially. 'Her sisters have arrived and I have been talking with them. I am taken with each of them, although I am not sure yet what their names are. They are all lovely.'

'Keep those musings to yourself.' Marcus gave a soft backhand to his brother's arm. 'Neither her father nor our own will accept another quick union today.'

'I have no expectations of those eternal ties.' Nathaniel took out a handkerchief and gave an exaggerated mop across his brow. 'I fear it would be the death of me.' He handed his glass to Marcus, then folded his handkerchief, putting it in his pocket.

Marcus returned the drink to him. 'I don't doubt you. How many days ago did I have no marriage in my future?'

'That special licence did not appear by itself.' Nathaniel took a hearty swallow, emptying the liquid. 'You must have been entirely too angry at Father.'

Marcus pressed his lips together, then gave a sideways glimpse at his brother, unwilling to discuss his true feelings. 'I was bored and tried to conclude what I had already experienced and what I didn't yet have. The choices were narrowed to a castle or matrimony and I knew of no castles to be had.'

'Nonsense. You're jesting again. You and I could have found a way to build a castle. Much easier than marriage from what I've heard.' He tapped the empty glass. 'Don't worry about tripping over me. I will locate some woman who will understand how I have been thrust into the streets and will offer me shelter.'

'Let me speak with Father. I may want you to stay and I may move.'

Nathaniel raised his eyebrows. 'You *will* have a little more trouble getting a woman to accept you've been displaced tonight.' He smiled. 'Tomorrow, yes. Tonight, no.'

'I'll leave in a few days.'

'If it is to Mother's, it might work. If you plan to live with Father, you'll disrupt his latest relationship. He usually has a new one every year or so.'

Marcus didn't speak.

'One other small thing,' Nathaniel added, 'you might need to be aware of before you talk with Father. When I told him of the marriage this morning, he asked if he was going to have a grandchild. Apparently, Robert has assured him of your deep longing to litter the landscape with little replicas of yourself, and now, for your safety, we have convinced Father that the woman has told you a child is on the way. You might want to break the news to her.'

Marcus moved sideways and stared at his brother.

'Oh, oh.' Nathaniel shifted his feet, increasing the distance between them. 'No fisticuffs permitted on your wedding day.'

Marcus spoke through clenched teeth, keeping his tone low so no one could overhear. 'Father will be furious at both her and me. Believing her duplicitous and me duped. I'll have to convince him otherwise or he will hold it against her.'

'Let him have his joy now and perhaps you can confuse him that eight or so months have passed when it is actually a year. That is the plan I would go for.' He turned to the refreshment table.

'Which immediately causes me to discount it,' Marcus said.

Nathaniel whipped around. 'Unless you do have a child on the way. You big brother, you. You example-setter. You married man.' He coughed, turning away. 'Almost choked on that last one. Hope it's easier for you to swallow.'

'No.'

'Let us pray for a miracle and you'll convince Father it takes some women ten or twelve months to deliver a child. You had best keep planning ahead.'

'I have no plan for tonight,' he said, 'but sleep.'

'Brother,' Nathaniel said as he moved closer to Marcus's side, draping an arm across his shoulders as if he could not imagine having to impart such knowledge. 'You are married. You do not even have to kiss her, but if you're given a treat, it isn't polite to refuse.'

'Nathaniel.' He used his wiser, older-brother voice. 'I do not like to do things halfway.'

'When I marry—if—' Nathaniel said. 'I do not want you to pick out my beloved.' Nathaniel dropped his hand from Marcus's back. 'The woman has addled you beyond repair. Next, you will be staying home alone with a proper night-cap on and scribbling poetry about daffodils. Or picking the petals from them and saying, *She loves me. She loves me not.*'

Nathaniel appraised Marcus and jumped back. 'Calm down. I'm your brother. Bad manners to kill a sibling today. You must wait.' He sped away to another guest.

Marcus surveyed the people milling in the garden, but his attention roamed until it stopped at his father, knocking back another glass. He'd probably had enough to be in a softened frame of mind.

Before Marcus could move half the distance to his father, someone gripped his arm.

He turned to see Tilly smiling up at him. He remembered her from their childhood. She was at Beatrice's first wedding breakfast as well, only she was permitted to be with the adults and they were the same age. She had dismissed him as they'd passed in the hallway, but later recalled him fondly at soirées.

As he turned to her, her touch didn't drop away, but she pulled herself closer to him.

The years had enhanced the girl he remembered. He took in the coiffure which seemed too thick to easily stay in place and the dress which showed her to perfection. Tilly was alluring, but to him, it was much more like the temptation of a deadly viper trying to finesse prey into the right location to trap it.

He recognised the promise she exuded.

'I must give you my salutations on your wedding day,' she said. 'And welcome you into our family and our hearts. My little cousin has done herself, and the family, proud. We are so happy…' She brushed her fingers along his sleeve.

He didn't know what she would have said next, because something pushed against his back and he shifted his feet aside, and Emilie popped into place at his arm.

He noticed the feigned innocence. 'Oh, I am so sorry, Marcus, I fear I couldn't be away from you a moment longer.' She reached to him to be steadied and, as he did, he realised she had moved him from Tilly's touch, and now her own hand rested on his elbow.

For a woman who'd not seemed to mind if he went his own way, she had a firm grip on him.

'Tilly, is not my new husband the most handsome man?' Emilie bunched her shoulders, as if shivering at the prospect of Marcus as a husband.

Marcus watched her. He could see no evidence of acting.

'He is.' Tilly gaped at him with no less fervour than she had shown before. 'But, somehow, I surmised you preferred Mr Westbrook.'

'I wished to make Marcus jealous.' Her lashes fluttered gently. 'I couldn't forget his magnificence.' As she spoke, she moved slightly against him.

'Cousin, you have had no man very deep in your intellect unless it is for someone you plan to use as a model,' Tilly said, daring disagreement.

'My dear husband, Marc, has been there.' Emilie's eyelashes nearly caused enough breeze to fan him.

The adoration disconcerted him.

Emilie filled her lungs, letting the wonder of her good fortune show.

Marcus gazed at his too-serene helpmate and glanced across to the narrowed stare of her cousin.

'And how are you to make me trust such nonsense?' Tilly asked, her mouth twisted into a grimace.

'What difference does it make? We are married.'

Tilly glared at her cousin, not letting go of her topic. 'When did he tell you of his fascination with you?'

'That is an indiscreet question,' Emilie said. 'A tale for only our ears and one we will remember fondly.' Emilie turned her adoration back to him. He ascertained she was making sure he wouldn't dispute her words.

'And the billiards room was not an ambush?'

'We had, perhaps, both presumed we'd be surprised. I did want a wedding that people would remember,' she admitted. 'Did you not hear of the special licence he had ready?' She pivoted in his direction. 'Magnificent.'

'The planning was elaborate,' he said. 'For weeks I had dreamed of nothing else but you at my side.'

Her fingers skimmed her throat.

He pulled her hand to his lips, gave her a kiss and said, 'Sweeting, we should not talk of this. It might make your cousin blush.'

He released her and she turned to Tilly. 'I must be the luckiest woman to have a man such as Marcus. He is handsome. As the elder son, he will inherit his father's lands. He is all a woman could want and, I must say—more.'

She warmed to her subject. 'So many women have conspired to catch his fancy and now to be aware that his affections, his very being…' she touched over her heart '…he has put at my disposal so that I might continue to create the paintings he loves.' She turned to him and devotion shined. 'He so admires my watercolours.'

She smiled, a superior one. 'He married me

because of his rapturous feelings when he admires my works. He adores my art.' She beamed at her cousin. 'Among other things.'

'You have done well, Emilie,' Tilly said, wryly, 'and now I will converse with your mother and let her know how happy you are as she is under the impression that the events were different.'

'I could not share the secret of our fondness for each other,' Emilie said. 'It was dear and I relished having it as my own. We wanted a short betrothal.'

'Are you…?' Tilly inspected the area of Emilie's stomach. 'So you were both forced into marriage by the prospect of a child?'

'No,' Emilie said. 'But, when I have a child, I should hope it has Marc's eyes.'

Marcus took her hand, raised it to his lips and spoke. 'I should hope it has your eyes.'

'I should hope you both don't get your wish and it is limited to two eyes.' Tilly frowned at them both and made her way to Emilie's mother.

Emilie peered at him. 'You are good at this.'

'I'm a husband, now. It's what we do.'

'Ah…' She nodded, swaying against him. 'Now I understand why women are warned about the Westbrook men and why they don't heed it.'

Marcus clamped his teeth together. Westbrook *men*? He would have preferred Emilie to have only referenced him. He didn't like to be reminded that she'd first written to his brother.

He wanted to ask her if it mattered which Westbrook man she'd obtained. But he didn't. A woman, on her wedding day, would be a fool to answer the question with any name other than her husband's.

Or exceptionally honest. And that integrity would certainly darken a wedding celebration.

He caught his father as the older man reached the refreshments. Seeing Marcus, his father grumbled, 'I need this more than you.' His father moved the glass closer to his body. 'But you obviously know the direction to Fortnum & Mason as I have seen the bills.'

'Will you walk with me?' Marcus moved to indicate the path through the middle of the garden and away from the guests.

As soon as they were enough distance from the others, his father stopped and spoke to him.

'You could have chosen anyone, son. Anyone,' the older man said. 'I know she is appealing and, I admit, I'm impressed with her awareness of the traits of males, but her father is a cleric. True, her mother was the old Duke of Kinsale's eldest child and she does have that. But the girl has been raised a cleric's daughter.'

'She is from a good family.'

'So-so.' His father fluttered a hand in front of him and both continued on the path. 'Blast it. You could have done better.'

'I did well enough.'

Both paced along, their hands locked behind their backs.

'No, she is definitely not of good enough family. A backwoods cleric's daughter.' He inspected the sky. 'And even if she is a duke's granddaughter and the current Duke of Kinsale's niece, might I remind you, not every stallion and prize mare produce good offspring.'

'She will be fine, Father, and if not, I will deal with it.' Marcus knew he would be dealing with it.

'She sounded as if she does know what to expect from life. That her eyes are open.'

'My eyes were half-shut as I said my vows.' Marcus heard the truth as he said it. 'I need to open them now so that she and I might truly learn what we are made of. So, I ask you if I might move to Stormhaven where my grandfather was born?' The weight of his marriage loomed heavy in his mind.

He had married on the spur of the moment, the future shrouded to him. It had taken a few minutes of vows and the veil was removed. But he had not been able to risk losing her to anyone else.

'That house? It is nothing but a few sticks.' His father stopped and faced him, exasperation evident. 'I could not let my lowest servant live there. That low-life piece-of-tripe valet of yours will not stand for living in such a place. You will have to leave him behind.'

'I will let him stay at the town house if he so wishes. But I plan to go to my grandparents' old home. I might leave as soon as possible, but I have not discussed it with Emilie.'

'No woman would live in a dung heap such as that.'

'Workmen could make it liveable. It might take years, but I'm up to the task.'

'Son. Have you taken leave of your senses?' His father held Marcus's arm so he couldn't turn away.

'Yes, when I saw a woman at a soirée and I had marriage on my mind, and I could not shake it lose.'

'Forgive me. Forgive me. I shouldn't have done it. I should not have pushed you so hard. I will not do the same with Nathaniel.' He changed course. 'On the other hand... Nathaniel. He should be pushed.'

One thing his father would never learn was how to reverse a decision. How to consider the wishes of others, as well as his own. He'd been taught to put himself first from birth and it was beyond him to do otherwise.

Then Marcus hesitated. Had he not been raised the same as his father?

He contemplated Avondale.

'If I stay here, I will lie with her, I will produce children. I will gamble without caring whether I win or lose as neither affects me. I will spend evenings and nights at gaming clubs. I will find new women to amuse me. That is all the substance I will have.'

'I do not see much wrong with that lifestyle. Many men are happy with it. I am one of them.'

'I want my life to change.' He perused the gardens, hoping he might some day have pride in ones he had planned. 'The past few years have been a blur of revelry that mean nothing to me in the morning. I would like to build more than gambling memories and not lie with women who have their hand in my pocket when they smile at me.'

His father glowered at the grass. 'Obviously you haven't been choosing the right ladies. A woman worth her coin makes sure you never feel her hand when it is in your pocket.'

'It is there, nonetheless.'

His father stopped and raised a brow. 'It is better that the hand be in your pocket than at your throat. Those are the choices a man has when he is deciding between a wife and a mistress.'

'Mother is not like that.'

'Doesn't mean your bride is a retiring miss.'

'Emilie may care for watercolours and drawing and oils, but at least she cares for something. It is not my title or the finances. First, she chose Nathaniel.'

His father put his hand to his forehead. 'I cannot believe you said that.'

'If she were blinded by a title or funds, she would have chosen me.'

'It doesn't matter if a woman is after you for funds or title. You will always have those things. They aren't going away. You have nothing to lose.'

They reached the end of the garden. His father turned, but Marcus reached out a hand to stop him from going back to the breakfast.

'With respect to you, those are important things. They are my heritage. But they are simply heritage. Nothing I can claim as my own creation. An act of birth, nothing more.'

'You would prefer a birth in the stews?' his father groused.

'No. I wish to test my mettle. I wish to be alive. I wish to see what it would be like to create something. To build something. To have earned my place on earth.'

'We can't all be Wellington. Even Wellington didn't start out with all the glory. He once was the Honourable Arthur Wellesley, an earl's son, not the firstborn might I remind you. Nor even the second. You can involve yourself in politics if you want substance. You have a chance to progress into it—it's there for the taking.'

'Before I can make decisions that will influence others' lives, I have to understand what matters. Right now the recommendations I can make to others would detail drinks, theatre and gambling hells.'

'Those are useful experiences. Those are living experiences. You were educated at Oxford. I don't understand what all the bother is about.' He paused. 'Did that valet of yours give you these ideas?'

'No. I have not said such a thing to him as he would possibly leave my employ.'

'I'll tell him.'

'Father.'

'It is that woman, then. She's addled you. She has no sense of the challenges an heir bears and no anticipation of the trials you'll encounter.'

'Emilie has no knowledge of this. I wanted to give her freedom to pursue her passion. Something I do not have and could not give myself. But I could easily give it to her. We've spent few occasions together.' He studied his father's reaction. 'Very few. No true intimacies. None.'

'Blast it.' His father sighed. 'Do you mean that she isn't going to have a child?'

'She isn't.'

'That was my reasoning,' his father said, 'that she had ensnared you with her femininity.' He scowled. 'Marcus, if she has ensnared you in some other way, you are in a mess.'

'I give her the freedom that I cannot give myself.'

'The money to repair your grandfather's lands will cost more than many nights at the gambling table and more than a woman can take from your pocket.'

'You want an heir. Emilie is not with child. I do not have to lie in her bed if I stay here. No heir for you.'

'And I might prance through the twilight wearing a toga.' His father laughed and patted him on the back. 'Are you trying to bargain with me, my son?'

'I am merely musing aloud.'

'When did you begin with these country plans?' his father asked. He examined Marcus.

He told a half-truth. 'Not long ago.' While he'd waited for the cleric, he'd watched her fidget. Some part of her seemed caged. Trapped in herself and in a world that did not fit who she was.

While she'd paced the room, she'd picked up a vase and studied it, browsed at a picture on the wall, meandered through the room again, examined one side of the frame, then picked at a speck of dust on a chair arm, then continued, arms crossed.

The older women had grumbled, asking her to be still, but Lady Semple had taken Emilie's side, hugged her and said her farewells. Lady Semple did not want to be present when the others arrived, particularly his father.

When he'd watched Emilie's restlessness and felt his own, he'd decided it would be best for both him and Emilie to go to the countryside. And if not best for the both of them, then she could stay behind and splatter colours about to her heart's content.

'She didn't beguile you with a siren's tricks?'

'No. She likely tossed her book of siren's tricks into a fire.' All Emilie wanted was a paintbrush, not a husband. 'If her parents hadn't forced her hand, she would never have agreed to the marriage. Which makes me more irritated than I would have believed.' He lowered his voice. 'You could say our families brought us together. A disarranged marriage.'

'Parents.' His father squinted at Marcus, lips grim. 'They keep ruining the lives of their children.'

Marcus chuckled. 'I would agree.'

'Marcus, if you were not the image of me and if your mother were not the woman she is, I would swear you are not my son. What if, underneath the exterior of this artist, you discover a heartless woman who grows more detestable as the days pass? Not everyone has your mother's tolerance and, remarkable woman that she is, I can hardly endure her.'

'Tolerance,' Marcus said. 'Mother obtained it by sheer force of her strength.'

His father didn't answer.

'Do you mind that I'm not planning to follow your path?' Marcus watched his father.

'No.' He laughed. 'But you will have to prove that to me.'

'I will.' Marcus let the silence grow between them, his own quietness making the words more emphatic.

He would prove to his father that he could travel a different path from the one laid out for him.

As a child, Marcus had often not seen his father for weeks that stretched into months when he had known his father was in London. He had once seen him with a strange woman on his arm and he'd heard so many rumours they'd bored him. His father said fidelity was limiting himself to one mistress. And Marcus suspected that, on occasion, Avondale fell short of that goal.

'What of Stormhaven?' Marcus asked.

'Take it. All that I have is yours. And anything I can do for you, you have but to send me a message,' he vowed. 'But I will not plough.'

'I would not ask you to, Father, as I would like straight furrows.'

His father laughed again and, for the first time Marcus could remember, his father hugged him.

Then they turned and went back to the breakfast, and he heard Lady Beatrice's laugh.

'I don't understand why she chose Lady Beatrice to discover us,' Marcus said. 'Except the woman speaks with everyone and can get a message across the country faster than anyone else.'

'That girl is her niece. Emilie is Lady Beatrice's niece.'

Beatrice had done the portrait of his mother. But he'd not really made the connection until now. After all, the artist was married to the Duke of Edgeworth's brother.

And Emilie was the Duke of Kinsale's relation. 'But Emilie is related to Kinsale.'

'Lady Beatrice is the old Kinsale's youngest daughter. I thought you knew that,' his father said.

'I know of her as Edgeworth's sister-in-law.

The woman who painted the infamous picture of her husband.'

'Your mother chose Lady Beatrice as her portraitist because I had Thomas Lawrence for mine. That set your mother against Mr Lawrence. And, she put the finished paintings on different sides of the room.'

'I noticed.' That fact hadn't escaped him.

'Emilie sounds like her aunt from my view,' Avondale continued. 'Edgeworth does love his brother and accepts Lady Beatrice into the family, but she's Beatrice. I cannot imagine what it must have been like for her husband when he saw that engraving of himself in the newspaper. Naked. Except for a leaf or some sort. I heard it wasn't in the original. I recommend you don't take off your clothes near Emilie in the light of day.'

Marcus bade farewell to his father and the guests and, giving Emilie no chance to argue, gave the driver directions to his town house and helped her into the carriage.

She sat across from him, fanning herself. 'It has been such a busy day, and well, night. It is like a week all wrapped up into one day. I am certainly amazed at your constitution, Marcus.'

'Don't ever paint me naked, Emilie.'

'You have an admirable form and should be proud.'

'No, Emilie. No.'

'But my aunt has a proud painting of her husband. Everyone's seen it. It was the talk of London for months. Did it somehow pass you by?'

'A copy of the engraving was tacked to the wall at the club until the Duke saw it and ripped it to shreds.' He took in her reaction and didn't see the shock he anticipated. 'Have you seen it?'

'Not the engraving. The one that is framed at my aunt's residence. She put a handkerchief over the most private area and showed it to Mother and me.' She squared her shoulders. 'It is an astounding piece, but I do not believe it has the depth of your mother's portrait.'

The carriage interior was silent.

'You are already planning to restrict my art.' She peeled her gloves away.

'Can I be the one happy this time, Emilie, and there will be no naked likenesses of me?'

'I give you my solemn word that I will not paint you entirely naked.'

He would take what he could get.

The carriage rolled to a stop and he helped her disembark. He extended an arm to indicate she precede him into his town house.

Inside, Robert took Marcus's hat.

She spoke to Robert. 'I shall be having a few

things delivered over the next few days. Please get me at each delivery.'

Robert stopped and slowly rotated to Marcus. 'This is—has been—a bachelor establishment. I am a valet. We have no butler.'

'Just let me know when each delivery arrives.' Emilie continued up the stairs.

Robert acted the part of having a sword and falling upon it.

Well, the first hours of a marriage were an adjustment.

Chapter Eleven

Marcus sat in his study and Robert put the novel he had read on to the shelf.

'I did appreciate your inviting me to the wedding breakfast, but did not attend as they depress me so,' Robert said. He pulled at his waistcoat, ran a hand to brush his hair back and checked his teeth in the mirror.

'I am married.' Marcus stared at the ring on his finger, next to the family ring that his father had given him.

'I am aware.'

'The ring is tight.'

'You have been married how long?' Robert turned, examining his profile now in the looking glass. 'Enjoy.'

'It has been splendid.' Marcus could not mistake the unease in his stomach. He scowled at the brandy bottle in front of him. 'Did you know she's Beatrice the Beast's niece?'

'Certainly.' Robert looked down his nose. 'That is your attraction to her. You searched out someone who'd dismay your father.'

'No.'

Robert huffed. 'And I am a virgin.' He rummaged through the bookcase, moving things aside, pretending to straighten them, but checking behind each item. 'May you partake of the most deliriously happy wedding night, as the joy will not endure. I have never wed and I am constantly reminded of the evils of marriage. Particularly when my sister informs me of hers,' Robert said, pulling out a bottle. 'Found it.' Then he ambled away. In a few moments he returned.

'The new addition to your family has rung for dinner to be taken to your room. Would you like a tray there as well?' Robert turned to him. 'And what have you done with the good cigars?'

Marcus ignored his last question and answered the first.

'I told her we should sleep tonight as we want the experience to be the best possible. I will be in Nate's room. He's staying at Mother's for a few days.'

Robert paused. 'Are you certain this is the way you should start out?'

'No.'

Robert didn't move.

'Would you be willing to move with me to the country?' Marcus asked.

Robert shook his body, as if shaking off a feeling of doom. 'I could.'

'We will not have suitable accommodations.'

'You could move somewhere lacking suitable accommodations?' Robert didn't close his mouth after he spoke. He stumbled, grasping for something to keep him upright.

'Robert, could you not play-act that you are a valet?'

'Possibly not. It is more fun to play-act that I am at least a duke. I do not aspire to be King. I know my limitations.'

'Do you mind, Your Grace, to play a game of patience with me?'

'Sir, on your wedding night?'

'I am not in the mood for billiards. And I fear my true gambling is limited to matters that require no funds.'

'How am I to play patience with you?' Robert asked. 'It is a game to be played alone.'

'You drink my wine for me. Smoke my cigars. You may as well play a game of cards for me.'

'I enjoy the wine and cigars. Patience, eh.' He grimaced, reached for the cards and moved to sit near the game table, putting the bottle near his hand. 'But I will play your games so you may complete your wedding night.' Robert began dealing, holding the cards extended so he could peer at them.

'I do not expect to complete my wedding night, either.' Marcus reached to take the bottle. 'And for some reason, I keep comparing this to the days of my little dog long gone. That started out well, but didn't end on a good note.' He exhaled. 'A good dog Gus was. At first.'

'Gus was everything you've said—I'm sure. Unfortunately when you had him it was between my tenures with you. I was working with a different animal—some child that incessantly whined.' He squinted at the cards, then held one at his chest as if keeping a secret from himself.

'I see your plan.' Robert ignored the game. 'You intend to keep her guessing. You'll control the household that way.'

'No, Robert. She hardly knows me. In fact, I would say she's a stranger to me. Albeit, a fetching one.'

Robert slapped one card on top of another. 'I feel it in my bones that this will be a disastrous union. You must hire a butler straight away because I am so concerned with your needs that it will be impractical for me to take on more tasks.'

'I have always gambled, Robert. And don't expect me to add a butler.'

'You never gamble. You make mistakes and call it that.'

Marcus watched the cards. 'I am not certain that Emilie cares anything for me. In fact, I was surprised when she told the cleric she would marry me.' That moment had emblazoned itself in his mind. 'I thought she'd changed her mind.'

'If you want someone who cares for you, I have found the path to a woman's heart is quickest and sweetest by avoiding marriage. In truth, they detest it as much as men do. Show me a rich widow who wants to marry and I'll show you…' Robert stopped, deliberating on his next words. 'I'm trying to imagine a rich widow who wants a husband. Perhaps she might need a valet to help her get over those delusions…'

'Stop thinking about other people's marriages and help me prepare to move to Stormhaven.'

Robert dropped the cards, letting them flutter to the table, and rose. 'We are surely not going to that disgrace where your grandparents lived. It was in poor shape years ago and age is as unkind to houses as it is to people.' He went to the mirror and inspected his hair. 'Blasted shingles keep falling off the roof.'

Marcus didn't answer directly. 'Tomorrow, determine if any of the maids will go with us. Nathaniel will remain here, so the staff can stay. But we will need trunks packed, food prepared and perhaps tools purchased. We will need wagons loaded. I must employ workmen. I would like Emilie to have trained servants as I am not sure she can adjust to the demands of a household easily.'

Robert returned, lifting the cards he'd dropped, the rest of the deck in his hand, and he stared at the table. 'Do you know at which point your senses disappeared? Did you feel them leave your body? Or did you wake and discover them gone?'

'I suppose they slid away, a little each day.' Marcus reached out to turn over a card.

Robert pulled another card from the deck and peered at it. 'If I were you, I could envision a better way to spend my honeymoon.' The older man didn't stop his concentration on the cards. 'I will wake you in the morning and let you know if you have won any games.'

'Thank you, Robert. See that the maid checks on Emilie. Also have the maid remove some clothing from my room so you can bring me something to wear in the morning.'

He headed to Nathaniel's room.

The next day, he awoke as his door opened. Robert didn't knock.

'You won many games last night,' Robert said, cheerily, but then his tone changed to chagrin. 'But you cheated.'

'I cheat every game you play for me.'

'What is frightful is that you still lose.'

'Do you feel the least wobbly from the brandy?' Marcus asked. His skull was banging soundly. Wellington's cannons couldn't have pounded louder.

'No,' Robert insisted. 'I am of stronger stock than you young lords who must groan and lie about all day with damp cloths plastered to your foreheads.' He tossed a pair of trousers on the bed. 'Now, rise and dress yourself. You have a duty to do.'

'The sole duty I am interested in would not require trousers.'

Robert shrugged away the words. 'A sour miss is scowling the rooms this morning and it would be best suited for the two of you to be together, so that you might rapturously observe each other—or at least prevent her from speaking to me.'

Marcus contemplated the trousers flung across the bedcovers.

Robert reached for a shirt and cravat and held them at the ready.

Marcus took his time dressing as he knew Robert didn't like to wait. As soon as he had tied Marcus's cravat, Robert held the brush in hand and, after Marcus donned his coat, with a few swift dashes, took the specks from it.

'She's in the sitting room.' Robert tossed the

brush with a clatter, then aligned it perfectly beside the shaving kit.

Marcus searched Emilie out and found her, poised with a pad of paper in her hands, determination on her face, ankles crossed.

Her chalk stopped in mid-air.

'Good morning.' He dipped his head in acknowledgement. 'I must talk with you before I go out. I'll be getting supplies and staff arranged so we can move to the country.'

She dropped the chalk into a container. 'That will be a good thing. I do not like this establishment, although I am content to make do.' She turned as she surveyed the walls. 'Not a well-lit room in the place. I can hear carriages pass. I would prefer forests and sunshine and cooling breezes.'

She deliberated on her sketchbook, picked up a pencil and her elbow began to move, quivering while she filled in the shades. 'Why did you marry me, if you do not plan on having an heir?'

'Emilie. Do not presume for a moment I don't intend to share your bed. I fully expect to make my presence known and for you to have no complaints whatsoever in that regard.'

'Oh.'

'But yesterday was eventful. Additionally, it was a trial for you. You married. You spent your first night away from your parents and we'd been awake most of two days. That was no time to begin anew. Nevertheless, before I fell asleep, I did recall your reaction to my physique.'

Reaching up, he tapped one shoulder. 'Move over, David. You have competition.'

He saw a flash of humour.

'Well, I'm not immune to the male form. Artists can be passionate people on occasion.' She inspected the ring he had put on her finger.

'You don't sculpt, do you?' he asked.

'Not yet. I long to learn.'

He hadn't promised her the opportunity to sculpt. He wouldn't accept any marble in the place. He imagined two statues of himself, both naked, perched grotesquely on pedestals at each side of an entrance to a room at the British Museum, with Emilie reigning supreme as she waved a carved rod, indicating points of interest. Oh, that would be thrilling for the men at White's.

'I want to move to a country estate. Stormhaven lives up to its name. Last time I saw the acreage, it appeared to have been a true haven for tempests and is in sad disrepair,' he admitted. 'It will take years to correct it. But you can spare no expense in decorating it. It's been in my family for centuries, yet no one cares for it.'

He walked to her. His senses collided with each other, each one fighting for dominance in their awareness of Emilie. Arousal flourished. With a light touch, he brushed an errant lock of her hair back behind her ear.

In that moment, he understood art. When she moved her neck or her torso, even the slightest, it seemed that the world flowed through her and that she was the centre of everything. A painting of the world and Emilie moved in the hub, spokes of life surrounding her.

His fingers trailed down, touching the softness of her earlobe. The delicate curve of her jawline. He inhaled the scent of fresh morning soap. His lips parted.

She let her chin move within his touch, not resisting at all, but melding into him. She stared at him. 'No one cares for it? It's been abandoned?'

'Where do you want to live?'

She slowly moved her gaze to him.

'I prefer—not here.' The words broke the spell of their moment together. 'Robert is unskilled as a butler.'

'He's a valet,' Marcus corrected her.

'I promoted him.'

'He's my valet.' He delivered the words very softly and with complete assurance.

She deliberated on the spine of her sketchbook. 'Based on your appearance, he is a talented valet. He has no skills as a butler, anyway. Keep him if you must.'

'Thank you.' Mark delivered the words just as his father would. He caught the similarity in tone and couldn't take the words back, and didn't know if he would have.

He turned briefly, his feet facing the exit, but he stopped. 'Then are you pleased to move, Countess?'

'Oh.' Her chin moved up. 'I haven't been addressed so formally before. That sounds... suitable.'

'I would say you are accomplished already at being able to direct your designs as a peer would.'

'That is indeed thoughtful of you. And I must return the compliment. You are every moment Avondale's heir.'

The words moved like a drop of winter's brandy that had missed warming his throat, but had splashed at him from above and leaked down the inside of his shirt at his back.

'Lady Grayson. I am not happy with the excesses I follow. Gambling bores me. Drinking is no solution because I do not like the things I say when I am dissipated. I feel I reveal too much of myself to near strangers and I do not like it. I require substance. To know my mettle, and not gauge my personality by the enjoyment others expect.'

'For this you married me?' She pondered the statement, but then relaxed. 'Well, I am an artist.'

'To me, that is not as important as you might suppose it is when compared to the way you see life. I married someone I once saw when we were children. Then the other night, you consented to marry me and I knew that was the singular opportunity I would have to take a different path from the one I had always foreseen. I had hoped...' He shrugged. 'I do not know exactly what I had hoped for.'

He could not put it into words for her. She'd never understand. He could not see all the colours and he knew they were there. He'd discovered them by accident on the day he'd first seen Emilie.

She rose and didn't stop until her skirts brushed his legs. 'You remember me as a child?'

'You were playing some nonsensical game. I'd been at a window and saw you running to the trees, and wondered what you were doing and investigated.'

'I seem to remember you now.'

He pressed his lips together for a half-second before replying. He shrugged the words away. 'I noticed you. That's all.'

One soft finger touched his temple, moved

down the side of his cheek to his throat and slid down the front of his shirt. 'I couldn't miss you now. You were made for inspiration.'

He could not be in her grasp. Then he realised he was a tad late for that. He had to get her out of his reach.

'I have to get workmen situated so we will have a roof. Terrible leaks.' He turned, taking a step. He couldn't acknowledge, even to himself—particularly to himself—how tempting she was to him. She fascinated him. He tried to ascertain why and all that his mind could unlock was an image of her.

Then she closed the distance between them. She examined him.

They stood like two strangers at a ball, ready to begin a dance, both aware of the music, yet not sure if the composition would lead them together or apart.

'When we were children,' she said, words slow, 'you were the boy…the one who spoke with me the day of Beatrice's wedding.'

'I had to stay with the children and I didn't like it. You challenged me to a duel and called yourself a highwayman.'

'You were too old to be with the children and I knew it. I picked you to rob.'

'You stuck a stick at my waistcoat.'

'I did stop short of running you through. With

a stick. Which likely would have broken. I requested you to play highwayman with me, but you dismissed it as beneath you. I was too young for you to really notice.'

He put his hands on her shoulders and brought her closer, his fingers trailing until he had both palms at her cheeks. His thumbs grazed her lips. 'I noticed you. Your dress was all flounces and your hair had bows. The frills overpowered you in size, and yet not in spirit. You saw none of the fripperies. You enjoyed the sunshine and the lemonade and ran among the oaks.'

She touched him. His stubble was freshly shaved away, yet she could feel baby-fine hair where his lips began. Perhaps he had a tiny scar, so small as to be invisible if she were not so close, running in a straight line along his cheek. His lips. His mouth felt softer than her own. So delicate. A contrast to the rest.

He grasped her sides, sending rays of warmth into her.

Marcus took up all the space in front of her, the scent of shaving and fresh linen mixing with what might have been a hint of brandy.

She waited.

His lips touched hers, so gently that it would have knocked her off her feet had he not been pulling her closer.

She'd not felt herself move. She'd felt nothing,

nothing but Marcus's lips and the wonder of a kiss unleashing so much wildness inside her that she would have never deemed it possible to feel.

He pulled her against him, crushing her into his body, finding her mouth, tasting her and embracing her as if their lives depended on it, but instead of feeling consumed, or captured, freedom blazed within her. And then he stopped, pulled back and waited until she could think who she was and where she was.

'And then we married at dawn.' He pondered his words. 'The hour you chose for a duel and which ended up a wedding time.'

She could say nothing. How could you when Michelangelo's marble came to life and spoke?

'I want a fresh start,' he said as he moved towards the door. 'For myself.'

'For us?' She didn't want the distance to grow. 'I am satisfied with the man who stands in front of me. I did not expect a perfect union, or, in truth, a long one.'

'A fresh start for me. What if there are only a few times in a person's life that they can truly change the path of who they are and become who they are meant to be? And what if this is my last chance?'

She turned to her sketchbook and opened it, inspecting a page. 'My destiny was to have been the same as my grandmother's and all my female ancestors. To have that journey, I would only have had to notice the men of my father's parish. I'm fortunate not to have those constraints. Some day you will go your separate way and our lives will remain intertwined through our children, but not our hearts. Our marriage began flawed and will end the same. I accept that.'

She fixed her attention on him and she inspected his features, amazement creeping into her words and raptness in her gaze. 'But you are perfection.'

Perfection, she called him. She observed his exterior. Much like everyone else in society did.

And she was *fortunate*.

He was as lost to her as he was to himself. 'I'm little more than a cutpurse who lives in a fine world. I take what I covet and leave the rest behind.'

'The marriage?'

'Yes. I took what I wished. You were more entranced with Nathaniel. And you shouldn't have been.'

'He was charming. You should not say such unkind things about your brother.'

The words stilled Marcus. But he chastised himself. She couldn't be blamed. She'd been straightforward, sending the note to Nathaniel. She'd not met his brother that night, but had stayed away.

He'd signed Nathaniel's name to the missive inviting her to Hatchards. She'd arrived. He couldn't blame her for that. She'd brought her mother. 'I would not deny you your art, and you must understand, I will have this chance.'

'And you don't care if I paint?'

'Not at all.'

'Then I cannot care how you choose to spend your days. That would be unfair.'

He had to leave the room before the heat of it choked him.

At the door, he called out, 'I will be getting workmen and staff for Stormhaven. The residence may take some industry on both our parts.'

He would end up like his father with too many mistresses to remember if he did not change.

Yet he was out on the street with a horse, getting his boots scuffed, while chasing after some madness that could bring him no ease.

He stilled. Perhaps his father chose the women for his ability to forget them. Who knew? Avondale had claimed once, in a moment of utter foolishness, that the new woman he had charmed had given him happiness. He'd ended his search for feminine perfection. He'd found her.

Marcus had held his fists behind his back and

wished his father well before crashing out the door and going back to university.

The next meeting with his father, they'd not spoken of anything but horses, and then after university, someone at a club had nudged him, angrily, and claimed Avondale was having a new dalliance with the man's sister.

Marcus had commiserated and learned that the novelty of his father's true love hadn't lingered as expected.

Marcus didn't even buy his boots from Hoby, because that was his father's bootmaker. He refused to follow in those footsteps and bachelorhood was the safest path to that. He could let Nathaniel marry and provide the heir.

But in simply a few days, Emilie had entered his world and he'd dashed headfirst into a marriage.

The ink had hardly been dry on the special licence and he'd not given himself occasion to weigh his actions, because if he had, he would still be single.

But Emilie.

That day at Hatchards had sealed his fate, tamped it deep with the paperwork, and he'd invited Lady Semple and friends to finish the negotiations.

Now he had the rest of his life to sort out, and

was seeing no colours. Only the clouds in the sky and a smattering of rain.

He stopped, pulled himself on to the horse and planned the chores he needed done before he could move.

Carpenters.

Marcus had ridden to the near ruin years before and the sight of it had caused a knot in his chest. The place had scarcely resembled the site of his grandmother chasing him, flapping her bonnet at him, saying she had to get the galloping horse out of her house. He'd loved running into the room and neighing. Even when she couldn't get up, she'd rail because someone had seemingly let a horse indoors.

The memories pushed him forward while he found a carpenter who needed work and knew of a few others who could help with the repairs.

When he returned to the town house, he'd wanted the first face he saw to be Emilie's, but Robert met him at the door.

The valet had a firm set to his lips and his mouth moved silently before he spoke. 'I presume you had a pleasant day.' Robert took his coat.

'It went well.'

Marcus walked over, seeing Emilie's sketch-book where she'd left it behind. He flipped through it, seeing sketches of her mother, her father, her sisters, and then one of his brother, Nathaniel. He ground his teeth together, turning a page. There, with a few lines, was another drawing. A few lines, no more. The likeness of his ring in the corner led him to believe the likeness was to be of him.

But it certainly wasn't filled in.

Robert grumbled, pulling Marcus's attention, and he dropped the book.

Robert bunched the coat in his hands.

'Could you speak to your wife? Perhaps move her and keep us here?' Robert asked with an unusually gentle tone.

'Not likely.' Marcus spoke casually, standing perfectly still, hoping the situation was not too severe. 'What did she do?'

'She does not treat me with the respect due to me,' Robert said, draping Marcus's squashed coat casually over his arm.

'As the valet or the Duke?' he asked.

'Neither.' Robert ground out the word and motioned for Marcus to precede him up the stairs.

Marcus waited.

Robert continued. 'I do not even want her to speak with me. I am your servant, not hers. And she orders me for no reason.' He held his bearing high. 'I am a valet. Not a lady's maid. Valet. Is that so hard to understand?'

Marcus refrained from mentioning the many stretches Robert hadn't seemed to understand he was a valet.

Robert made his voice a falsetto. 'Get me some water, Robert. Adjust the window. Bring me a shawl. Take the shawl to my room. Sweep the floor in front of my dainty little feet.'

He faced Marcus, and shuddered. 'She even followed me to my bedchamber and didn't go away when I didn't answer. Highly inappropriate. She opened the door.' His voice increased on the last word. 'I was on my bed reading—*reading*, Lord Grayson—and she commanded me to get her a glass of water.'

When he finished the recital, Robert couldn't contain the movement of his arms. Marcus's coat was flapping about. And he knew that Robert rarely addressed him as Lord.

'Water. *A glass of water?* To ferret out my chambers took her much effort and she didn't even want the water that I got for her. I graciously forced myself to get it because I wanted to please her so she would leave me be—and she dunked a paintbrush in it.'

'I will get her a lady's maid.' Marcus's voice flowed lullaby smooth.

The valet forced words past his lips, enunciating each one. 'I have sent a servant to wait on her, but that unwelcome person still seeks me out.' Robert ran a hand through his white hair. 'This isn't the turn of events I expected. You have married in haste and I will repent in leisure.'

They went to the stairs.

Robert continued, affecting a woman's voice as he followed Marcus. '"Open the door a crack. No, that is too open. No, that is too closed."'

As they topped the stairs, Emilie waited, listening, and Marcus gave her a slight smile.

When Robert saw her, he said, politely to Marcus, 'May I get you something, Lord Grayson?'

Twice, Marcus thought, *twice Robert had addressed him as Lord Grayson. The man was upset.*

He stared at Robert for a brief moment. Robert had a most calm demeanour, but a few strands of his hair were sticking straight up and that was not something Marcus had seen before.

Emilie glared at Robert and Robert looked over her as if she were not there.

'Marc.' Her head was high. 'The servant...' she pointed a finger at Robert '...threw a book at me.'

Robert glared at her. 'It is not fitting for you to be in this *servant's* bedchamber and I was merely bouncing it from the door in frustration in the hopes you would notice said door and leave.'

'You were disgraceful,' she said. 'To throw a book.'

His voice was calm, eyes serene. He spoke softly. 'I didn't have a dagger.'

Chapter Twelve

'Marc.' She turned to him and her arm reached out so that she nearly thumped Robert.

The valet raised his chin. He held Marcus's coat as a matador might hold a cape and fluttered it towards Emilie.

'How can you allow this?' Emilie cried. 'You must defend my honour. You must send him packing at once. You can easily find someone to replace him.'

Robert gasped.

Marcus ran a hand through his hair. 'I would like some help in the sitting room, Robert.'

'I would most like to help you, Lord Grayson. Anything you might ask is a joy for me to do. I live to serve you, as I have done practically since—' he swaggered '—your birth. You were the most superb charge a tutor could have.'

The minute they both were alone, Robert shut

the door and wilted. He thrust himself into the wall, crashing against it.

'Are you replacing me?' Robert asked. 'Has that woman bewitched you?' He turned to Marcus, a catch in his voice. 'I did save your life.'

'I have no plans for sending you away, Robert. But it would be best if you could get along with Emilie.'

Robert lifted Marcus's coat and brushed the dust free, but he was doing it with the force necessary to dislodge boulders. He muttered, 'We have not seen yet if you can get along with her. I assume she dabbles in the black arts. That is the only way I can fathom this disaster.'

Marcus settled in the chair that moulded around his frame from the many hours he'd sat in it. He inclined as far back into it as he could and turned to ease the tension in his neck. 'I will tell her to treat you with respect as you and I have known each other for many years.'

Robert trembled as he took out his anger on any object which dared to cling to the coat. He picked at the wool.

'It is understandable she's unfamiliar with the town house, a new husband and servants. I would think you could help her adjust.' Marcus tried to make peace. 'You are irreplaceable, Robert. We have blood ties.'

Robert's anger disappeared and he seemed pleased with the coat. 'She upsets very easily.'

'Do not make things worse.' Marcus cocked a brow. 'You'd best pray to watch your words with Emilie.'

Robert huffed. 'I did not mean to upset her. I may have mentioned that you had been confused about whether to put Nathaniel's name or your own on the licence, but I would have never done so had she not pushed me to the end of my tether six times.'

'Do not mention the licence again. Neither to me nor her.' Marcus glared at the older man. 'I will not let you go. But I will empty a chamber pot over you if you do not watch your speech.' Marcus knew his next threat to Robert would have to do with cigars and brandy. Robert would listen then.

'Your lordship…' Robert shuddered. 'I fear you have condemned yourself by bringing a haughty bumpkin into this household who does not appreciate you or the fine things you provide.' He mocked her voice again. 'Things here are "*not as pleasant*" as she is used to. There are more birds in the trees there. The grass is of a deeper green. The sky is a deeper blue. To hear her speak, the insects part to each side of her as she glides above the grass. To have this woman ordering me about… This woman whom you graced with marriage. A woman you went out of your way to provide a special licence for and take great care with her reputation, which would be enhanced by her nearness to the Westbrook family.' Robert spoke through gritted teeth. 'I do not know if I can keep peace in this household. The honeymoon is *over*.'

'Robert, please, for me, try to appease her, or I will move and leave you both here.' Marcus touched a hand to his knee.

Robert sputtered. 'I would not stay. I wager she and Nathaniel would get along well, but I would not remain. I will search you out. And give you a reporting.'

Marcus focused on Robert. Why had Robert, who favoured him above Nate, thought Emilie would get along so well with Nathaniel?

'What rubbish.' He heard her voice before she entered the room.

She held a book up. 'This is nothing but rot. You are reading this filth?'

Robert's book that he had got from the Huddleston's man.

'My pardon.' Robert followed behind her, reaching over and slipping the book from her hand. 'I'm reading that masterpiece of literary accomplishment.'

'I will never act as this fish-brain describes…
Ha. And, I repeat, *never*. It is a book on how a
woman should manage a household.'

'Leave, Robert.'

'Farewell.' Robert bowed and obeyed the
command, holding the book to his chest. 'I endeavour to study this and take notes, in case
they are needed.'

She went to Marcus's desk and picked up the
ink bottle, studying it. 'The servant refused to
even read the list of paints I needed. I had no
funds to give to the maid to purchase them either
and the shopkeeper would not give her credit.'

She put the paper down and picked up his led-
ger book. He rose, reached out and took it from
her hands. 'Make your list. And I'll see you get
enough to last you.'

She took the stopper from the ink bottle, then
plopped it back on.

'Ah. I can do that.' She rubbed her palms together. 'I'll get plenty and have extra for a likeness of Robert, a true portrayal.'

He could imagine that any representation of
Robert she created would incite an explosion.
He'd best get them all to the country as soon
as possible. It wouldn't do him any good to see
either her or Robert on the scaffold. He'd have
lost both a wife and valet, and no one would be
happy.

Much like today.

'You must not let Robert come with us to the country.' She wafted by him. 'He is rude.'

'My dear, he will be moving with us. And you must be pleasant to him.' He suspected Robert was more unsettled by Emilie's lack of gratitude for her new place in the family than concerned for his own permanence.

'You would choose him over me.'

'It is not a choice,' he said. 'I have you both.' He had a part of her, but such a tiny part that he wasn't sure it mattered.

He stretched, yawning, but she was out of reach of his fingertips. He felt his body ready itself to join her.

He ground his teeth together and observed her. The longing turned to insistence.

'Robert is too forward,' she said.

'He is very forward.' How could she speak of Robert? Of all the men in his family, she ignored only one.

'He drinks your brandy.'

'He smokes my cigars and, if he sees a shirt I have that he likes, he orders one for himself and I am billed for it.'

'Does he have a hold over you?'

'When I was a child, Robert saved me at the risk of his own death when he threw himself between me and a runaway horse. He jumped forward, pitching me aside, and could have died when the hooves hit him. He had been my tutor a week and had told me to stay inside to finish my lessons. I didn't. He followed me.'

'That is valiant.'

'My first tutor was perfection. Perfection. Until I heard a thump in the night and found him pushing a maid against the wall and her crying out for help. I didn't understand. Father hadn't been home for weeks so I couldn't expect his help. I ran to get the butler, and he tossed the man out the door. My parents were informed and my mother brought Robert to me as a tutor, without my father's agreement. There was a tremendous row. But then he rescued me the next week and Father accepted him well enough.'

'You will not dismiss him.'

'No. Besides that, he is my mother's half-brother. Before my grandfather eventually wed my grandmother, his mistress had a child. Robert was the child and my grandfather and grandmother recognised him as family.'

Robert had never lived within the household, yet on occasion he'd been discussed as a family member.

'He is not to mention the reasons of our marriage to either you or me again. I warn you he may forget. You can speak to me and I will correct him.' Marcus understood that sometimes his uncle did speak too bluntly.

Emilie appeared to accept Robert's birth without question, more concerned with her own marriage than his grandparents'.

'He is not to mention it to you?' she asked.

He could smell the mix of roses with a hint of turpentine—Emilie—which almost annoyed his nose but pleased the rest of him.

'No, I do not like to be reminded of it.' Even his mouth changed as he felt her move towards him.

The surprise of it caused him to release his hold on her hand and she pulled away.

'If he could have died to save you, then you cannot send him packing.'

'Emilie.' He spoke with the command of generations of the peerage and his voice didn't rise, but could have carried a great distance.

She stopped at the sound.

'I have to sort out who we are to be. Who I am to be.'

'You are the future Marquess of Avondale. That is plenty for one man.' She spun away from him. The door shut behind her and the gentle click of it sounded like a death knell to him.

She'd said it didn't matter to her who he was, because he was Marcus Westbrook, the future Marquess. He believed her. He was the man who gave her the paints and brushes and would take her to the country and let her have her way.

Now he knew how the victims of the cut-purses felt.

Chapter Thirteen

The bouncing of the vehicle jarred the uneasiness inside her. The corset had been tied snug and it pinched with every movement of the carriage. With each jostle, she tensed her feet to keep steady.

Marcus had flicked a glance in her direction, but he'd not said anything when she'd chosen the opposing seat in the coach, facing the road behind them.

The trip loomed in front of her and she dreaded their arrival.

She hoped she was up to the task of instructing the housekeeper, or that the servants would handle things well enough that no one needed direction. As one of Avondale's properties, Stormhaven would be elaborate and beyond the status Emilie was accustomed to.

But not as much as the marriage was. She'd considered the plight directly in front of her when she'd agreed to marry. Not the future. She'd not reflected beyond her work. Her mother had complained that the scent of oils would be the death of Emilie, but she'd not listened. Nor had she thought of it spinning her into a maze that had no escape.

She had yoked herself to a man who would be in society—and she would be expected to comport herself as a countess. Her insides seized. She'd not considered that when she had agreed to the marriage.

But Marcus—at least on appearance—would be a jewel in any artist's crown.

He wore his clothes so well. She held herself firm when the carriage jostled them together. The heat of his skin caused her leg to prickle. The aliveness of him. Touching him gave her more feeling than when she viewed a masterpiece.

She watched the dust they were leaving behind, swirling about like fragments of her soul escaping.

Her husband rode across from her. Silent.

At first, he sat much like a general on a venture into a new mission might appear, hair trimmed neatly at his ears, his coat and clothing pressed. Tiredness in his face.

'You really look nothing like Nathaniel,' she said.

His glare didn't change, but his attention

snapped to her, causing a warning, although she didn't know why. 'That night at the dance, when I confused the two of you, I can't understand how I did it. Except, I had been examining the painting and I didn't want anyone to know that I had tears in my eyes. I couldn't look at anyone directly. To be observed crying at a dance would have been disastrous. No one would have believed it was because of the art.'

Then he reclined back and stretched his legs. His face softened. 'Art makes you weep?'

'Some art. And I cannot explain why. It just happens.'

'I've never felt that way.' His quiet words were revealing about him, not meant as a criticism of her. He returned to thoughts only known to him, but he appeared less like a general on a mission, even with his arms folded, and more like a man on the way to sleep.

During the trip, the bounces had moved Marcus into the middle of the seat across from her and she'd confined herself so they would not bounce into each other.

Finally, he shut his eyes and relaxed.

His knee bumped against hers.

She didn't know if he remained awake. Apparently, he'd fallen asleep because his features softened and his leg angled against her skirts.

By the curve of his lips, he was having a pleasant dream.

His knee bumped her again.

He gave no indication he had noticed, but his leg tipped a little more against hers.

The road smoothed. His knee bumped hers and it was definitely not a fault of the road.

She held firm, but inside, her stomach tumbled more than the carriage wheels.

He peered out from his lashes, the sides of his lips rising higher. 'Pardon.'

'You could tell the driver to slow,' she said to him, 'if he is driving too fast. The jostling appears to be keeping you awake.'

'I like to be jostled. In the right way. And I like to be kept awake.' A companionable glint followed the words.

So, he liked to be kept awake.

'Don't let me disturb you.' The carriage moved and she steadied herself by putting a hand on his knee—moving it so he couldn't rest his leg against her. Her palm burned with the feel of the skin beneath the trousers. 'I wouldn't want to keep you awake.'

His eyes opened wider. 'We disagree on that.'

She took her hand away, leaving behind the heat of his skin, but not the increase of her heartbeats.

His lids closed again, but he had a half-smile.

Exactly as she would render him. But didn't dare. Oh, that was a lie. She would dare.

'You've really not been jostled properly, Em. I beg your forgiveness.' He kept his lids down.

She moved closer to the edge of her seat. 'One wonders. About things. Just in passing.'

'One does? What does one wonder about?'

Heat flamed in her cheeks.

His smile widened a second. 'You mean… *that*?'

'I would not know what you are referring to.'

His leg touched her knee. 'That.'

'You are purposely jostling me.'

'Husbands do that to their wives. On occasion. I've heard. Rumours.'

'Should you trust rumours?'

'It depends.' The wheels covered a lot of distance in the time it took for his eyes to fully open. Nothing moved inside her. 'I'd like to have faith in that one.'

'I am concerned.' She interlaced her fingers.

His gaze didn't falter from hers. 'Don't be.'

He sat straight, then moved his upper body closer to her and put his hand on her knee, and rested it there. She couldn't swallow, but she didn't need to.

'We're getting a late start, Em. But it's not because I don't want to hold you. I do. And it's not because it will be unpleasant. It won't.'

'Are you certain?'

'Yes.'

Marcus remained so close the heat from his body caressed her. 'Kiss me.'

The kiss began slowly, but instantly moved into something more, melting her. He put his hand on her waist, holding her, letting the moment linger, combining their movements with the carriage and holding them together as one.

When it ended, with less effort than a twist of his wrist, he tucked her beside him and pulled her close, her hands snug between them.

She let herself lean into him and he held her upright. She grasped his waistcoat to remain steady and it didn't work.

'Marc. Carriage,' she pulled back to whisper against his cheek while his lips trailed the skin of her neck, tasting.

'Carriage club.'

Where had she heard those words before? Then she remembered something she'd overheard the men boast about and she kept his waistcoat bundled in her hands. 'Yes.'

'Later.' He muttered an oath. 'I would never— Not the first time. Maybe the third or fourth.' His lips swept her cheeks and found her mouth. She savoured the warmth of the kiss, and his caresses, both with his mouth and his hands.

Her nipples hardened and he brushed a palm

over them. 'We are too close to the end of our journey.'

She kept her eyes closed as she acquiesced, 'It wouldn't be proper to do such a thing in a carriage.'

'I suppose it isn't,' she heard him say into her hair. 'Not for the first fortnight after a marriage. Then, the rules change.'

The carriage bounced and she reached out, holding him to steady herself.

He moved his jaw against the soft skin of her neck. 'I am very busy right now getting to know the feel of you. A man must know the taste of his wife's skin. The feel of her breasts and the scent of her hair. No true husband would leave a treasure unexplored in front of him without unearthing the passions they could share. And you will have some things to discover as well.'

She grasped his waistcoat buttons. His waistcoat was no true barrier, except, it was. She undid one button, then continued.

He reached to hold her other shoulder, rubbing soft circles, brushing the fabric of her dress against her skin. She slipped her hands under his waistcoat and snuggled close.

The coach rocked them together, easing Emilie's fears. The pads of Marcus's fingertips soothed her as he cupped her close, erasing the uncertainty of what the next nights would bring.

'We're almost there, Em. We must put ourselves back together.'

The carriage slowed and she fumbled at the buttons on his waistcoat. The closures seemed much smaller than she remembered and the fastenings much larger. His hand tangled with hers and he kissed her while she finished with the buttons, and the wheels below them stopped.

Then he opened the door, jumped to the ground and didn't give the groom a chance to help Emilie, as he reached for her himself.

Before she touched the road, he grasped her waist and swirled her around, putting her lightly on her feet. She stumbled into his grasp and he took up her vision.

'I will make this right for you. For us. For our children. Don't be upset by what you see. I'll make it better.'

Emilie's ears rang with the words Marcus had just spoken and overtook all her other senses. *Our children.* The words splashed against her and it wasn't that she was upset by the thought of motherhood, but the task daunted her.

She'd never taken any part in the direction of servants. Or marriage. Or anything more than the blending of a few colours. That she could do. Everything else would be new.

Except, she scrutinised, Stormhaven. The ancient structure hadn't weathered well.

An estate loomed in front of her. The columns of the front portico were braced by timber, shutters were missing and there was little to recommend the abode but the flowering vines that climbed over it.

A dwelling that had been ignored and abandoned, to return to the earth. She'd never seen such disrepair.

Once, the home had held children's laughter and the scents of baked goods and memories of Christmases and celebrations and maybe even anniversaries—until it had been forgotten.

She'd expected imperfections and faded walls inside. Not this. Not a grim monument to the past, crumbling back into the earth.

Then she understood. This could be her salvation. This would not be a universe of soirées. No one could entertain here. No one could question a marriage. Or tell her this was too far above her. This was a blank canvas. She swallowed. The abandoned structure was perfect for her. A place she could find her own direction and live comfortably without censure.

Just the right distance from her family that she could see them on occasion, yet far enough so her blunders would be ignored. A place where children could roam and no one would shout at them for laughing too hard or hiding in the cupboards.

Marcus hadn't moved, waiting. She turned to him. He studied her, lines at the side of his lips, jaw locked.

'The forests. The leaves. Such variety. Amazing.' She touched his forearm. 'I cannot believe you have brought me to such a perfect place. And it is perfect, Marcus. It really is.'

She couldn't tell him the reason behind the perfection. No one would sneer at her for her choices in the fabrics of the house, or the splatters of pigments she might spill when mixing them, or the errors she might make in dressing the children.

She studied the acreage, shading her brow. She'd seen neighbouring homes along the way, but now she could see the land as it had first been formed. No one would condemn her here for ambling about with a canvas, or question why she was not roaming the rooms insisting a maid scrub or polish or clean.

She stole a peek at Marcus and the expectation of her disappointment remained on his face.

'I'll have all the space I need for roses and lilacs. The scents inspire me.' She could not let him suppose her unhappy with the estate. She couldn't. This would be a perfect place for her creativity. True, the house was in disrepair, but the woodland appeared glorious.

Then she stilled. She bent her knees slightly and gave a bounce. 'I hear a chicken cackling. I am so glad the chickens are already here. And a colt.' She pointed to the animal tied to a tree. 'It's a beauty, if you get past the fact that it's all legs.'

She moved to pet the foal, noticing that it was skittish. The animal ran to the end of its rope, but calmed and nuzzled her hand when she approached.

Hugging the colt's neck, she hoped some day she would be able to ride it into the fields.

The little one was as new to the place as she was.

She'd never had a horse of her own. She was pleased, but to suddenly have a pet, and the whole estate, and a husband she didn't know, daunted her. She'd married and there was no going back. It was what she'd blundered into, but she'd never foreseen the upheaval. She'd been plopped down in the middle of somewhere she'd never seen, with a man she hardly knew.

She embraced the colt again, so Marcus couldn't see her.

She'd tried to show her contentment with the land, but her insides quivered. This was the house she was to be a wife in and, while the structure fitted her—or would—she didn't know how the aspect of being a helpmate would suit her disposition.

She'd struggled not to cause rows with her sisters and some days only hiding away kept the harmony.

Emilie remembered her plan to create as she wished and she'd gained it. But, in her considerations, she'd blurred away the time from the vows until the husband became wearied with her.

Stormhaven she could live in. It had a roof and walls.

But the husband. He'd stood so stern while examining the area. And they might as well have been a universe away from everything she had known.

True, he'd been glorious in the carriage, but he'd known exactly what he did to her and she'd moulded into him because to do anything else would have been impossible.

Marcus came with the acreage and he scowled so, only envisioning Stormhaven as a ruin. Oh, heavens, she would be destroyed if he took her back to the *ton*.

She'd wanted her paints and now she had them, plus more than she bargained for.

She stole a glance at him. Marcus regarded the house as if it were a calamity, and she looked at the colt's eyes, sensing unease, and tried to soothe it, fearing it sensed her worry and Marcus's displeasure.

If only he hadn't appeared so stern. The soirées had been such a trial for her, but she'd managed, knowing the efforts would soon be over. Now she had a respite from them.

No man she knew would take on a structure such as this. So many cracked and broken windows and so much effort needed. She would not blame him if he wished to return to London, but, oh, how she wanted to stay.

Marcus had watched Emilie. Then he followed the direction of her gaze. The house appeared to be undergoing a demolition, not a renovation.

Rotted boards. He'd never seen so much decayed wood. Boards for repairs lay scattered about, but not the forest of felled trees the repairmen would need.

He saw disrepair upon disrepair. His father had been right. This was no place to be. Blooming thistle had taken the place over and he could scarce see the entrance.

Weeds had been stomped into routes the men had created, but no actual repairs were in evidence. A wagon remained to be unloaded. Supplies were askew in every direction. He could only pray that the few rooms he'd instructed to be attended to first had been taken care of.

He would have to send Emilie and Robert back to London. They would not be able to bear this. He couldn't tolerate such a tumbledown residence.

Emilie stood, hugging the colt's withers, and concealing her face.

He'd not anticipated her putting on such a brave front.

Robert moved to him from the other carriage loaded with supplies, staggering after his boots touched the ground. 'We will all die. The house will collapse on us. The two of you can be buried together. I will aspire to be interred as far away from this as possible.' Robert blew a puff from his mouth in such a way that it touched his eyebrows.

Then he beheld Marcus, paused and groaned.

'Sir.' Robert stared at Marcus's waistcoat. 'They were properly done this morning when I dressed you.'

Marcus realised his buttons were fastened askew.

'I pray you will teach her how to put things back as she found them,' Robert grumbled, reaching out.

Marcus threw Robert's hands away and re-fastened the buttons.

He strode to Emilie, clasped her arm and pulled her snug to his side without looking down.

Blast it. Blast it. Blast it.

He should have waited before bringing her to Stormhaven. He should have burned the monstrosity and started afresh.

'Get the stack of boards out of the road,' he shouted to the men. 'Put them behind that decrepit heap.'

He kept her tucked close and ordered the wagon to be pulled to the back door and told Robert to get the maids organised.

The lead man for the work crew, a man named Jonas, rushed to Marcus.

Marcus gave orders rapid-fire, anticipating half to be forgotten.

He paused, mid-sentence. They would all go back to London. Everyone would understand.

She quivered at his side.

He inspected her.

Eyes, dark, alluring, stared at him. No tear streaks. 'I like the house.'

Marcus dismissed Jonas and bathed in the sight of the one delightful thing on the estate.

'Please,' she whispered. 'It needs windows replaced. A board or two, but they're already here. You said you wanted to be away from a life of wagering and drink. This is a chance for both of us to pursue our passions. Give it time.'

'There'll never be enough time to right this disaster.'

'Look around and commit this view to your memory,' she said. 'The cracked glass, the rotted boards, the lumber strewn about. Remember the sight of it now. Then, after a week, a month, a year, pull that sight out of your recollections and compare the progress you've engineered with it.'

He searched into the past and remembered the images of his grandparents and the games he'd played in the dirt. No one had reprimanded him for destroying the gardens or returning to the sitting room soaked from falling into a pond.

This place could be returned to its glory and fulfil him.

He squeezed her close. He wouldn't have to send her to London and hear his father's opinions. He wouldn't have to risk falling back into his old lifestyle.

He savoured a feeling and he investigated what it was. Something he'd not anticipated. And then he understood. He might care for Emilie. Not just desire her. Not just support her. But he might grow fond of her.

'Come.' He offered a hand. 'We must find you a room. I've had the workmen correct the kitchen and two bedchambers first. They should be the most usable.'

* * *

They were to select a room for her? She didn't move at first. Then she trod fast enough that his arm fell away from the caress. But at the door, she stopped.

Marcus shoved the door open and Emilie didn't want to see if he might carry her over the threshold, or forget the tradition. She rushed ahead.

Inside a stairway greeted her. She didn't even turn to the kitchen, but went upstairs to the family quarters. She needed a place of her own, a space of her own, and a chance to feel at home.

She went to the family rooms. First, she went to the biggest chamber where his trunk rested and there was a bed with a fresh covering on it. Oh, that was a mistake. The bed was large.

Then, she went to the next, a smaller one with new fabrics hanging from the four poster. All the wood gleamed. The room smelled as a lady's room should smell. Dried flowers? She didn't know. She liked the scent of it. A soft scent that made her think of a sanctuary or harbour.

She walked down the hall, inspecting the interior, aware Marcus followed.

One dust and dirt-filled room held a cheval mirror, cracked, and she stopped for a moment and brushed some of the dust away to peer into the glass.

'Gracious,' she said, when she saw her reflection, with tendrils of hair hanging loose. 'Why did you not tell me?'

She examined the glass after straightening her hair. 'I'm no different. That surprises me.'

'What did you anticipate?' he asked.

She pressed her hand to the mirror. 'I expected I would look older. Married.'

She didn't appear married to him either, but more like a woman who could stop his heart without any weapon but herself. He must be on guard and not let a shapely vision spiral him into a trap with no release.

She shouldn't bend towards the mirror like that. Her derrière pointed in his direction and her skirts were hardly full enough to be proper, and with the mirror and her bottom in sight, he saw almost as much of her breasts as he had seen in the carriage.

Her mussed hair and rumpled clothes somehow made him want her more.

Marriage had its moments.

She turned to him, wary and unsure.

'Among all this ruin, I see you,' he said. 'And I'm thankful for that special licence and the chance to partake of your aspirations.'

She didn't believe him, but she accepted his words.

Next, she moved from the room to the next one which was the smallest room, a corner room, which smelled of musty dirt and animal meanderings. 'I simply must have this chamber.'

He pursed his lips. 'You might get fleas if you sleep in this room.' It was as far from the biggest one, the one with his trunk in it, as she could get. 'Besides, your things are at the other end.'

She took no notice of him, but conceded, 'I'll have my things moved.'

'Wait.' His voice demanded attention. 'Why do you want this room?'

'Did you notice the view? You can see a small lake and a stream.' She spoke as if he had no imagination at all. Then she held out her hands, palms up. 'And the light in here is brighter than in any other. This is the best room of all for sketching.'

He tapped a board on the floor with his boot. The board was curled up. 'Did you not see the floorboard you could stumble over? The broken glass in the windows?' He took the edge of the door in both hands and moved it sideways, not to and fro. 'The door which is not even held by one good hinge?'

'Easily fixed.' She spoke to him as if she could not believe he saw those things as problems.

'The bed.' He pointed to the thing which was barely bigger than that a child might sleep in.

'That thing is full of rats, birds' nests and insects.' He sniffed. 'And the room smells like a wet dog's fur.'

She sighed. 'True. The mattress will not do.'

She went to it and began to tug at the feather bed. A scrap of cloth came loose in her hand. 'Could you help me put this out? Perhaps we can hold it together enough to carry it outside to be burned.'

He went to the bed and helped her pull the foul-smelling thing from it. He was sure animals had fared better in it than any human had on top of it. 'The one next to my room has been replaced.'

'I noticed.' She tugged at the feathered lump. 'Then I should have no trouble having the same done here.' She grunted as she moved through the doorway.

'Why do you want to sleep so far from me?'

'The light. You are welcome to move closer.'

'I don't need the light.'

He waited, unmoving. 'There is a new feather mattress in the room next to mine. Sleep on it until this room is ready for you. I will have someone begin on it tomorrow.'

He wouldn't force her to move closer and he refused to move his things to her.

Stalemate.

He'd heard that chess was not a game of pieces, but a game of territory.

He looked at the walls. There could be a lot of territory to wrangle over if they chose.

A wife should be near her husband, or at least be receptive to the thought. But he understood she didn't really believe herself a part of him.

He wondered if, in her mind, she'd made a list of wifely chores to look over occasionally and check off.

'Thank you, Marc.' Happiness flowed from her. The gratitude resulted from the chance to be alone and separate from him, but he couldn't shut his mind to the woman who stood before him and who had repeated the words of commitment to him.

Her eyes sparkled, hints of jewels. She'd never smiled at him so. No, he was sure of it. He would have remembered it. He swallowed. A temptress gazed at him.

'I'd like to be friends, Marc.'

He already had a friend he could discuss things with. Robert. Hell, even Nathaniel.

He wanted—not a partner exactly. Not a new acquaintance. Not exactly a companion. Not anything he could put a name to.

But he could put a face to it.

He wanted an Emilie.

He'd fallen into a whirlwind of Emilie and he hoped he could catch himself before he hit the ground.

Robert waited at the bottom of the stairs and watched as they brought the ruined feather bed down.

The valet raised an eyebrow and followed them outside. 'Sir, the servants' quarters are disgraceful. The best room reeks. I must move back to town immediately. I fear that I am not of enough constitution to bear this insult to my senses.'

'Robert.' She dropped the end of mattress. 'I would so hate to see you leave, but I am sure Marc would lend you the carriage this very moment.'

'I was merely jesting.' Robert assumed a malevolent stare, which faded as he addressed Marcus. 'I live to serve you, in whatever circumstances you provide, milord.' Then he stalked away, turning a corner to the servants' area.

'I don't know why he doesn't like me.' Emilie winced. 'I merely mistook him for a butler and that is an elevation over a mere valet.'

'Mere valet?' Robert snapped back from around the corner, glowering. 'No one has ever insulted me such,' he sputtered, then disappeared, a clattering noise assuring them he'd gone.

Marcus took Emilie and drew her to him. 'He is more to me than a valet.'

'I know he saved you.' She glanced behind her to make sure Robert didn't listen. 'Your clothes are perfection and I'm sure he is responsible…'

'Just because a person has a certain title, it doesn't mean that is all they are.'

'Like wife?'

'Or husband.' Marcus dropped her touch and strode away.

Wife. A perfect example to her that a designation shouldn't hamper a person's status.

Well, he was not a mere husband. He'd never felt less like a mere husband. An appendage?

He imagined her introducing him to a friend, right after she mentioned her supplies and how camel hair could make the finest tip for colour on canvas. Assuming she remembered he was in the room.

At least she would not call him Nathaniel.

Blast it. He could not see hues and now the few tints surrounding him were grey and murky.

Outdoors, he examined the world and then turned back to the structure behind him. No wonder he'd preferred the night hours. The darkness had few hues and he saw the same as everyone else in the dusk, and better than most.

Before sunset, Marcus sent the workmen en masse to the study, with cloths and a broom, bucket, water and soap. Like a crew of sailors, they made the room shipshape, or at least clean. Then he had a work table moved in for a desk and things set up.

Emilie heard the bustle and, after the men departed, she arrived with a list of more things she needed. She stood near Marcus so she could use the lamplight.

Robert came in, holding a nearly empty glass. 'You shouldn't drink alone, so I'm here to share a brandy with you.' He spoke to Marcus. 'Perhaps a cigar later after the lady has retired.'

'It has been a rough day, but not all of it was bumpy,' Marcus admitted. 'The place has decayed rapidly in a few years.' He pushed his chair back on to its two back legs. 'Although I can see the potential of the acreage and don't expect it to need much work. I don't estimate those tasks to *jostle* me too much…but just the right amount.' He interlaced his fingers behind his head and met her eyes, and she blushed. The blush hit him full force and nearly knocked the air out of his lungs. The night was so close.

Robert coughed as if a frog were in his throat.

'I am anxious for tomorrow,' Emilie suggested. 'I intend to go to the pond and see if any fish are in it. One of the workmen said the pond I see is not the same as the one further afield. He said he has lived in this area always and there is one that I must see and it is—'

'You are not to explore the woods alone.' Marcus laid a palm flat on the table.

She gulped as if he had said he was going to lock her in a dungeon.

The room was silent.

'Emilie, I do not want you hurt, or lost, or falling and breaking a bone or any number of things which could happen to you in the woods. Your safety is utmost.'

'Marc, I'll be a short distance from everyone. You'd hear a shout if I were in danger.'

'I think…not.'

He noticed Robert giving her an uppity scowl.

'Robert will accompany you.'

Robert spewed the brandy so forcefully that Marcus had to wipe his hand. 'Robert,' he chastised.

'Sir.' He rose to his full height and took on the bearing of a valet. 'I cannot go traipsing the countryside as I have many duties to attend.'

'Besides waking me in the morning and drinking brandy at night—what, pray tell, might those duties be?'

'Well, if you remember, I once saved your life.'

'And you may be called upon to save Emilie's.'

He put both hands over his eyes. 'That might be the death of me.'

'I will *not* have him in the woods with me.'
Emilie jumped to her feet. 'It is not *proper* for
a lady to be in the woods alone with a man who
is not her husband.'

'I assure you, Lady Grayson—' Robert's nose
jutted up '—you never have to worry about my
conduct with you.'

'Robert,' Marcus stated, 'you *will* accompany Lady Grayson whenever she is afield. And
you—' he fixed his attention on Emilie '—will
gracefully let him accompany you. And neither
of you should throw anything at the other.'

'It is more inspiring to walk in the woods
alone,' Emilie said sweetly. 'Inspiring. Magnificent. Magical.'

'The lady is accurate,' Robert added quickly,
moving to stand in front of Marcus so he could
press his case. 'And I believe she is a capable
woman and would be able to extricate herself
easily should any unpleasantness arrive.'

Emilie moved so quickly that she was now
between the two, facing Marcus.

'Blah.' Emilie stretched out her arm. 'You
know how dear painting is to me. It is the muse
inspired from my soul. I must be inspired. I must
create. And how can I do such a wondrous thing
if I am in the presence of…' she looked over her
shoulder '…blandness?'

Robert hissed.

Marcus was tired. He pushed the chair from the table, stood and fixed both of them with a stare and raised his voice. 'You will accompany each other when Emilie is in the woods.'

'Blah,' Emilie repeated, crossing her arms.

Robert's nose elevated as if he were the highest of the peerage and he looked at Emilie. 'I can see your point, Lady Grayson. I am too bland to be in the presence of such greatness as your painting. I am entirely without appreciation for muddy colours swirled on canvas that are supposed to invoke the viewer to rapturous incantations.'

Emilie raised one brow. 'You would not know enough to appreciate Lawrence or Michelangelo's art.'

Marcus stretched to his full height.

'Robert, help me in my room. Now. Please.'

Marcus walked out and Robert followed.

The second the door clicked shut, Marcus turned. 'Do not bicker with Emilie.'

'She started it,' Robert said, with his hand still on the door. 'She always does and you always take her side.' He sniffed loudly, shoulders lowered.

Marcus stared at the valet, waiting.

'You have been the son I never had. Now you bring in another individual to the household and you are expecting me to be her lady's maid.' He gulped. 'I had fears about the day you married and I went against my better judgement to help you meet this woman in the billiards room as you'd shown no preference for any woman before her. Then all the peace I had is gone and we are living...' He regarded the structure. 'In near rubble far beneath either of us. Particularly you.' Robert turned his back. 'I could always go to Nathaniel...' Robert's knees bent and he wilted.

Nathaniel? Blast it. Not Robert, too.

'I need you here.'

Robert's shoulders shook. He didn't speak.

'You are not her lady's maid,' Marcus added. 'You are my valet. And this is an important trust I place in you. You have guided me like a father. And you will keep Emilie safe.'

'That is a tall order.'

'You are up to it.'

'Barely.' Robert touched fingertips to his forehead. He sniffed again. 'She is not the woman I had expected you to marry and I cannot forgive that she chose Nathaniel before you. If only I had destroyed that first letter.' Robert inhaled and while still on his feet, he stumbled towards the door, body weaving. 'I had no expectation it would lead you to her. Nathaniel, I would not have minded if he'd wed her. But, you, sir, I had hoped...'

Marcus waited, unable to let himself react.

Robert puffed from his nostrils. 'But in all fairness, sir, you could have married the brightest bloom, the highest luminary, and I would not have deemed her your equal.'

After Robert exited, Marcus opened the window, feeling the coolness. So much for sending Robert away.

Robert thought him above the stars. Emilie thought him nearly as exalted, but beneath the last drip from her paintbrush.

He took off his shirt and threw it at the nearest wall.

He tried to remember each moment when he had seen her as they grew. He'd noticed her from a distance and she'd always seemed lost in her own imaginings when he tried to capture her attention. She'd not noticed him until the unveiling, and then, not truly until after she had spoken with Nathaniel.

And now they were to start a journey together, but not united. Two separate individuals travelling on the same road, but barely in the same vehicle.

She'd accepted the house and it had caused contentment deep inside him. He'd been ready to tell the men they were going back to London and might return, or might not.

But then she'd liked the house.

He'd planned a marriage—a joining much

like two countries who united so that both might profit, much like his parents' without the profanities and mistresses. The larger country would protect and finance the smaller, and the smaller would provide support troops, plus manage their care.

He'd not liked his father's dalliances because he'd found them weakening, particularly as they were well known. They'd undermined the country that his mother had created.

As Marcus grew, his father would not be with them this week, or that week, but would stop in and arrange their lives to suit him, and then he would be on his way again.

All his childhood, Marcus had felt that if his family had lived in the same home together, it would have suited them all, except his father. One cog in the wheel had caused all the disruptions.

Marcus wanted to live near his wife. He had the town house for winter. He had Stormhaven for summer. They would exist together and there would be no discordant cogs.

He slipped off his boots and lay on top of the covers, bringing about the scent of clean crisp linens and a hint of lavender. It reminded him of womanliness and when he envisioned a woman he could only see one. Emilie.

The door shut in the room next to his. Marcus

waited until the sounds quieted, then he rose and moved forward, searching out his wife.

Without knocking, Marcus entered the room. Emilie was in bed, but the lamp blazed beside her, her attention focused on her new portfolio, her hand sketching with deft strokes and her concentration rapt.

He saw the moment she became aware of him. Instantly, she closed the book she sketched in and slipped it behind the bedside table, still holding on to her pencil like a talisman she couldn't release.

His feet were bare on the rug and he crossed the room, moving to her side of the bed.

He grasped the pencil, taking it from her grip, and dropping it beside the lamp. 'You have nothing to worry about.'

'Marcus,' Emilie said, regarding him. 'Everything has changed.'

'Except us.'

'Especially us.'

'Don't think about the past or our future, or even tonight.'

'It's not that straightforward for me.'

He clasped her fingers. 'This is one night. You don't have to concern yourself about it, you only have to feel. Tonight is for you.'

'Do you mean it?'

'Completely.'

The moment the words were out of his mouth, he regretted them. He was going to be up all night—stiff as a pike—and she would ask at that point to draw him. That would not be the pinnacle of his life.

He took one of her fingertips, kissed it and hid a sigh, because Emilie seemed as stiff as a pike also, but for different reasons.

He examined the small fingers clasped inside his larger ones. He wasn't going to come second to art. Not his lovemaking. No. That would not work well in the long run. Not even for a month.

Or a night.

He took her forefinger and held it to his lips. Long. Graceful. Kissable. He caressed her hand with his face, letting his jaw rest against it, manoeuvring it to hold him close.

Then he moved her over and reached around her, tugging her near, soothing her. 'You studied me, but grant me the same desire.' Whispering, he asked, 'You wouldn't put a masterpiece in front of me and tell me to ignore it, would you?'

'Me?' she asked. 'You think that of me?'

He slipped down the shoulder of her chemise and backed away enough so that he could bend to kiss her. She was the great works all combined in one.

Then he took off his trousers and slid into bed beside her.

Chapter Fourteen

Emilie gazed at her husband. In his appearance, she could see power and strength, but reclined beside her, he relaxed, appearing at peace with the world.

As his hair brushed against her, she scented masculinity, a leather, soap, woollen and skin scent—a potent scent she'd not known before.

With the fingers of his right hand, he caressed the shoulder he'd exposed earlier when he'd lowered her chemise to her upper arm. She moved slightly so that she was turned more towards him and his left hand moved across her back and pressed them close.

His hands overpowered her with their tenderness.

With all the force of her own nature arguing with her, she pushed him away and reached for his chest. She had to touch him. She had to feel the muscle, the energy in him. The beating of his heart and the vibrancy in his skin.

She lived through the movements of her hands.

He pulled back and gazed into her eyes before his lips closed over hers and blocked the world away.

Marcus explored her skin, tracing her and bringing need alive.

'Em...'

She heard him groan out her name and she loved the sound of it on his lips. No one had ever said her name as Marcus said it and no one ever could.

His teeth grazed her neck, sending shivers throughout her arms and legs and leaving her unable to comprehend anything other than the moment.

Her fingers caressed softness mixed with hardness and absorbed the steamy heat of his skin.

She touched him carefully, awash with the sensation something so simple, yet with more complexity than she could measure, created inside her. His other arm was around her, pulling her tight against him, and she surrendered easily, comforted by his presence.

He wasn't at her side to make the night long.

He was there to ease her into a world of the two of them and make the journey easier.

Emilie studied the contours and curves that led from Marcus's neck to his jaw and her finger followed her gaze.

She skimmed the stubble appearing on his chin and opened her clasp so she could embrace more of him. His lips rested soft in her hand and he put a kiss against her.

She continued on, exploring the skin over his cheekbones, the slope of his nose, and retraced her movement to graze the softness of his earlobe. She intertwined her fingers in the tendrils of his hair, again amazed at the delicateness contrasting with the rest of him.

She didn't think—she existed—existed as if she would only ever feel this moment and it would last her to eternity.

He moved closer into her reach and absorbed her hand, as she immersed herself in him.

She didn't ask—his response had given permission and she swept a nail to the edge of the sheet, and pushed the scant piece of the fabric away, but she could not completely unveil him.

When she touched the coverings, he stilled, waiting.

Searching his eyes, she knew he accepted her perusal of him, but she couldn't move the sheet away. The fabric rested, baring his shoulders, but covering him as modestly as Moses had been.

But Moses was marble and Marcus wasn't. She heard the moving fabric and looked in time to see it slide completely away from his body, revealing something she'd never seen in any piece of artwork, or imagined.

She reached to pull the cover over him again, but he stopped her.

He moved the sheet to conceal his hardness. 'I didn't mean to startle you.'

'You didn't…exactly.' It was enlightening. Overwhelming and overpowering. And all she'd imagined.

She spread her palm and reached down where the sheet ended and leg began. Hairs curled under her fingertips as she moved from his skin to rove over the sheet. She swept her hand up, remaining on the covering, and then tugged the cloth free again.

Resting her palm against skin, she again brushed her hand over him, almost above him, but close enough so that her senses could translate the touch into form for her.

She spread her fingers, rubbing over his hard nipples and tracing the contours of his abdomen. His skin was muscled, just as the statues had been, only it was alive, warm, and the hair gave texture to her touch, then receded as she found his maleness.

He didn't speak and she understood the connection that two people who made love could share. The moments of vulnerability and discovery.

'I could never get tired of this,' she said, aware of each intake of air and the soft exhalations he made.

'That's why there are so many hours of darkness,' he said. 'So we can share moments like this.'

'But you were made for light. At least…' she paused '…for my light.'

She committed every place she touched to memory. It would linger inside her for ever, yet awareness began afresh with each stroke.

He closed his lips over hers again, lingering, tasting and beginning the slow descent into something he could not return from. Just as he felt himself going too far, he stopped.

Taking control, he traced her body, lingering at her lips, her breasts and her hips.

Then he snuggled her close to him and swept lower, caressing her, finding her pleasure and stroking it until she cried out, and he experienced the moment through her gasps. Waiting, he lay against her, intertwining their legs, content for her, but awash with contained emotions inside himself.

His forehead dampened so that when he moved, her hair attached to him and he untangled from it.

When her breathing softened, she relaxed in his embrace.

He savoured the togetherness and the memory of holding his wife near, and the closeness of sharing a pillow. Waiting, he let her snuggle into him and use his body as her refuge.

By morning he expected to strengthen the bond they had started and make love to her fully.

'I would like to draw you,' she said sleepily.

The words hit harder than any direct blow. They speared him. Their lovemaking hadn't made her realise that there was more to living than she could ever find at the end of a pencil.

'I want to be your husband, not your model,' he said.

'You can be both.'

'I suppose I could. But I don't want to be.'

'These moments meant nothing to you?' she asked, fully awake now.

He palmed her cheeks and kissed her, another one of tasting and even surrender, but only a surrender into the kiss, not into something he couldn't risk. 'This isn't enough to build a family on.'

'Did you not like…me?'

'I don't know the masterpiece to compare you to, but it's true you are a Venus, or an Aphrodite, or whomever pleases you to be the most. You are unequalled and none could top you. I must consider my place in the sum of what matters to you.'

'You don't want me to paint after all?' Her jaw tensed.

'I cannot say that now, can I? I promised you and I meant it. You could not be happy without creativity. I know that.'

Emilie was an artist. He'd once heard it said that artists developed a bond with their subjects. But he wasn't going to pose for Emilie to find out. Marriage was a different attachment and he would have love or keep the distance between them.

He thought of his parents. Now he understood their relationship better. It was easier to be away from someone who hated you, than to be married and living under the same roof. His mother could survive easier by detesting his father than trying to be considerate. And by instigating fights, his father felt vindicated by not being with his family.

Hearts. Lovely things. He should be like Nate

and lock his away. He already had the box for it, resting under his bed—the lone object there.

He kissed her goodnight and moved back to his room.

Marcus woke, aching for Emilie but not willing to bend to become less than a man. Bright light streamed into the window.

Waking fully, he would long for her the entire day. But making love to her had rewarded him.

He'd explored his sensations through her instead of experiencing them fully himself.

Whether she had grown closer to him in the night, he wasn't sure. But he became closer to himself.

He'd brought his wife to pleasure and he hoped it had brought her to something else, a realisation that he wasn't just a detour on her journey, but part of the destination.

Marcus rang the bell to alert Robert to bring the shaving water.

He'd waited a quarter of an hour when he realised that Robert would not be shaving him that morning. No matter, he ran a palm down his jawline, feeling the stubble.

He went to Emilie's room, the bed made perfectly. It no longer bothered him that the rest of the place was a shambles. He rang the bell for a maid to bring him the warm water Robert always had simmering in the kitchen when Marcus awoke.

Donning a dressing gown, he waited in the hallway for the maid and told her what he required.

He returned to his room and, within minutes, a pitcher was brought to him. The girl was new and, from the steam rising out of the jug, Marcus realised it hadn't been mixed with cold to bring it to the right temperature.

Well, he would not miss shaving one day so much.

He had a new journey before him.

Stormhaven would become a home, a woman would be beside him and within a few years he would remember this as the day he started anew. He moved to the top of the stairs and began his downward descent.

The stair tread buckled under Marcus's boot and he grasped the banister. He would have to have that floorboard mended immediately.

He strode into the kitchen. No one was there. Dishes were scattered. He saw cold bacon on a platter and took a bite.

Outside, the sun beat down on him. The thuds of hammers mixed with the sound of a saw being pulled through wood.

A wagon rumbled to the gate, bringing more

supplies. Jonas dropped the handsaw, rushing over to help with the unloading.

A man who'd just arrived with the wagon ran to him, holding out a letter. 'My pardon,' he said to Marcus. 'I'm to give you this.' Then he went back to the workmen and they began to remove the wares.

Marcus opened the letter. From his man-of-affairs. The two maids he had hired, sisters, had taken another job. He had another prospect and would send her as soon as possible, if she would consent to move to the country.

Marcus put the paper in his waistcoat pocket. They would manage.

Emilie and Robert emerged from the woods, Emilie swinging her sketch pad. The cook followed along behind with the handle of a small wooden box in her hand.

With each stride, Emilie kicked her skirts in front of her. Then she caught a glimpse of Marcus and she brightened.

It was as if he saw her for the first time, ever, and her gaze was for him only.

Emilie marched right up to Marcus and she beamed.

Oh, it would be so worth it. The responsibility of getting the building in order and creating a place for family would mean the world to him.

'Lord Grayson,' she said, waiting. Then she touched his wrists, sliding her hands down to grasp both of his. 'I sketched in the most beautiful stag today. An outline, but it should be one of my better works. When I finish, I'll show it to you. Perhaps I'll place it over the mantel.'

'This is getting heavy, Lady Grayson,' Robert complained.

She turned to go into Stormhaven. 'I must get Robert settled before he complains again, then I need to get the colours started.'

Robert trudged by Marcus, the easel under one arm and a bundle of supplies on the other side.

They moved through the doorway and the foreman of the work crew called to Marcus. Inwardly, he berated himself for the fairy tale he'd created in his mind earlier. He'd perceived that one night with Emilie and she would fall into his arms, profess love for ever and they would continue on as the master and mistress of the grand Stormhaven estate.

She would see that canvas was only fabric—it didn't have a beating heart. That he stood before her and—

What nonsense. She would ask him to move aside as he was blocking her view.

Marcus, feeling bearish, forced himself not

to growl at the workman, and worked silently beside them, instructing what he wanted, then taking guidance from the foreman on how to get the details accomplished.

When the supply wagon arrived later in the day, he finished work and returned to the house. The cabinet had arrived. 'Take it upstairs. Turn right. Second door. The library,' he spoke to the men unloading it.

Marcus moved in line behind the workmen, supervising their delivery.

Inside, Robert's stature changed when he noticed the wares being delivered.

'Ah.' Robert watched the procession. 'Lifeblood.'

Robert limped along, following the wares.

Emilie turned to him. 'Is my new easel there, Marc? You know I must have a new easel. The old one is too heavy for Robert to carry.'

'I am not a pack mule, Princess Emilie,' Robert retorted. 'Drink helps in periods of hard survival.'

Marcus noticed the case of brandy and told the boy to put the bottles in the cabinet.

Marcus needed to keep the peace, and the liquor cabinet might help. Assuming he bartered judiciously. He followed Robert.

Marcus heard Emilie following and wondered if a conflagration would ensue.

Robert rubbed his palms together. 'That is a beautiful cabinet.' Then he caressed the grain of the wood. 'Beautiful. I will fill it.' Robert spoke in ducal tones to the boy and the boy looked at Marcus with raised eyebrows. Marcus's agreement was the solitary sound in the room.

He went to the older workman and held out his hand. The man put a key in his palm.

Robert saw the key and his shoulders dropped. 'A key?' he asked.

'Yes. Surely that is fine with you. We would not want anyone making off with the brandy. And my cigars are to be delivered to me and I will put them in there as well.'

'You cannot be serious. You hardly like brandy and you complain of the smell of smoke in your clothes.'

'The cabinet will be locked. You can discuss it with me later, but my mind is set.'

'How am I to follow after her—' he thrust a finger at Emilie '—with a dry throat?'

'You are capable.'

'I will perish.' His head rolled to one side and he put a palm on the door as he staggered from the room. 'I may have to seek a post elsewhere as I cannot live like this.'

'I will miss you so, Robert.' Sunshine sparkled in Emilie's voice.

He stood straight again and Marcus saw Robert turn back, speaking softly to Emilie, and she responded, with a gasp, following him.

'And that is not why we need so much brandy. No one has to be sotted to look at my drawings.'

The delivery men watched the doorway as the two left, then one looked at the other and said nothing.

'Let's get the rest of the wagon unloaded.'

After the supplies were put away, Marcus joined the crew to help with the barn. The roof needed a lot of work.

The sounds of hammers and saws, plus a few moments of the workmen jesting, were the interruptions of the afternoon.

The older one watched Marcus. 'My son can travel from London and help us.' The man glanced to the windows. 'He'd prefer carpentry and the fields. Not indoor work.'

'Yes. It'll go faster.'

'And if you don't mind my saying so, milord, you have a face like a line of wet washing.'

Marcus helped lift a new brace post into place.

'Marriage isn't for everyone,' he said.

'I believe those two are not adjusting well to it,' the workman who'd spoken earlier said.

'They are getting along,' Marcus said. 'Friendly now compared to the first few hours of my marriage.'

'Truly?'

Marcus shrugged. 'Well, a dagger was discussed.'

The man's jaw dropped and Marcus chuckled.

The post went into place. Marcus kicked it with the sole of his boot to see if it would hold, then left the men. He could imagine the conversation they would be conducting.

As he walked to the yard, he saw Emilie outside setting up her paints. Her back was straight and she had paper hung on an easel. He could see a paintbrush in her hand and colours in the other. He saw the rinse cup on the edge of the easel and Robert stared over her shoulder.

Robert didn't have to accompany her after they returned. She was in plain sight. Safe.

She put the tray of colours on her lap, pulled the cup to her and rinsed her brush.

'What did you say?' She turned to Robert and as she moved, she dropped the cup on his boot.

'I was complimenting your unusual use of colours. And I thank you for washing my boot.'

Marcus watched as Robert flicked the water from his boot in her direction.

'Lord Grayson,' she called as he strode by. 'Might I have a word with you?'

'I would like to have a word as well, Lord Grayson,' Robert called. 'And if you'll remember, I saved your life once.'

As he got to the top of the stairs, Marcus slowed long enough to reach above where a crack in the wall stored the key to the liquor cabinet. He walked into the library, then realised Emilie was close on his heels.

He unlocked the cabinet and pulled out a bottle.

'Robert has ruined my painting.' She arrived behind him, Robert just beyond her, and held the work up for Marcus's review.

He moved towards her. 'Shush,' he said. She didn't seem to comprehend. He kept moving towards her and she backed away, still listing Robert's faults.

He snagged her waist, and in the moment her lips closed, he placed a kiss on them.

Robert held both palms up, ducked his chin and turned away. 'I have nothing to say except I believe I will retire. There is entirely too much affection in front of me.'

The valet made good on his words and Marcus remained with Emilie.

Robert was right. Marcus did have an affection for her. It crept into him, and resided, bringing so many other potent things with it.

He refused to let his mind wander, tamped away his thoughts, and went off to the fields.

That night, he noticed he didn't have a glass in his room. He didn't know why there were no glasses unless Robert had removed them on purpose. No matter. He went to the cabinet and returned to his room.

He drank slowly, and not much, as he didn't want to be foxed.

A knock on his door. 'Goodnight, Marc. Pleasant dreams.' She didn't enter.

Marcus forbade himself another drop. If he did, he would stumble and her arms would ease his descent, but increase the speed.

All their lives, his father had raised Marcus to be the bearer of the family heritage. Nathaniel hadn't had a problem with it. When Marcus had wondered aloud about meaningless encounters, Nathaniel had been untroubled, remarking that Marcus could have all the responsibility and the conscientious women, Nathaniel would take the unconscionable ones.

Then Marcus viewed the women Nate preferred. They laughed loudest, frolicked longest and had the *joie de vivre* that Lady Semple had mentioned.

The beauties of the world always spied Nate. Nathaniel never had to seek them out, but Marcus noticed the marriage-minded ones tended to discover him first. The frivolous ones initially sighted Nathaniel.

True, Marcus simply had to glance into the bevy fluttering near Nate, single someone out and she would dislodge herself and flutter right to him.

Emilie had mistaken him for Nathaniel at the dance.

When Marcus had singled Emilie out, she'd still written to Nathaniel.

At the time, it hadn't mattered. But now it ground like glass shards into his consciousness.

He reflected on the women he had entertained before he married. Those women he had not chosen. The quiet, docile, gentle women who listened with grace to his every word. They'd been all but invisible to him. Emilie, he could see. But he wasn't sure it was enough.

He stared at the ceiling he could not even discern in the gloom and he desired—every fibre of Emilie.

Her perfect body which he had felt once and that touch had sealed his fate. He didn't know how he could resist her, but he kept telling himself that his hands had lied to him. She had not really felt like the first day of spring with the magic of a rainbow. She had not really felt so incredible that he could still imagine the press of her skin against his lips.

He would make a new world for himself, even if he might be the solitary one living in it. And it would be with this roof over him.

He would fight for it, as soon as he worked out how one armed oneself against beauty and feelings. Then he realised. Soldiers. A man could not fight a battle without soldiers.

Chapter Fifteen

 ⟡⟡⟡

Emilie sat on the edge of her bed, swinging her foot. Marcus had barely recognised she was alive since he had made love to her. She'd thought it would have meant more to him. He appeared to have forgotten it. He spent more hours with the stablemen than he did with her.

She had asked her new maid, Mary, where he went and had discovered he joined the workmen in the old cottage, staying out as late as he might at a gambling hell. And Mary told her the men wagered and drank and boasted of their pursuits.

She'd waited, alone in her room, with her flower portfolio to sketch in.

She had delayed her journey in the mornings so she might eat with him before he worked in the fields and he had acted as if she weren't there. Oh, he had said a few pleasant words, such as 'Good morning' and 'That was a delicious meal', but he had not even noticed her at his side more than he might a footman.

He'd spent hours in the servants' area making notations in a book. Robert had followed along, giving advice, and Robert had given Emilie a smug, self-satisfied, kiss-my-coattails grin.

Emilie moved to the top of the stairs and paced in the hallway. Marcus. He could not be so blind. She touched her waist, grimacing as her hand rested over the tight fit of the corset. She'd had the maid someone had hired from the village give her an extra tug or two and she felt strapped inside the garment. Even wasps would be jealous.

She touched her hair carefully. Extra pins and she'd let the maid spend an hour on it. If Marcus didn't return soon she'd be having the vapours, her scalp bruised from the pins, her breasts pushed up to her neck, suffocating from dollops of perfume—for nothing. A dead, odd-shaped pincushion that smelled good.

Marcus. What if he'd married her with the expectation that she would have the same talents as her aunt Beatrice? What if he'd only wanted her skills?

He'd brought her to a place filled with inspiration. He'd made love to her, but restrained himself, and he'd kept further from her after their intense moments.

He saw her as nothing more than a resident in Stormhaven. He spent time at the barn, the pens, and concerned himself with making sure the estate was perfect.

What if his intention was to create a life that was nothing more than a reproduction of the scene inside his mind? And the figures inside it were kept at a distance to prevent them from disrupting him?

She would have to show him that she was flesh and blood.

The door opened. Her husband had returned for his evening meal.

She swept down the stairs, serenity in her movements, chin high—practically forced so by her corset—and she planned her pace so she arrived at the bottom as Marcus did. She gave a twist of her hand, moved wide and saw her mistake. She lost her footing and stumbled towards him, crashing into his middle.

The *oof* she heard was not her fault—her balance was off from getting stuffed into the dress. He jumped sideways, catching her, then carefully propped her up.

'Emilie.' He put her firmly on her feet and increased the distance between them. He kicked at the stair treads, testing their strength, as he put her aside. 'I thought the crew had repaired that broken wood. I'll have Jonas inspect it immediately.'

'You don't have to concern yourself, Lord Grayson,' she said, speaking so softly that he might be entranced. 'Sadly, I stumbled.'

He studied her, then waved a hand in front of him, clearing the perfume. 'I do not care if you have brandy early in the day. I know you saw where I hid the key. You don't need to cover your breath with perfume, but you shouldn't drink so much you cannot get down the stairs.'

He shook his head. 'Tell Robert to see that a maid brings you one of his concoctions in the morning and it will help the pain you'll have. For now, try to sleep it off so you don't hurt yourself.'

One must do what one could. Her demeanour almost dripped adoration at him. 'Lord Grayson. You are so correct. Might you help me to my bed so I can rest safely?'

She hadn't seen the maid watching until he motioned to the woman. 'I still have the mud of the fields on me. Mary can see you safely to your bed.'

'Yes, miss.' Mary dashed into view. She'd pummelled Emilie into the clothing. The woman almost lost her fight with laughter.

'Very well,' Emilie said sharply. She turned, grabbed the banister and marched up the stairs as quickly as one could who'd been halved in the middle.

At the top of the stairs, she passed Robert.

'Lady Grayson,' he said. 'This mere valet will be taking himself off to bed. Should you need anything, please don't hesitate to ask one of your maids.'

The next morning, Marcus saddled his horse and rode before dawn. He'd taken to the roads, putting distance between himself and Emilie. The daylight hours were long, but the nights were unremitting.

He returned to the barn, but sent Jonas to fetch him breakfast, even though nothing seemed palatable.

He wanted Emilie as a true wife, and a united home. Not two individuals sharing a country. He wanted something few people truly experienced, judging from the world he lived in.

If he so much as hinted that their relationship must come before anything else, he could feel the resistance. *You promised*, she'd say. And, yes, he had promised that she could always paint. But he hated the image of himself drowning and her suggesting he wait before being rescued until she'd captured his expression.

He made himself wait.

* * *

Emilie heard a noise as she stopped at the open door to Marcus's room. She peered inside. The maid was making the bed.

Emilie strolled in. Marcus's best boots hung upside down on a boot rack. There was a definite hint of leather.

The woman raised her head briefly, but bent back to her work.

'He is very tidy,' Emilie told the servant.

'He is the tidiest person,' the woman admitted. 'Not like most high-born people—I've heard.'

Emilie went to his wardrobe and opened it. She looked at the folded garments.

She rifled her fingers among the clothing. Another scent caught her consciousness. She picked up one of his shirts and held it to her nose. She could smell Marcus as if he were in her arms.

The maid coughed.

'Lord Grayson is truly a wonderful man.' Emilie put the shirt back in place. 'I notice because he is my husband and I have a most critical eye because of my studies.'

'Aye,' the woman agreed. 'He could make any woman forget herself.'

Emilie tensed.

The maid laughed, then continued. 'Except me, of course. I've got my own man to tickle my fancy at night. He can't sleep without tumbling me—course I don't really mind.'

'Yes.' Emilie shut the door of the wardrobe. Such base talk from a servant. She had not been properly trained. 'Lord Grayson is the same.'

The woman's face was as serene as the pool on a windless day, but the fish were laughing from under the water.

Emilie perceived the bed and wondered how it would feel to sleep beneath those covers. Her own were lacking. Lacking Marcus. They'd been so much more inviting when Marcus was in the bed. She'd planned on many, many more nights like that, and that plan had evaporated in the morning mist.

'Lord Grayson has magnificent shoulders.' Emilie's fingers followed the woodgrain of the wardrobe.

'Yes, he does,' the maid said, innocently.

The woman was unfit for her job.

Marcus had revealed his man-of-affairs in London had been unable to hire anyone willing to move on short notice, so he had found people who lived near by. He'd informed her that if she truly wanted anyone but Robert to leave, he would let them go. But the work would remain. Emilie would need to assist, as he had assigned strict duties to each servant, and he'd been unable to employ anyone else. The cook was no longer allowed to mix Emilie's paints, but had to attend to meals.

The maid interrupted her thoughts.

'When I took water to the men yesterday, Lord Grayson was returning to the barn. He'd removed his shirt and he's very muscular,' the maid continued as if unaware of Emilie's scowl. 'Water was dripping from him,' the woman said, rubbing her hand over her arm in an uncalled-for manner, 'which somehow didn't look unpleasant.'

'Do you not have washing to do?' Emilie asked.

'A lot of it,' the woman answered. 'Paint does not scrub out quickly.'

Emilie shrugged. 'Well, you must get to it and I will take the men fresh water. I am sure Lord Grayson will not mind.'

'Are you certain?' the woman asked. 'It's refreshing for me to take the men a treat.'

'You have too many duties.' Emilie turned away. 'And I need to see how the work is progressing. The pens are of extreme importance to me and it will give me a chance to check the livestock.'

'Very well,' the woman spoke softly.

Emilie got the pail and ladle, filled the bucket with fresh water from the outside pump and walked to the barn, where the men were replacing the roof.

Marcus perched on the roof with the men and she didn't see how he kept from tumbling to the ground.

Forcing herself to remain calm, she waited, watching his shirt outline his torso as he moved and the lines of his trousers as they hugged the muscles in his legs. But, he was perched precariously on that roof.

Finally, he spotted her and moved to the ladder. The others followed.

After they had got their fill of water, the men returned to their work, but Marcus remained beside her and put a hand up to shade the sun as he inspected the repairs. Emilie turned to retreat, but Marcus took hold of her arm and pulled her closer. 'Are you here to see me?'

'No. I didn't want Mary to see you.'

'Mary? The maid?'

He brushed at her cheek, which surprised her, and anticipation rose. When Marcus beheld her, she felt unique. Enchanting.

'Yes. She mentioned seeing you without your shirt.'

'The afternoon was hot. We'd visited the pool to cool off and removed our shirts there,' he said. 'None of us expected her to be about when we returned.'

She held the bucket at her side. 'I think you should only be viewed by an artist.'

'I agree.' His fingers trailed her arm and his lips moved so close she thought he would kiss her, but he didn't. 'One in particular.'

Marcus schooled himself to be firm. No matter how much he wanted her for that moment, he wanted her more for a lifetime. He wanted so much and he wasn't sure she was capable of giving love.

He could see the hues in her cheeks, the contrasts of light and dark in her eyes.

He couldn't stop himself. His hands slipped to hold her waist, unmoving.

'Do you miss Nathaniel?' he asked, quietly.

'No. We did speak, but not for long,' she said, words straightforward. 'He wouldn't enjoy the farm.'

'No. He wouldn't.'

She rested against him, tipping her head to his shoulder. Everything about her tantalised him, except her one true love.

'Marc, I was so wrong about you.'

'When?' He braced himself.

'I judged you a rake.'

He didn't speak. Never would he have dreamed he could stay from Emilie's bed. The control was important to him. He wouldn't become his father if he could resist these moments with Emilie.

'I was a rake. I'm not now. Never again.'

* * *

Stabbing desire invaded Emilie.

Never again.

Never.

Again.

Marcus probably spent his nights in his chambers reading pious works. Goodness, he had agreed quickly enough to the marriage when she had compromised him. She remembered his trying to send her away and he had smelled of brandy. If not for the drink, she doubted he would have fallen into her arms.

She suspected Robert had somehow tricked Marcus into the whole of it. Robert could be scheming.

From all she had seen of Marcus, he had few wanton yearnings about him, but when they burst forth, they overwhelmed her. Their first night had been glorious. Sublime.

'What's wrong, Em?' he asked and his knuckles brushed against her cheek.

His arms encircled her.

She was enveloped in his scent, his strength and could feel the beat of his heart.

But, he didn't press himself against her and she realised he didn't fancy her as a woman, but as an artist. He slept alone because he wasn't tempted by her.

He had told her at the beginning that she could

paint, and now, now she understood why. He had simply wanted to become her patron.

She could have screamed. She had married and had become his property and he had abandoned her for labour and toil.

She could create landscapes to her content. Her days were of her own design.

Except she wanted to rip the buttons from his clothes.

She tightened her shoulders and looked at him. She put her palm flat, and ran her fingertips over his cheeks.

'Marc, I fear you work too much,' Emilie said.

'It's keeping me alive, Em.'

She thought of her flower portfolio. She had purchased it to sketch blooms in, but instead, she'd drawn Marcus on the pages and those moments had saved her. 'I understand.'

'Much to be done,' he answered. More than he'd anticipated. But it was saving him, he could feel it. Each day his body strengthened and he tired, and he fought temptation by instructing the crew. He'd insisted their job hadn't been finished until they shared a card game, and wagered the next day's jobs. The gambling lasted long into the night, with tasks changing hands many times. He relished the same camaraderie he'd had in his clubs and no one here had questioned his orders the next day, but ran more quickly to get them accomplished.

In London, he'd been one of the pack—here he was the leader. Jonas looked to him for guidance and Marcus provided that without hesitation, learning and commanding at the same instant.

'You have men to do the work.' Emilie wavered, uncertain.

She no longer reminded him of the waif he'd once seen. This woman needed to be comforted. Held. Reassured.

'You must let the others do their duties,' she said, breaking the spell inside him that had weakened his resolve.

He saw Jonas watching. Marcus called the man to his side. A soldier. Reinforcements were needed.

'Yes, but I learn more about it if I am helping. It's why I must live here. And the work is done better if I am involved. I make the decisions and understand the how and why of it.'

And the work helped tire him and take the frustrations of need for her and pound them out with a hammer or grasp at one end of the saw. The workmen's foreman was becoming a friend to Marcus and he understood Marcus's need to keep busy.

She stayed beside him. 'My father doesn't work much physically. Your father doesn't.'

'That was expected of me as well, but…' he shrugged '… I like it.'

They were near the pens and Marcus heard the foreman catching up to them.

'I must check on the colt,' she said, walking to the pen. The horse cantered to her.

'Do you have any questions about the livestock?' Marcus asked. 'Mr Jonas can answer.'

She patted the horse. 'No.'

Marcus watched. Jonas coughed.

Marcus appraised the foreman and Jonas handed him a hammer. They both walked away.

Marcus tossed the hammer up and caught it by the handle on the descent.

'I can ask the men to stay on for a few more weeks,' Jonas said, 'but they're anxious to get back to their families.'

'The two from the village will provide enough assistance for us. As soon as they finish the house, let the others return to their homes.'

'Everything will fall into place on the estate if the work is continued,' Jonas said. 'With the hands working, and your ideas, there will be a lot of labour ahead.'

'I'll have years of getting the place's appearance to my satisfaction,' Marcus answered.

'What better do you have to do?' Jonas asked. 'You? A newly married man? A wife inside who fastens her eyes on you every time she goes on a walk to her painting and then returns several times back and forth during the day, and sometimes sets an easel up where her face is right in line with whatever you are doing. Yes, carpentry is very important, milord.'

Marcus glared at him.

'You can give me the hammer,' Jonas said, reaching out. 'My workers will complete the barn.'

Marcus composed himself, kept the tool and went back to work. He was building something, only he didn't know if it would fall to the ground in the first breeze.

Robert avoided him, but Marcus didn't care. He preferred it. The valet personally held Marcus responsible for Emilie's presence. And he hated the restraints on the brandy.

He had heard no shouting. No one had found him to tell him the outrage of the day. He might sleep well if he could ignore the summer heat permeating his bedchamber. He had to believe that in a few days, maybe even tonight, Emilie would come to him.

The thought of her in his bed made him ache with longing. If she didn't come to him soon, he would go to her. He couldn't wait much longer.

She would have to realise he was flesh and blood and alive. Desire pounded in his body, and with each strike he'd made on a nail, he released tension, but not the longing.

He was exhausted from the work and that helped a small amount. Still, he fought to sleep.

In the night, Emilie knocked on Robert's door.

'Robert,' she whispered, holding her candle and turning the latch and sticking her head inside. 'I need to stargaze. The night is bright and it is so perfect, plus the temperature is hot and I cannot sleep.'

'Go get that man upstairs to indulge your fancy.' Robert sat up. His hair was mussed and he even wore a nightcap. 'I am not watching the skies.' He waved her away, snuggling back into his pillow. 'It is full of inadequate drops of light and they generally do not move much and they never sing or frolic. I see no reason to watch them.'

She held up a bottle of brandy. 'I was going to take this with me.'

She saw the defiance fade and he wet his lips.

'Now that I am awake, it is too hot to sleep. The heat in here is much too oppressive. Let me dress while you get a cup. I will meet you at the servants' door.'

He nearly beat her outside.

'See, Robert, how the heavens surround us.'

She spoke after she filled his glass and sat on the ground. An owl hooted in the distance.

'I will search for them as soon as I have finished my brandy.' He held it out from him as if he could see inside the contents in the darkness. 'I see the heavens in it. I mean no offence, Lady Grayson, but I cannot tell one star from another. I am here because of your bribe and, I must say, that was thoughtful of you. How did you get Marc to release it to you?'

'He didn't hide the key very well and he knows I am aware of it. He has accused me of drinking too much of it already and I haven't touched it until now.'

She hid a yawn. Staying awake until she knew Marcus slept hadn't been easy.

'He hid the key well,' Robert complained.

'It is—' She stopped, her hands behind her in the grass, and leaned backwards. 'It is hidden.' She toed off her slippers.

'You will not tell me?' He snorted. 'It's not that you care to imbibe.'

'I won't because Marc won't believe either of us if we say that we were broken into and robbed of our spirits.'

'I cannot conceive of anything else in that dilapidated mess a thief would deem worthy of his time. That heap of boards,' he grumbled. 'And the countrified maids all have their farm-bred noses stuck up.' He stopped. 'I shouldn't have let Marc have such a hand in selecting servants. The boy has no idea of what a house needs.'

She laughed. 'It is a fine estate, or it will be, Robert, after the spate of repairing. And you are the lone servant who does nothing.'

'Which goes to show how poor Marcus is with hiring. He is far too understaffed. The maids should have reprieves for mischief. Lightness. For staring at glowing spots in the heavens with you. Give me another drink before I die.'

'If you die, I will bury you with a landscape of mine in your hands,' Emilie said.

He grabbed the bottle from her. 'That concept will keep me alive.'

She laughed and then laughed even louder when Robert glared. He put the glass on to the ground and tossed the cork in her direction. She batted it away.

In his bedchamber, Marcus stirred. The weather had cooled, but the night gave no respite. He dreamed of her again as he did whenever he slept. Over and over, but this time it was the sound of her laughter that had awoken him.

He imagined her smiling and then he remembered her curves. She might have the heart of an artist, but her own shape was of a Venus.

She probably could not sleep either. He would

check to see if she might like his company. He wanted the length of her beside him, to feel the touch of her against him again, wrapping each other together, letting the warmth of their bodies soothe away the temperatures of the night.

He could not plan a proper seduction of her heart with his mind tied around her warmth.

Marcus walked to her room and didn't knock. After all, he was the master of Stormhaven and she was the mistress. He missed her more than the cool temperatures of the night, or anything he'd ever longed for.

Once he unleashed her passions, fully bringing her to an awareness of the moments they could share as a couple, surely she would see beyond her paintbrushes to her husband.

When he entered her room, he stopped, not believing what he saw.

She was not in her bed. He strode across to pull the counterpane up and looked under it, even while being completely aware she was not in the bed. How dare she not be in her bed? Nor his?

He strode to his room, pulled his trousers on and went downstairs.

He opened the door to Robert's room and saw the empty bed. He was as awake as if he'd been dunked naked in snow.

A hint of burning candle wax touched his

nose and he realised the laugher he'd heard hadn't been a dream. The sound had been from below his window.

He opened the outer door and gently closed it. He moved barefoot, silent, and walked as if not to disturb smoke.

Voices carried to his ears and he went towards them, but he stayed in the shadows to conceal his presence.

Chapter Sixteen

Marcus could see Robert, glass to his lips, and could hear Emilie talking. He discerned her outline, as she reclined on the ground as comfortably as any nymph.

Darkness had intensified the world, bringing earthy scent mixed with summer blossoms to him.

'You must learn to like the stars, Robert.' Emilie's voice carried to him. 'They are night magic—their sparkles. It is the theatre of the heavens. We have crickets, frogs and owls for the orchestra. Wind is the applause when it rustles in the leaves. We are the audience and have the same seating as Roman emperors or kings of the past.'

He knew he risked being seen if he moved closer, but he had to investigate the stars. He wanted to see them through her eyes.

He gazed overhead into the immenseness.

The night infused him with wonder and he realised he stood in a different spot in his existence than he had ever been before. The stars were the same, but he was no longer looking at them from the view of a child, or of a man who had nothing better to do than laugh away the hours of the night. He studied the phenomenon of the heavens above and realised the marvels didn't stop at the end of the stars, but also reached to the people around him and his daily life.

'And next you are to tell me that I can make wishes upon them and they will come true.' Robert spoke.

'What would you yearn for, Robert?' She sounded genuinely interested.

'I fear I cannot say. Your ears are too delicate.' He swirled the liquid in his glass.

'Robert. Is it worse than what you said when I bumped you with my easel?'

'You dropped it on my injured toe. Now they're all sore, thanks to you.'

'You have ruined three pictures now. The first one you fell on to. The one of you as a shepherd gathering brandy bottles. The one of your nose. I insist you must stop.' Her words had a lulling quality, almost fading away.

'You had barely begun that last dabble,' Robert stated, calmly. 'And, it was not developing into one of your better ones.'

For a few seconds, neither spoke.

'I liked it.'

'I could tell as you spat out oaths at me. Now, that was not appropriate for you to say. You sounded as if you have no upbringing. Did you learn that speech from Marc?'

'Goodness, no.' She straightened. 'I don't think he would even know how to say those words.'

'I think he would,' Robert admitted, refilling the glass. He took a moment to examine the stars. 'As he has repeated them loudly to me and added his own variations.'

'Mmm…' She stretched back again, her chin to the heavens. 'He does not talk much with me.'

'I'm sure he's told you that nonsense about listening to other people instead of speaking honest words.' Robert ambled over and tapped her shoulder with the bottle. When she turned to him, he handed it to her, offering her a drink. She declined.

'Yes. He has. He is near perfect, is he not?'

'No—and Nathaniel was your first choice,' Robert grumbled. 'You should have seen the grief on Marc that morning after you cavorted with his brother. He told me about it, but had no notion of how he sounded. He would have fared better if someone had kicked him in the abdomen. I thought he might be catching some odious ailment and I feared for his safety.' He took a sip. 'Not yourself, of course. Another odious ailment.'

'I selected Nathaniel because I didn't hold out much hope for him.' She pushed her toes into the grass. 'Marc— I don't know. I thought he detested me. And besides, he was… I could not figure out Marc—and who would want a husband with his own notions?'

'He's more sensible than Nathaniel. I assure you.'

'Yes…' She paused. 'Yes,' she repeated as she stared overhead. 'I did end up with the better of the two. In fact, he's— That was my mistake.' She laughed. 'I didn't want a husband, but got one. Unfortunately, he is too honourable.'

'Marc?' Robert choked.

'Yes. He is not the same man I'd heard tales of. He brought me to this place and I see deer daily and the birds are fascinating, and I do not have to go to parties and I have the stream— which I like. But he is not behaving as expected. I never dreamed he would stay here.'

A breeze blew Marcus's hair and he moved sideways, dislodging a pebble. He froze.

Robert whispered, 'Did you hear that? Something in the woods. What if it is an undead spirit?'

'Robert, ghosts are more afraid of you than

you are of them.' She sighed. 'I will not let them steal your brandy.' He heard the resignation in her voice.

'Lady Grayson, if I were not so thirsty, I would spill this on you. Accidentally, as you always do, of course.'

'I have never hurt you on purpose.' She sounded affronted. 'And you did ruin my work.'

'The last one was an accident,' he said. 'I really did fall. I hold you responsible for it, also.'

Robert faced the sky. 'These stars are dull. They ought to move about to give more interest. Yes, they should wander about.'

'*They* do. They move all night.'

'If you drink enough…'

'Not another bottle, Robert.' She tapped at his feet. 'The one is doing you too well. I will need you all day tomorrow.'

Robert cocked his head. 'You are not the usual sort Marc courted. Not the feminine variety. He's often remarked to me how he adores a woman who sways when she walks.' Robert groaned. 'And feet. Of all things, feet…' Again, Robert groaned.

Marcus's jaw dropped. He'd never said any such thing to Robert.

'He has spoken many, many hours of the beauty of a woman's ankles and how he loves to count each toe,' Robert continued. 'It brings him to rapture. Feminine feet.'

'Toes? Feet?' She picked up a stick and tossed it into the woods. The object crashed to the ground.

Robert jumped, then relaxed as he realised what had caused the sound.

'Nonsense,' she said.

'Whatever you say, Lady Grayson. I miss London, but I can't leave Lord Grayson. He needs me and someone has to take care of you.'

Emilie gasped.

'Do you not go along with that?' Robert knelt down and settled beside her. 'You paint. You take no notice of the household. I'd wager you're no different from how you were last year, or the year before or the year before that. Some people mature. Some people just age,' Robert said. 'I cast no stones. I compare you to myself.'

'I'm not flattered.'

'You shouldn't be.'

'Does he mention marriage or his opinion of it?'

'Lady Grayson, how would I know?' He grunted. 'Yet, it is my job to know these things. I so envisioned you to be much more like the woman Marc mentions in his private papers.'

'What woman?' Emilie's tone sharpened.

'She is not real.' Robert let out a loud yawn.

'You woke me to ply me with drink and question me. Now get it over with so I do not have to listen as much tomorrow when I am with you. I don't know why you couldn't realise I will need more drink then.'

'You mentioned a woman…'

'In Marc's list,' Robert added. 'The List.'

Marcus let out a slow exhalation. Robert was lying through his sotted teeth.

'What list?'

'I'm not to know of it. But since he was a child, Marcus has kept a list of what he foresaw as necessary in a wife. It may not be in the box under his bed, of course, but I suspect it is. He has always hidden it from place to place. And I don't know for sure where it is now, but he mentions it to me incessantly. I know he would not leave it behind. It is hidden somewhere within these walls.'

'What did he have on it?'

'This is good brandy, Lady Grayson. Might I have the location to the key?'

'No.'

The silence reached a crescendo.

'What is on the list?' she asked.

'I fear, for all the drink in the world, I could not divulge it, as I have never seen the document. It is something Marc has mentioned to me repeatedly—his list of what he concludes is perfection in a helpmate—and when I catch him scribbling on it, he hides it from my view. He read a paragraph to me once and said he has updated it as he matured. Once he may have said in passing how much he admired a woman and I saw him writing after that. A retiring woman. Compassionate to his family. Generous to servants.'

'Do not assume I believe anything you say.'

'Well, I may have added the part about being generous to servants—and for your edification, I do not deem myself a servant to Marcus, but a companion. I am a confidant. A mentor. Almost before he was out of his governess's arms, I was there for him. His first word was "No". His second "Mother". And his first full sentence was "Robert, fetch my cravat."'

'Robert, be serious.'

'You know, Lady Grayson, tying a man's cravat could bring the two of you closer. He and I have had many deep conversations while I have dressed him in the morning.'

Marcus tensed. Robert had best keep his confidences.

'What do you speak about?'

'Well… Let me see…'

Marcus involuntarily made a fist.

'We've talked about his musical abilities. His deep appreciation for good boots. And that is where I learned of his fascination with women's feet and his comments on the list he has. Perhaps he has it stored in the box under his bed.'

'Can you get me the key to the box?'

'I could. But I won't. Unless you give me another bottle to ease my conscience. I would not even ask Marcus about his inventory of the perfect woman if I were you as he will tell you it does not exist.'

'Marc is more private than I anticipated.'

'He would enjoy a journey to the pool with you. I should be ill in the morning.'

'You are trying to get out of going yourself.'

'Yes. Marc should have to go with you. The two of you need to spend daylight hours together as it enhances the night-time hours.' Robert stopped the glass halfway to his lips and turned to her. 'Trust me. Just trust me on this. You'll never see the heavens the same as you would if Marc were with you. You must insist upon it. Look lovingly at him. Brush against him. Your skills in flirtation are non-existent. Work on them. Get him to go with you. Surely you can discover some womanliness somewhere in you. Or borrow some. Don't expect to find any from the maids here.' He finished the glass.

'Oh, and one thing you must know about Marcus. Don't mention the puppy he lost as a child. He hasn't recovered from the loss.'

'Tragic,' she said. 'To hold something dear and lose it.'

Marcus filled his lungs. She had no idea. And Robert—Robert had taken on the role of a matchmaking mama.

'He is so beautiful that I can forgive him for ignoring me. He should be allowed the licence only to be admired.'

Robert sputtered and choked, and she moved sideways to make sound thumps at his back.

Beautiful? Marcus's attention locked on to the word. Emilie had just called him—not handsome—but beautiful.

Several times in his past women had chattered on about how handsome he was and it hadn't meant anything to him.

Emilie, his wife, had said he should have the right to be admired. She saw him differently than anyone else ever had.

'Stop, Lady Grayson,' Robert snapped as she continued to thump his back, recapturing Marcus's attention. He moved from her ministrations. 'If I am dead, it will be hard for you to drag my body along through the forest with you and I am sure you would have to do that. Even in death, you would not let me escape.'

'Of course not. I am so pleased we are friends now, Robert.'

'Lady Grayson, you are becoming the daughter I never had and would abandon. But blood is thicker than brandy,' he muttered. 'Thankfully so. Because I like brandy. Wine is good, too. Don't forget. And I like puddings. Cook has been dreadful about that.' He stretched and pushed himself to his feet.

'Thank you for enjoying the stars with me, Robert.' She stood, then twirled around, gazing above.

He grumbled, 'Do not mistake my loyalty to spirits as admiration for the heavens.'

'Robert, you must help me further my connection to his family. I have met Marcus's mother, but have only spoken with his father during the breakfast. I suspect he didn't think me appropriate for Marcus. I might invite him here so he can truly get to know me.'

'You'd best be careful of that. His father pushes Marcus and doesn't see the true value of him.' Robert considered. 'But now since Marcus is working about the place and wed, his father might respect that.'

'Should I invite his sister or Nathaniel?'

'No. I think you should concentrate on yourself and Marcus. Why didn't you suggest he stargaze with you tonight?'

'When Marc is near, my brain gets jumbled. I can't see past him to paint, or enjoy nature.' She sighed.

Marcus understood how a painting would feel in a museum if it were secretly alive and waiting to be admired and the visitors walked right past it to shout out in awe at the marvellous sculpture of a tree.

'He prefers to spend more time with the renovations than me.'

'He might be sorting himself out. This is as new to him as it is to you.'

'But it's his ancestral home.'

'It's your home, too, Lady Grayson.'

'It's all strange.'

'And he's your husband.'

'It doesn't feel like I've married. It really doesn't.'

They strolled closer to the walls and Marcus returned to his room, suddenly chilled by the night.

Emilie didn't feel like herself near him, but she'd said no such thing about his brother.

In the middle of the night, for a simple conversation, she had sought out Robert before her husband.

And she didn't feel married. His father had once said the same thing to him.

The next afternoon, he was close to the barn when he saw the two returning from the woods, loaded down with an easel, a lunch basket and the day's supplies.

He heard Robert clear his throat.

She changed her path, progressing towards Marcus.

'We had a fine session today, even though Robert was so slow his shadow kept outrunning him. Lord Grayson, do you want to go with us tomorrow?' Emilie asked. 'The butterflies are in full force and the wildflowers are entrancing.'

'Yes, Lord Grayson.' Robert propped the easel on to the ground. 'I have never seen so many glorious butterflies. The woods are thick with them. Flora and fauna abound. The stream is refreshing. Well shaded.'

'A picnic?' Emilie asked. 'A picnic would be delightful. Robert could stay behind in your place to help the workers.'

Robert sputtered, gaping at Emilie. 'Or I could supervise the household staff from the comfort of a chair.'

'No. Thank you for the offer.' Marcus turned away, picked up the nail he'd dropped, and returned to his hammer. The two took the hint.

As far as performances went, it wasn't bad. He tapped the hammer on to the nail head enough to hold it in place and completely set the nail with one pound.

He stared at the iron against the wood.

He had strength he didn't know he had.

Taking another nail, he set it, then, with a swift blow, he finished the pound.

He had a family, like it or not.

Surveying the estate, he picked another nail.

He looked at the structure of Stormhaven. He needed to expend as much effort on the inside as he did the outside. He had the strength.

Emilie watched her husband from the window. 'I fear Marc may have taken a taste of your brandy. I am certain the bottles were not exactly as they were the night before. He's ill.'

'I have no sympathy for him. He had a number of my brandy bottles at the side of his bed this morning and one was uncorked,' Robert grumbled. 'I will not work for a man who drinks to excess.'

Emilie took her flower portfolio and opened it. On the second page, she stopped to study the drawing she had completed of Marcus's hands and sighed. They were holding a lady's glove.

She touched the paper and the feeling of Marcus's skin overwhelmed her, but immediately it faded. The page lay flat. Without pulse.

Then she leafed through the other pages and closed the book, taking it to her room.

Marcus's bedroom door was closed, but she peeped inside and took a quick meander, enjoying the masculine feel of the space. Oh, the room was precious—scented with shaving soap and leather boots and all the best parts of a man. She imagined Marcus's profile again and fanned herself. She would get nothing on to paper if she kept daydreaming about him.

She drew her breath in.

Well, she could draw. She exhaled. The flower portfolio saved her. In it, she could devote herself to creating. She could sketch herself contented, or as close as she could be without Marcus in her arms.

That night, Marcus imagined he could still hear her sweet voice as she bargained with her enemy and his friend over his private details. And, dear Robert, the man who had been a part of his days more than his father, was leading her along like a puppy on a string.

He went to his frock coat and took the key from the pocket. Reaching beneath the bed, he moved out the box and unlocked it, putting the key inside.

He took the letters and began to read them, one by one. A few letters from his mother, one from his father expounding on the heir's duties, a few from Nathaniel that he now wanted to rip up and the ones Robert had written to him when he was at university.

Shoving them back into the box, he remembered burning the other letter that had changed the course of his life.

The one from Emilie to his brother.

Ah, he should have kept that one. He used the heel of his boot to kick the container back under the bed.

Even with ire in his heart, he was not immune to her. The anger went no lower than the waistband of his trousers, and below that everything else disappeared but the burning he had for her. What had she done to him? How could he be so mad for a woman who would use him without mercy?

Chapter Seventeen

'Emilie, I don't want to concern you, but I fear Robert may have found the key to the brandy?'

'Really?' She gulped and rubbed the neck of her dress. 'Don't be angry with him, Marc. I am sure he meant no harm.'

'I am not the least upset, Emilie. Robert is long in my heart and deep in my confidence. If he felt he should have a swallow or two, how could I mind?' Particularly if the cabinet now contained bottles filled with water or tea. Cook enjoyed concocting potions. Beetroot juice added colour. He imagined Robert's astonishment when he discovered that fact.

'Marc.' She touched his arm and then hugged him. He gave in to the moment, relishing the exuberance he could feel.

He forced himself away. Away from the innocence and zest of Emilie. She'd been sheltered by her parents. Something he didn't think he'd ever experienced. His earliest memories were of his parents' fights, instructions of duties and rules for ways to behave in society, and efforts to grow quickly enough so he could escape.

After the wedding party where he'd seen Emilie, he'd determined he would be included with the adults and, that night, he had taken Nathaniel and they had slipped out into the streets.

Two hours later, Robert had found them inside a tavern, but he'd watched from a distance. Marcus never knew when Robert withdrew. The carriage waited, empty, at the door, when Nathaniel and Marcus departed and the groom jumped down to help them.

Marcus's life had changed, he'd been propelled into adulthood.

Now he wanted substance and stability.

'I have a surprise planned for you.' Emilie scarcely controlled her anticipation.

'You do?' he asked, quietly. 'And what sweetness have you prepared for me?'

'You will like it,' she whispered.

'I am sure I will.' The sense of foreboding wasn't new to him.

'Your father may come to visit. At least he has been invited. I've sent a cousin of Mary's with a letter requesting him to journey here.'

'He will be unlikely to arrive. Carriage trips pain him.'

'Robert said not to do so. But I've told Robert we are to have guests and he must be on his best behaviour.'

'He agreed?'

She nodded. 'I had to promise that he could select the meals as he thinks I'm giving Cook too little supervision.'

'What did the letter say to Avondale?' he asked.

'That you are the best son a father could ask for, and that you have followed in his footsteps and he should be proud. And I invited him to please come soon as we have missed our family. He sent a note back with the messenger saying he will be here tomorrow.'

'Could we not have waited a few weeks, or months more?' he asked softly, then, before she could reply, he continued with another question. 'Who else did you invite?' Instantly his mind went to Nathaniel, her first choice.

'Don't concern yourself. I will be the best daughter by marriage that your father has ever seen. I will make certain *all* the servants are on their best behaviour. I will do you proud.'

'Wonderful,' he said. 'And who else did you invite?'

She stood proud. 'Mother.' Then she pursed her lips. 'I considered that carefully and had the messenger wait for the second message.'

He'd not acquainted himself with her parents and the thought concerned him. He should have written to them to reassure them that their daughter was well and being taken care of. When her mother arrived, he would beg her forgiveness.

Marcus would have preferred to have communicated that by post, but Emilie needed her family. He wasn't so certain about needing his own father.

He knew he had made few efforts to do the one thing his father wanted most—produce an heir. Perhaps that would not be discussed. And, perhaps the visit would go smoothly and perhaps Emilie would not talk with Robert under the stars.

Marcus contemplated the visit. His daily affairs would be secret unless his father talked to Robert, who would tell him that Marcus had not been travelling down the hall at night. Or, Emilie, who would say she didn't understand why people had to spread such lies about Marcus being a rake.

'Emilie. In the future, you must consult me before inviting my father.'

'But it's your family. And your father will take the tale of how wonderful we are doing back to London and it will ease everyone's mind.'

'Did you invite Nathaniel?'

'No. But I can.'

'Do you miss him?'

'Of course not.' She twirled her fingers. 'He has a gift for creativity and he doesn't even care. I like him well enough but he has squandered his gift.'

Emilie appeared so innocent.

He remembered the innocent eyes of his father as he stood faking astonishment at his wife's accusations that he was publicly humiliating her. How could she dare say he was infatuated with any woman? And the discussion had progressed downward over the years until Avondale had told his wife that love was for fools. His mother had agreed, and had told his father that applied double to anyone who cared for him.

The denials always sounded loudest when his father was the guiltiest.

Emilie inclined closer, the rosewater scent of her surrounding Marc. 'But I did invite your father and am planning a wonderful dinner. Robert has told me the man doesn't give you the respect due and I will convince him that you are an industrious son whom he should be proud of.'

She clasped her hands together. 'He should be proud of you, Marcus. You're an exemplary son. You are restoring a family home. And you will carry on the Westbrook traditions.'

'I won't carry on as he did.'

Emilie's stricken appearance alerted him that he'd used more force in his words than he'd meant.

He could not tell her. He could not tell her of the ever-so-polite hatred between his parents. Of the ways they had sniped and snipped at each other, and how they had insisted on sending the children to the nursery so they could speak privately, but his mother's shrill words condemning his father carried through the walls. Then Avondale would leave and not return for months, once past Christmas and on to the next.

His mother had incensed his father by inserting Robert in as a tutor when the first one had been sacked, but after Robert had saved her son, she refused to consider anyone else.

His father had lifted the flag of surrender, which had surprised Marcus.

He'd really not presumed his father to care that much.

He needed to tell Emilie about his parents, but she remained a stranger to him. He had no one to blame but himself. And her passion that must always come first.

Much like Avondale's mistresses did with him.

He was outside when his father's carriage rolled into the yard. He strode to meet him.

He watched the older man exit and glance at the roofs.

His father's jaw was set and he took his time contemplating the surroundings.

'A lot of work is still to be done,' Marcus admitted.

'Yes' he agreed, 'but I can see the work has begun on the old dung heap. Stormhaven is in better repair. Have all the windows been replaced as needed?'

'Yes.' Marcus examined the exterior, noticing the work that remained. 'The men removed a fox from the house before we got here. I have not told Robert as he would be unwilling to sleep here, nor have I told Emilie because she might have suggested we were amiss for not keeping the pet.'

'Sounds as if you have it all under control.' Avondale didn't move, still examining the house.

'I would hardly claim that.'

'Did you direct the note Emilie sent?' His father's voice was low. 'I was concerned as she stressed how much you missed me. I told you this country experiment would not work. It is not healthy.'

Marcus laughed. 'It has not proven fatal, yet.'

'You do have some mettle to you.' His father pulled his timepiece from his pocket and examined it. 'Got that from me.'

They walked to the entrance and the door opened instantly, with Robert standing aside. He wore proper livery and bowed to Marcus's father. 'Your hat, sir?'

Marcus saw his father back away and glance again at Robert. Robert didn't seem to notice. Marcus had no idea where Robert had obtained the clothing.

His father gave Robert the hat and they walked to the sitting room.

Emilie entered, wearing a stunning blue gown that swirled at her feet. Her hair was twisted up, waves of it flowing down into even more curls.

Marcus had never really cared for art and never would, but Emilie surpassed anything he'd ever seen on a stage, in a painting or in a museum.

His throat constricted.

Then she directed her attention to his father. When she greeted Avondale, but hardly spared a glimpse at him, a tiny part of Marcus collapsed inside himself, but he shoved any resentment away.

His father returned the welcome and kissed above her hand.

Emilie spoke, her voice cultured. 'I am so honoured that you could visit us. I have been so happy waiting on your arrival.'

His father nodded. 'I am pleased to be invited.'

She twirled as she moved to tuck her hand around Marcus's elbow. Her perfume had even changed. She no longer wore rosewater, but something that reminded him of an exotic location and dances with flowing silks.

He inhaled, trying to keep the scent of her inside him and the feel of her warmth preserved in his memory.

'This is the loveliest estate I have ever seen.' She glowed.

Marcus looked closer. She wore kohl and something else on her cheeks. Her lips were different. He could see they were deep red.

'I know this wonderful home needs improvement, but I love it so much. Did you grow up here?' she asked his father.

'No. Stormhaven belonged to my father-in-law. I have always lived in London.'

'Well. You can visit often and as long as you'd enjoy. You mustn't miss a visit to the farm.' She tipped herself closer to Marcus. 'We have a colt who will make a fine stallion.'

'I'm pleased to hear that.' His father brightened. He respected good horseflesh.

'And we might have a little one soon.' Emilie continued. 'I am hoping.'

'I am proud to hear that.' The older man beamed and clapped a hand on Marcus's back.

Marcus swallowed. It was improbable, to say the least.

'Yes,' she added, sparkling. 'Bluestocking is going to have a calf. Our first baby born on the farm.'

Marcus saw his father examine him from the corner of his vision.

'Yes, Father. A calf. A pleasant addition to our quiet country home.'

'I didn't know you were happy about that, Marc.' She patted his arm. 'I didn't even realise you'd guessed Bluestocking was going to have a calf. I was saving the surprise until tonight.'

Marcus closed his hand over hers, then lifted it to his lips, bringing her closer. 'A lovely surprise for my father.'

The older man searched their faces.

'Are you faring well, sir?' she asked, leaning towards her father-in-law. 'You seem at a loss for words.'

'I'm doing fine,' he added. 'I was taken aback by your invitation. I had determined the two of you would still, be, um, happiest alone.'

'No, no, no.' She waved an arm. 'We so love visitors. Marcus is skilled, working at the barns,' she said, then Marcus saw her pause and stumble to correct her words. 'He manages to get a lot done, without forgetting his status as your son. He is a credit to his noble birth. Very much your heir.'

At some point he would show the blackened thumbnail and the calluses on his hand to his father.

'I see.' His father's mouth sagged.

'Perhaps we can go for a walk after we eat, Father?' Marcus suggested.

'My back is sore from the carriage ride, mayhap later?' He strode forward. 'Just a catch in it, nothing serious.'

'Yes, that would be wonderful to tour where our gardens will be,' Emilie agreed. 'You must see our flock of chickens. We have three kinds and some are more sociable than others. Unfortunately, I didn't get them when they were chicks so we are not as close as I would like.'

Robert waited solemnly in the corner of the dining room, whisking out a chair if needed. Pouring wine instantly. Marcus bypassed the decanter and found the bottle, then observed the label, reassuring himself the drink had been taken from Cook's cabinet.

He noticed his father shaking his head gently. 'Marcus, you seem to have worked a miracle.'

'I can take no credit for the household, Father. It is in Emilie's hands.'

Robert stiffened more, if that were possible. 'And, of course, Robert is invaluable.'

The valet's chin rose, the edges of his lips firmed, and he exuded serenity.

'Emilie, is that how you see it?' his father asked.

'Marc is the mastermind behind the transformation,' she assured him. 'He brought me to this lovely place and lets me enjoy the forest, and I can explore all day with my easel at my side. I direct all improvements for the livestock pens. Can you imagine a more captivating endeavour than that?'

'No… I cannot conjure such a delight.' His father studied Emilie. 'Your happiness seems genuine. I thought you might be displeased with the constraints placed on you. Especially in this forsaken wreckage that is a blight.'

Marcus didn't move a muscle.

'This is a glorious property.' Emilie reassured him. 'The repairs needed are immense, but not insurmountable. It has been a dream come true to stay here with Marc. But, let us sit to discuss it. It will be a treat for me to have two such handsome men at my table. And it will be nice to spend more time with Marc as he works so…' she paused, precisely selecting each word '…industriously supervising the hands when he

is not…' she looked to Marcus for the right word
'…perusing ledgers or literary works.'

Marcus doubted the two books he had in his
room constituted literary works, but they were
fine reading.

'He directs the workers a substantial amount
in his studies of becoming a great leader.' She
shrugged, raising a palm out, then touching her
chest. 'Of course, that steals him away from me,
but I must trust his judgement.'

His father inspected Marcus as if he could not
be hearing correctly. Marcus shrugged.

'Shall we eat now?' Marcus asked.

'Not yet,' Emilie said. 'I am expecting another
member of my family.'

He sat and watched as she kept a serene countenance. Her back straight and adoration shining
from her. He drank his first glass almost before
his hand had touched the stem.

Robert was immediately at his side to refill.
Marcus saw the other glass, and waited. Without a doubt, the night would continue as staged
by Emilie.

At that instant, Marcus heard the wheels
of a vehicle. Emilie, Robert and Avondale all
stopped.

Robert withdrew to receive the guests.

Marcus waited. Robert didn't immediately

return. Hushed murmurs sounded from the entrance.

Footfalls clattered in the hallway.

Marcus's mother burst into the room, parasol at battle-ready status and her chin lowered. Robert crept in behind her.

His father choked. Marcus rubbed his hand down the one side of his jaw and repeated the movement. He braced himself, shut his mouth and waited.

'What a delight to find you here,' she spoke to her husband.

Avondale stood, swallowed and shoved back his chair.

Robert took the parasol, after a brief back and forth. She didn't want to release the weapon.

She moved to Avondale and offered both gloves for him to kiss. 'Dearest.'

'My angel,' he said. 'It has been such a brief spell since I've seen you. You have improved with age. The years on your face always delight me.'

'As you have,' she said as she sauntered forward. 'Those jowls are the best I have ever seen.'

His mother stopped. 'I could hardly believe it when Robert informed me of your presence.' She moved away, turning to Emilie.

'And my dear daughter, Emilie. When Robert

said you were inviting *Mother* he thought that meant yours.'

'When we met in the past, I had taken you into my heart,' Emilie said. 'And I wanted my first guests to be my second mother and father.'

Marcus saw his mother's intake of breath. It took up her entire torso. 'Dear Emilie. What a pleasant compliment. I am awash with joy to be included in this day.'

His mother would play her aggrieved role to the hilt on occasion, but she didn't want to upset her new daughter.

Lady Avondale drew her shoulders tight and shaped the perfected row of curls at her temples. 'And you, Marcus, did you initiate any events of this wondrous gathering?'

'No. It was a surprise to me.'

She walked to him, extended her hands and he kissed above her gloves.

'It is always delightful to see my son.'

'You also, Mother.'

'Sad to admit, but I have a thundering headache,' his mother said, pressing the back of her hand to her brow. 'So I will not be good company.'

'The usual conversation.' Marcus's father arose. 'I can hardly believe it, the pain in my back has increased as well.' He gave a slight bow to Emilie and then questioned Marcus.

'Could you ask a servant to bring something to my room? I would not want to inflict my suffering on anyone and I have urgent business and must return to London.'

'Robert. Please show my father to a room to have a lie down. And, enquire of Cook afterwards. She has a remedy from the apothecary which will relieve pain.'

His father touched his hand to his back and limped from the room.

After his father departed, Marcus looked at his mother. 'Emilie and I have not spoken much of you and Father, and your devotion to each other.'

She laughed soundly. 'I'm amazed you haven't because that would be the shortest conversation on record.'

'I've had other things on my mind,' Marcus admitted. 'A marriage, a move and roofs that leak.'

'I have no problem with letting my new daughter know that all is not glorious in our family. Speak freely.' She moved to the glasses on the sideboard. 'Your father and I always have. It clears the air, but makes the throat sore.'

'You were both at the breakfast.' Emilie clutched Marcus's arm.

'Yes. But we spoke with guests. People that mattered. Not each other. Heavens, no.'

'Oh.' Emilie's mouth drooped. 'And, I so wanted to do well.'

'You have, my sweet,' Lady Avondale reassured her, waving a finger in the direction her husband had taken. 'It is that man who has erred.'

'I fear I'm ill also. This is not what I had planned.' Emilie squeezed Marcus's arm. 'Do you mind if I retire for a moment?' Her words wavered.

Marcus took hold of her wrist and reassured her with a smile. 'I'm touched that you did this for us.'

Emotions stirred and relief won. 'Thank you.' She lifted her hem and swept out of the room.

'So, are you the lone one without a pain?' his mother asked.

'I would not say that. But I'm used to the thrill of having you and Father in the same room.'

'More wine, Marc?' She held the decanter.

He looked at her. 'Did I ever tell you about my puppy, Gus?' he asked.

She poured a liberal amount in his glass. 'I saw the wound. And instructed the maid to bandage it. Gus had it in for you. I don't know how Nathaniel did it, but I suspected he took your clothing and taught Gus to bite it.' She pressed her lips so close they disappeared for a moment. 'He confessed later that it had been an accident and he felt horrible for it. And you were upset. I suspected you to have given the pet away and I didn't want either of you to find out what the other had done. You were boys, and brothers, an almost lethal combination.'

'That—' He remembered his mother's presence. 'That scoundrel.'

He downed the liquid in his glass and held out his hand for the bottle. 'I never suspected a thing.'

'Marcus.' Her voice soothed. 'I fear I also have pressing business to attend to and I will not be able to stay long and am required at home. The housekeeper is ill and…um… I will direct the staff in her absence. I will leave as soon as I've spent a few moments refreshing my memories and I'll return soon for a longer stay—when it is less crowded.'

'Please, Mother, enjoy your meal. Forget about Father's presence.'

'I don't know why I can't get over detesting the man so much, Marcus. I can't seem to put the past behind me.' She scowled.

'You have both been to several events recently and you've deliberated together on what Nathaniel and I should do with ourselves.'

'I try to be in the same room with him. But when I see him, the past jabs at me and it irks me to say a pleasant word to him, and returning to this place of my youth has stirred my emotions more than I expected.'

'I hadn't thought of that.'

'Nor had I. Please let Emilie know I will be pleased to visit longer before long and I won't be underfoot as I will be returning to my memories and building new ones with her.'

'I will.'

'I suspect I should commence some reminiscences with you as well, my son. But I would rather return later when Avondale isn't present. I was thankful I didn't know in advance when you were to be married so I could not dread the sight of your father.' She crossed her arms, a glass in her grasp. 'I forgave and forgave and forgave. It gets tedious. And I'm still forgiving him.'

She sipped. 'That's why you have Nathaniel and your sister, and no other siblings. I love all my children, but I could see him so strongly in you and your brother. I had to get past that, too.'

'Have you forgiven us for being his sons?'

'I try. I know it isn't your fault.'

As a youngster, Marcus had noticed the affection she'd bestowed on his sister and the reserve she'd meted out to Nathaniel and him. But she'd put Robert near them and encouraged them all to care for each other.

Marcus's father had pulled his sons closer as

they grew and it had worked out well enough for Marcus and Nathaniel.

'That was hardest for me. To see the image of someone you dislike when you look at your children. It wasn't so obvious at first, but as you and Nate grew, it nearly killed me, but loving you both made it a little easier to see your father.'

'Do you hate him?'

'I pretend to.'

She wandered closer to Marcus. 'And you? How is your marriage?'

'Better than yours.'

She smiled. 'Don't be like your father.'

'I'm not.'

'I fear Nathaniel will be.'

Marcus turned away from his mother. 'Some women term him *grand*.' He worried that Emilie did.

'Well, if he doesn't straighten up, I can assure you any wife will not see him as grand.'

Marcus withheld comment, moved closer and kissed his mother's cheek. 'Thank you for visiting.'

Robert entered and moved closer to his sister.

'Of course, I wanted to visit. Much of my family is here now.' She turned to Robert.

'Make yourself at home.' Marcus indicated Robert. 'He'll take you on a tour and show you the progress.'

Robert moved forward. 'Shall we begin, Lady Avondale?'

She agreed. 'I'd love to walk the same trails I favoured as a child. This will be the first occasion to view them with my brother.'

They departed and Marcus grabbed the wine and returned it to Cook.

Then he headed for the stairs.

On the fifth tread, his boot stopped. In that second, he was no longer in the shadow of his father, mother, his grandparents or anyone else.

He claimed his footprints, his family and his wife.

The others he could not control, but himself, he would direct.

Chapter Eighteen

Marcus's mother departed without returning inside.

Later Marcus coaxed his father out of his room and they had tea together. His father rose to the occasion, becoming the generous Avondale who could not utter an unkind word and could make the crowd around him erupt in laughter.

The sight pleased Marcus and he stood behind Emilie, a hand on her chair, and when she laughed, she leant sideways and his thumb skimmed her shoulder, and he didn't move away.

Another consequence of marriage he'd not predicted. A feeling of solidarity when in the presence of others. He wanted their hearts to be lodestones for each other and he didn't know if Emilie, with her inexperience, her comparative youth, could be ready to settle into such a restrictive role.

He doubted he would have five years earlier.

In fact, he was sure of it. He'd not been ready to accept responsibility, until he viewed Emilie engrossed in something that escaped him.

His father had gouged at him about heirs for many years and his mother had only concerned herself recently. But nothing had changed in him until he saw Emilie.

He never expected any competition when he selected a wife. And perhaps it was for the best she'd not fluttered around him.

When his father pushed himself to his feet, Marcus stood. 'Emilie, let us show my father the efforts we've made outdoors at Stormhaven before he leaves.'

He extended a hand and, when his fingers closed over hers, the feeling of phenomena invaded him even stronger than the instant when he'd looked at the stars.

He and Emilie walked with his father to the barn. Pride invaded him at the sight of trimmed paths and the sound of hammers.

Stopping at the pens, he waited as Emilie tugged on a handful of grass and held it out to the cows.

She moved closer to her little herd, indicating them as she spoke. 'You have already heard of Bluestocking. The one there is Josephine. That one is Blackguard. The other is Madame Heart for the marking on her side.'

'You named the cows?' his father asked her.

'Of course. If the horses are to have names, then I could not leave the cows out.'

'I've not named anything except the horses I've had. In truth, I had little to do with naming my own children.' He contemplated the cows.

'That's sad,' Emilie said.

'Marcus's mother and I began to part ways even before his birth.'

She paused and looked at Marcus. Neither of them spoke.

'My father and I picked the best bride and I could not have married a better woman,' Avondale said. 'Never question my assertion that I married the best woman to be my wife.'

'Perhaps grandchildren will bring you closer,' Emilie said.

'Although that is a nice hope, I doubt it.' Avondale's eyes discounted the suggestion.

Marcus pulled up a handful of grass and also held it out to the cows, and they wandered to him.

Avondale checked his timepiece. 'The woman detests me. You cannot understand the depths of contempt you can experience until you are forced into residence with a person.'

Marcus inspected his father, noting the grey brows, the silver temples and the straight bearing. Every fibre of him the man who believed the world should grant him the excesses he wanted.

'You have a big house, though.' Emilie reached through the fence and petted Bluestocking.

'Except the family quarters,' Marcus said. 'They are rather limited in size when Mother and Father are together.'

'Yes. Those walls close in on me. Particularly when my wife is between me and the door.'

'Be truthful to Mother,' Marcus said. 'She knows about the women. Accept that. Talk to her as you do me. Your grandchildren will know both of you better. I will not let my child visit you at your mistress's or any place but the family residence.'

Emilie's hand stilled. She withdrew from the livestock and watched Marcus.

'That's cold. You should care more for your mother than to force us together,' Avondale said.

Marcus refrained from saying he'd inherited his coldness from him. If his father continued his womanising, Marcus would accept that. If his mother hadn't been able to stop the so-called romances, then no one could except his father.

Avondale checked his timepiece again. 'We are not companionable.'

'Don't look for reasons you can't be true to her, find ways you can,' Marcus said.

'I swear you have different ways of looking at situations.'

'He does,' Emilie said. 'I'm thankful.'

'I wish you the best, Emilie.' Avondale stopped, looking at her. 'I hate to think of you having a marriage to be endured. My wife had already had our three children by the time she was twenty-five and we had essentially parted ways.'

'That is sad. For both of you.'

They walked to the carriage. Avondale clasped Emilie's shoulders and bade her farewell.

'Let me speak with my father a few moments more, Emilie.' Marcus nodded to her. 'We've a few old grudges to bury.'

'Then I must be on my way,' his father said, but he didn't get into the carriage.

Marcus waited until Emilie left.

He held out his palm and showed his father the cuts, scrapes and bruises.

'What happened to you?' His father regarded him.

'Work.'

Avondale grimaced. 'Labour is for servants.'

'I want to take this crumbling estate that was once the home of two people I cared for and turn it into something I can look back on for the rest of my life and know that I took part in the restoration. It is my reason for experiencing physical labour. In some ways, it is my chance to keep myself busy while I chart my course with Emilie. I never questioned that I wanted a marriage of faithfulness, but now I question if there can be more for us.'

'Good luck.' He turned. 'You'll be a better man than I if you can accomplish that.'

'If you had it to do over, would you have lived as you have done?'

'Don't ask. You might not like the answer.'

'I'd presumed for a moment you might regret the pain you've caused Mother.'

'I couldn't give her the connection she wanted.'

'Why didn't you marry someone to whom you could be faithful?'

'I've not met such a woman.'

'Are you certain?'

His father grunted. 'When Lady Avondale walked into your home…' He inspected his ring. 'I saw Emilie trying to please you. I grieved. I grieved in that moment for what might have been in my own household.'

'I will remain a true husband to Emilie for myself, if for no other reason than I refuse to take the path you've trodden.'

'That's easy for you to say now. In two years… In five… When she is more fascinated by the children than she is by you?'

His father had shown him, day by day, his

inconstancies. Marcus hadn't been entranced by the lovelies who'd ensnared his father. He'd been sickened by the pain his mother endured. He'd seen her efforts to repair, and lastly, the bitter acceptance.

He didn't assume either truly loved the other, but in the past, his mother had wanted a marriage. His father had wanted no part of faithfulness, commitment, or more than a Saturday night and a Sunday with his family. They wore on him after that.

'When Mother said she loved you, did you put as much confidence in it as you did the other women who said the same to you?'

'She was my wife. Wives say that.'

'Well, she doesn't now.'

A groom waited to assist Avondale into the coach, but the Marquess shooed him away.

His father set his jaw.

'I have been considering moving back with your mother. I thought if I might slip in on the opposite side of the house from her, then perhaps we might discover a friendship. Your mother… she is a remarkable woman. I wonder what it would be like to be friends with her.'

He raised his head and put a swagger in his words. 'And I will tell her it is all your idea as you have forbidden me to see future grandchildren if I do not live near.' He snorted. 'And when she starts writing volumes of complaints, you'd best back me up on that.'

'I will.'

The dust from the wheels had settled before Marcus stirred. He realised he stood at the threshold of the rest of his days and his behaviour would not just influence him and Emilie, but would even pass on to his grandchildren. Another generation would behold the same surroundings he'd toddled in as a child and, even if he were no longer present, they would see the same lands he viewed and he would have handed down to them a home better than he'd found it.

Yet, he didn't know if, in some way, he'd chosen Emilie because he'd not perceived her capable of loving him. The same as his father hadn't been capable of continuing a connection to one woman.

In some inner recesses beyond conscious awareness, perhaps he had tried to duplicate the union his parents shared—or didn't share.

The spectre of Nathaniel materialised before him.

He'd married a woman who had put both someone, and something, before him.

He'd doomed his marriage before he had purchased the special licence. If Emilie had fallen at his feet, professed love and assured him she would always be his, he doubted he would have gone forward.

Someone else would have caught his eye and he would have married her. Some other woman who didn't cling to him.

He retraced his memories of his previous romances. The ending had never surprised him. Perhaps the timing had. Usually he'd been surprised by the quickness of the parting, even when he requested the split. He'd ended relationships because he'd remained unready to commit to the vows.

He'd done like his father. He'd decided to wed and he'd found someone suitable who'd remain at a distance. But after the vows, he'd had a burst of clarity, not colours. No rainbows appeared.

He'd known his promise not to tread his father's path was on shaky ground and he'd had to shore it up. He'd had to rebuild himself.

Emilie hadn't comprehended what she'd settled for, but neither of them had. They'd each been content to form a union on the outside and a solitary existence on the inside.

Marcus's acceptance of solitude had evaporated when Emilie hadn't answered one question. One question. The cleric had asked *Will you take this man to be your lawful wedded husband?*

Marcus's expectations had crashed amidst the silence.

He'd accepted that she'd changed her mind. Everyone in the room would have held her at fault.

But then he'd looked into her face and he'd seen something he'd never seen before and something he'd wanted more than he could have imagined.

Then she'd answered, and at that moment she had altered him for ever.

'Marc.' Emilie waited just inside the door. 'I don't want a marriage like the one your mother and father share.'

'No one would,' he answered, 'except perhaps Avondale did at the time. He just did as he felt was his due, then the marriage settled into dust around him.'

'Did he love someone more than your mother?'

'Well, yes, I suppose he did. Himself.' Marcus drew a fingertip down the side of her jaw and summoned the memories of Emilie telling him that she must always paint and the knowledge of her putting her fascination above him.

Although, in all fairness, he didn't know that he could blame her. When he had asked her to marry him, he had offered her nothing of his heart and nothing of himself but a house and a name. And while he considered those of value, particularly his name, he didn't know if a woman should give up what she cared for in order to get a name.

He put his hand at Emilie's back and guided her into the dining room. Robert stood, examining the wine bottle.

Marcus realised instantly it was not the same bottle that had been served to them earlier. He would always hope to have Mary and Cook on his side and they appeared more than ready to do his wishes.

'Robert, you will visit Nathaniel for a few days. You can take my carriage. Today. That will give you an opportunity to search out your lady friends.'

'Ah.' Robert poured wine into a glass without paying attention. 'Lady friends…' He took a sip and choked. He looked at the glass, the liquid and the bottle. 'That was uncalled for.'

'Pretty weak wine, wasn't it?'

'Almost lethal.' Robert thumped the goblet into place. 'Both Mary and Cook hate me. You have them mixing this swill, don't you?' He studied the goblet. 'But they're matching the colours well.'

'Robert,' Marcus said, fixing the older man with a stare, 'should my affections begin to wander elsewhere from Emilie, you have my permission to give her full details as long as they are correct.'

Emilie gasped, turning to face him.

'Because I would tell you first, Emilie,' he said. 'Lies destroy more of a person than any pain caused by truths. Trust is the foundation of a home more than anything else and it is more important to have walls that bring you closer than ones you want to escape from.'

'Are you going to be like your father?'

'No. Nor do I wish to be like your parents, Emilie. I want us to chart our own course.'

'My parents get along quite well. They are devoted. We would do well to have a union like my parents have.'

He led Emilie away from Robert, taking her to the sitting room.

'Just from an outside view, and from the way you comport yourself, Emilie, I wonder if your parents have a marriage in which his service to the clergy comes first in his life and the children come first in your mother's life.'

'There is nothing wrong with that.'

'No,' he said. 'There isn't. But that is their marriage and each of them has something to put before the other. They both get on well because they both step aside for the other's priority.'

'You look at that as if it is a flaw. It isn't. It is love. That you love another person and you step aside for their happiness.' Her lips thinned and she left the room.

He wondered if he expected too much, both from himself and from Emilie. It would only lead to more dissatisfaction if he set his wishes higher than either could achieve.

Mental flaws could be just as destructive as physical weaknesses. He could not have expected his grandmother to chase him from the room when her knees were too weak to move.

Marcus retraced his steps to find Robert and entered the dining room.

'Did you not suspect how your voices under the stars might carry?' he asked, walking to Robert. 'As you and Emilie discussed me in the night.'

Robert deliberated. 'No, I was enjoying the brandy, and you manage to work out most things anyway. That woman is amusing and she is quiet when she paints. I was being friendly as you asked for us not to fight.'

'Well, you may both fight with each other as I believe I prefer that to your companionship.'

'You do not have to be so testy. I do not fight with her much. Her nonsense is amusing.' Robert took the wine glass, testing a sip again, before scowling. 'I must warn you, Marc, should you ever criticise her daubs, she gets clumsy with the paper.'

'You should not provoke her.'

'And she is innocent?' Robert sputtered.

'When she is truly, truly incensed, a light chuckle will make her too angry to speak.'

'Well, you must keep me informed of any future conversations the two of you might have as I don't want to be in darkness. I should have had a proper valet.'

'Marc.' His bottom lip protruded. 'You surely don't mean…'

Marcus didn't want to see tears. 'Robert, you know you are dear in my heart, but you are an imperfect valet and you have used that position to eavesdrop on me.'

'Thank you for saying I am in your heart. But I…' he sniffed and his words wavered '…hate to have failed you in any way. I am a tutor first and foremost, former thespian of the stage, and fortunate to be able to valet someone of your stature. The advice I give is a bonus because of my deep loyalty and affection.'

'To me or my brandy.'

'You. Certainly.'

'How does my brandy taste now, Robert?' Marcus said, his voice low.

Robert slumped. 'Exceptionally weak.'

'Enjoy. I shall not be purchasing any more soon.'

'Well, I know I could be a smattering at fault with the lovely lady you ignore and send me traipsing after, but perhaps you should ask to see the flower portfolio.' Robert's countenance changed and he stifled a grin.

Marcus stared at him. 'Her watercolours?'

'She has three books she uses.'

The reference to the notebooks ripped at Marcus's throat. He'd seen the picture of Nathaniel in the book she placed importance on. And he'd seen the lines on the page after Nathaniel. Just circles to indicate where features would go. If not for the completed family ring in the corner, he wouldn't have even guessed the sketch was of him.

Marcus studied Robert again. 'What is in the portfolios?'

Robert wet his lips. 'She only shows her two portfolios. Her family book, with all the drawings of her relatives and her sisters, and the one of Nathaniel and an unfinished one of you.' He grimaced away the words. 'Her sketchbook is full of whatever whim takes her at the moment. But she has a portfolio that she has told me is full of blossoms. It is her *flower* book.' Robert drawled out the word *flower*. 'No one is permitted to approach her when she is drawing *flowers*.' Robert interrupted his own snort. 'I suggested I might fetch a wrap for her when she went to check on the chickens she's so besotted with. The sketchbook was lodged behind her washstand. So, I opened it since she took no great pains to hide it.'

'And, what did you see?'

Robert bent forward, stretching his neck to Marcus, giving a wry smirk. 'Lord Grayson, nothing I haven't seen every day for the last ten or so years.'

Marcus glared, silently commanding Robert to speak.

'A drawing or two of you. Perhaps a hundred.' He scratched his chin. 'Flowers—' He sputtered, then muttered in laughter, 'It has been difficult not to refer to you as Lord Flower, but I fear for my safety if she were to hear me and I didn't foresee you would find it humorous either.'

Robert tucked his chin in. 'Silence about this has been difficult. You have no idea. This has been the hardest thing to remain hushed about and I was a base-born child. That was easy, compared to keeping silent about *Lord Flower*.'

'You are truly sacked.' Marcus spoke through gritted teeth. 'Now. I mean it.'

Robert clutched at his heart and stumbled backwards. 'You would do this to your uncle? The man who saved your life? At the risk of his own?'

'I will reflect on rehiring you next week when my temper has cooled.'

'Thank you. Lord Grayson.' He stood tall,

again the actor and the sublime valet. 'As you know, the good fortune of watching you grow from childhood into a man has filled me with the most pride I've ever experienced. You are, to me, all things family. If the situation arose again, I would sacrifice myself for you, as I prove daily in my dedication in keeping your Lady Grayson safe.'

Marcus levelled a gaze at him. 'You are not on the stage now.'

'Pardon, sir.' Robert slumped. 'I believe a valet should know his master so he can serve well. It is my job. And you promised me I could have the position for eternity.'

'I will pay you, but I might send you to stay with Nathaniel for the duration. My time with my wife is my domain and you are not to meddle, matchmake or attempt any efforts concerning it.'

He held himself proud. 'I have not…overmuch.'

Marcus put his nose near Robert's. 'And this list you mentioned? A list of the qualities I desire in a woman. Where is it?'

Robert retreated, lowering his stature. 'You overheard a simple jest between friends and a thank you to her for drawing the hideous picture of me as a shepherd with blisters on my feet.' Robert grimaced. 'That was not a nice thing for her to do.' He kicked. 'That was terribly unkind of her and she refused to apologise until I said I wouldn't traipse with her the next day as I would complain to you of sickness and I *meant* it.' He stopped on his way out the door. 'I will be returning in a week and please remember that I am your loving uncle and dedicated valet.'

Robert slipped away and Marcus paced the room.

Emilie had sketched him. He remembered telling her not to draw him nude and how she'd gasped at him when he'd removed his shirt.

He grinned. That might not have been his finest moment, but few memories equalled that one.

Her secretive moments. He'd sensed them.

He would have to open the portfolio of flowers.

Marcus waited in the sitting room, relaxed on the sofa, watching as the sun faded from the sky, bringing the darkness into the room. He held a bottle from the batch Cook had mixed.

'Do you not need a light?' Emilie spoke from the threshold.

'I'm fine.'

'Where is Robert?' she asked.

'I sacked him, for the moment.'

She clutched her chest. 'You cannot. You cannot let him go. He saved you when you disobeyed his instructions. He is an upstanding valet. And he has a limerick for every occasion.'

Marcus deliberated on her words. Surely Robert had not shared those poems?

'You will let him return?' she asked. 'It would be cruel to send him packing after he has sacrificed so much to be at your service.'

Marcus wondered what other tales Robert had shared with Emilie that had no basis in fact. 'He is at my home in London.'

'Is he returning?'

'I have told him I will think about rehiring him.'

'He's not a bad person. He's flawed. And you have to look past that.'

'Sage advice. Applicable to any of us, I suppose.'

She shifted on her feet. 'What is wrong? I should have asked earlier, but I didn't. I thought the visit with your parents would help, but now you have sacked Robert.'

'Do you want to share a future with Michelangelo, or me?' He brought the spectre hiding inside him into the room and offered it a place at the table. 'Or anyone other than me?'

'That's a ghastly question. I pledged to you and I meant it.' She halved the distance between them.

'Yes. You did. And I forced it. In a time when

you were struggling, I used your weakness to gain access to you. That was wrong and I am paying for it.'

'Marcus, you wound me. You wound me terribly to say that you forced my vows. You did not. I agreed. I know my views on marriage and I'm adept at making decisions for myself.'

He stood and moved so that the exotic scent she wore earlier in the day invaded him again. But he didn't sway.

'You didn't answer the question.'

'Artists are passionate people.' She raised a hand to the sky. 'I did not know how much until I married you. The feelings are stronger now than ever.'

'Artists don't have the sole entitlement to sentiments.' Emotions simmered inside him. He locked his grip on the bottle, then relaxed his hand and put the container on to the table.

'I have not changed my opinion of you from the first time I saw you,' he continued, 'or the second or the third. You have always been like a little flower. Or perhaps, a field of flowering thistle. Vibrant. Dangerous. Alarmingly enchanting and the blooms are petal soft, but you cannot get too close to the stems or you will feel too much.'

He departed, stirred with the same drive that could cause a sculptor to chisel at stone, hour after hour, with no promise that when the sun rose he would not examine his creation and see it as nothing more than a chipped rock.

But Emilie would never be less to him because he saw her with his head, his heart, and every part of him.

Marcus strode to his bed, removed the unlocked box and opened it. He again read the letter he'd written and placed in his waistcoat pocket, and added it on top.

Emilie,
I cannot see the colours of the world. Some colours blend so they appear drab to me, yet I suspect there is more to them.

I married you in the hope I would see the hues through you, but it is not so simple. If you desire to have a marriage, then you must come to me not as an artist, but as a woman. I will not walk along behind your art. I will be first, or I will not be with you at all.

You may let me know your decision.
Life is not about art. It is about love.
Marcus

Chapter Nineteen

Marcus watched the sunrise and returned to the house, not slowing until he rapped at Emilie's door.

He didn't wait for her to call out, but entered as she opened her eyes.

She pushed herself into a sitting position.

'Emilie, the box under my bed is unlocked should you decide investigate. I don't want secrets between us. And you should understand, I have no list of the many things I want in a wife. Only one. In the box.'

Sleep evaporated from her features. She smoothed the hair from her eyes and touched one foot to the rug.

'I'm working with Jonas this morning. I'll be back soon in order to take you to the woodland.'

'You're willing to explore with me?'

'Yes.' *Yes.* 'If you will consider the list.'

Leaving, he closed the door and listened to the sound of her getting out of bed.

He could not ever see her tousled again. He could not and walk away. If she saw something in him, as he'd seen in just those moments, he could not blame her for her fascination.

He imagined her in the room, dressing, and pushed himself from the door.

After leaving Jonas, Marcus returned through the servants' entrance. He didn't want to see Emilie just yet.

He went to his room, took the cold water he'd requested the maid leave behind and bathed in it, surprised that the drops didn't evaporate on his skin.

He would find Emilie and discover what she'd decided.

Marcus lifted Emilie's easel, the satchel and searched her out, beckoning her to follow him.

They walked along the trail Marcus had once raced as a child.

Breezes blew through the trees which canopied above them. He heard the sound of the leaves and noticed how it made the light twinkle upon the ground.

When they arrived at the stream, he slid the

pack from his shoulder and she turned away, lost in her own adventure.

'Don't rest now, Marc. Down the stream is much better. There is even a boulder there.' She spoke as if imparting a treasure's location.

He took the load back. He couldn't help smiling at the excitement she exhibited. 'Lead the way.'

And she did. She went along the edge of the brook and seemed to be taking an inventory of nature.

As they walked, he noticed the water skaters skittering along on top of the water. And she revelled being beside the pool, finding glory in the day.

'See.' She pointed to a large rock. The boulder's top was flat and it jutted wide from an outcropping. She could have easily sat on it with her legs across the top of it and dangled her feet in the brook.

She stopped. She reached to pull a shoe off and he noticed she wore no stockings. 'I think I have a pebble in my shoe.'

She hopped on one foot. 'Could you help me? I may lose my balance as I try to put the slipper back on.' She held her foot out, toes wiggling.

'Brace against the tree.' He rested the easel on the dirt, but didn't move in her direction. 'And you will be able to slip it on easily.'

She pressed her lips together and did as he said.

He had never seen a woman linger so when rubbing her hand against her foot to brush the grass from it. She near scrubbed the skin from her toes and held them towards him. 'Did I miss any grass?'

He pressed his lips together, hiding a smile, then answered, 'Those are five extraordinarily lovely toes. The best-looking toes I have ever seen.'

She smiled. 'You like them?'

'Of course. They are a part of you.'

He sat the parcel on the grass, opening the pack and removing the corked, never-touched bottle, and got a cup and poured himself a small drink while he watched Emilie.

She grabbed her skirt, twisted it as one might a hank of hair and pulled it up and held it out of her way. Then she knelt down, tucking the twisted part behind her knees, and letting her legs hold it snugly as she bent to cup her hands and drink.

He watched her wipe her mouth and stand. If he had come up on her unawares and not known who she was, he would have perceived her an exotic peasant. She fitted into nature as easily as the leaves on the trees.

'That is a good place to sit and watch the pool. I put my easel in front of it. But I don't feel like painting today.'

The trees shaded the edges and water rippled over pebbles to continue down the stream. He could see many stones and in places he could tell how clear the water was because he couldn't judge the depth.

'How deep is the pool?'

She put her hand to her waist.

'And you discovered that how?' he asked.

'The easiest way. My dress is heavy when it is laden with water, but it cools me.' As if to prove it, she waded into the water.

He turned to the side so he could see her. She seemed engrossed in some magic only she could identify. Butterflies flitted about and birds sang in the trees. Sunlight dappled, altering the patterns on the ground.

On the other side of the stream, she picked something up from the ground. He could not tell if it was a twig or some insect or something else. But she examined it carefully and held it up to the sun before carefully placing it on to the ground.

He'd married a sprite. A faerie. He had married the girl who played among the oaks.

Then he went to the largest trunk and lowered himself against it. He spread the cloth from the satchel and put the cheese, bread, sweets and dried meats on to it, eating as she explored the day.

He took a piece of the meat and savoured the meal, watching her.

When he had quelled his hunger, he wrapped the remaining food and stored it away.

She was on the other side of the pool, lying in the grass and paying him no mind, and he thought she might be asleep. Her bare feet were planted and one knee was rocking back and forth and the skirt of her dress was wet where she had waded through the water. She could have crossed without the water touching her skirt, but he was sure she preferred her own way.

Fingers interlaced, he used them as a cushion to rest his head against the oak.

He was sure she slept, until she slapped at her cheek as if something had tickled her.

She sat, covered a yawn and stretched. His breath caught in his throat. The dress she wore could not have been uglier. He was surprised anyone of her age would even own a dress of that making. But, when she stretched, his eyes told him the dress was not there and he could see the woman beneath.

She pushed at her hair, moving a pin out and sticking it back in. It made no difference that he could tell. Her hair moved as it wished, but so did she.

She waded back to him, raising her skirts, and he didn't mind the sight. This time, she lifted them much higher than needed and he appreciated it.

She sloshed back through the water and reached her hands out to him. 'Take off your boots, Marcus. If you cannot see the colours, then you can feel them with me.'

He removed his boots and stockings and walked into the water. The pebbles under his feet were carpeted in moss which wisped over his toes; the stones were rounded from centuries of water rushing over them.

Then he led her back to the oak. 'I have explored your pool, now sit with me for a moment.'

He wondered if she might try to seduce him. Or appraise him for a sketch. Both affected him the same.

She took the wine bottle, poured some in the cup, and quenched her thirst. Then she refilled the cup, offering it to him.

He reached out to her and pulled her on to his lap.

Wisps of her hair brushed him and he tried to keep his mind on her feet. He tried to imagine them for the opposite reason she would have assumed. He had noticed that they were tipped with mud and he had not even realised that mud could stick to the feet of a woman. None he had ever known would have let mud near their feet.

But Emilie didn't mind at all.

She passed the cup to him. 'My hands are full, Em,' he said, teasing her.

She took his chin, put the cup to his mouth and tilted, watching him carefully.

The touch of her hand made his heart go soft.

He grunted from his throat to let her know to take the cup away before she choked him, but he knew some droplets had escaped his lips.

He swallowed.

'You could kiss away the wine,' he told her. He put a hand at her temple and released two hairpins, letting her hair tumble over her shoulders. He wove his fingers into it, enjoying the silken threads, combing the locks, letting them fall to her shoulders, and then repeated the movement.

'If there is anything you want to know—ask.' He lightly put his arms around her. 'Ask me the questions you'd like answered. You may not always like my response. But I vow to tell you the truth as I know it. To become one person, we cannot lie to each other. We must speak honestly, so beware of enquiring if you don't want to hear the truth.'

She snuggled against him. 'Why do you not lie with me?'

'I am sure I had a reason, but at this moment it escapes me.'

'Is it because…?' She hesitated. 'Is it because I am somehow different from other women?'

'You are different from other women. I know that well. But not in the way you surmise. Your body is perfect, at least as I remember it. It has been a duration since I have touched it and I have not even begun to learn it.'

'Then why?'

'We need a marriage before we share a bed. I want you enough for that.'

She touched his cheek and, when her fingers moved over his lips, she stilled and he kissed her hand.

Studying Marcus, she added, 'Art is a language I comprehend. And you should not dismiss a language because you can't fathom it. Painting gives me a chance to look at everything closer. To study it. To feel it. To see if I can recreate it.'

'But if you captured me on a canvas, it's but one layer. One side of me. The outside. You could have more, Emilie.'

She was the only person he'd ever wanted to share his thoughts and his dreams with. The only one he wanted near him every day.

'You cannot understand my nature and I savour life more if I recreate it. I look at the moments of animals behaving freely and sometimes like humans.'

'Because they leave their mates after a season? Is that how you see it?'

'No. I want to be a part of your heart, Marc, always. And I want the game of life. To play. You did the same in London with the nights at the club. But this isn't idle play. It is what we are meant to do. To live as fully as we can, along with the earth.'

'I recognise what it means to you. I didn't sense it would matter to me to come in second in your love. But it does. I will not be only someone who stands aside and provides a place for you to pursue something else. I rationalised that was enough, but I know now it isn't. I worked hard not to have a marriage like my parents and then orchestrated one. I love you and want you to love me.'

'I cannot stop painting. That would be senseless. It would mean nothing. And you cannot care if you would suggest I give up something I love.'

'I ask you to add more love to your life. I wanted to become a better man. A man of substance. And I feel that I am. But you don't want me to change. You want a plaster cast of a man whom you can pull out when you need him and put him away when you are done.'

'Isn't that what everyone wants in a mate?'

'Not me. I'm reminded of a black widow spider who might kill her spouse after they mate. It is all well and good for her—she has her pleasure, her family and a nice meal.'

'That is a horrific thing to imagine.'

'It is how I feel we are progressing. First, I wanted a marriage and didn't mind that you would be dancing along with your fancies in the clouds. I don't mind your creativity. But I want to be a person for you, Emilie. Not a husband who provides shelter and supplies. Not a model for your sculpture plans.'

She rose and turned to the water. 'What if there is no more to me than this? What if I am a person to dabble at paints and that is all I am?'

'One heart cannot beat alone in a marriage.'

She touched both hands, clasping them over her breasts. 'I can feel you in the wind and in the water. You aren't only the muse for my passion,' she said, 'but my inspiration.'

The wind ruffled her hair and she stood alone and proud. 'You are the man to be the other half of me and I'm the other half of you. Together we will each be more alive. Our hearts should be the halves of each other. Not two halves of a marriage. Two halves of one beating heart.'

He must hear the answer and he must believe he came first or he would never achieve the satisfaction of marriage. He must believe it and so must she. A lie would get them no further. He stood. 'Tell me. Do I come first?'

'Yes. You are first. In all ways. I love you. Beyond the depth I have felt for anything. You are inspiration come to life for me. You surpass creation by more than I could ever foresee. You are the ultimate masterpiece.'

No. She was the masterpiece.

'Em,' he said and found the hooks of her dress, but he stopped. 'Are you ready to study me again, or perhaps jostle me?'

She grasped his arms, pulling him closer.

He touched the hooks of her gown and they fell open in his hand.

This was not what he had in mind. He slipped his hand down her back and found the ties of her chemise beneath the dress, but he didn't untie them.

She gave a happy sigh and wriggled against him.

His tongue roved the skin at her ear, moving to her neck, and she shivered in his arms.

'Em. It pains me to say this. It does. But I would prefer our first—the first time we unite completely, to be in our chambers...' he kissed her ear and she shivered against him '...as husband and wife. As partners.'

The kiss sealed both their lips, until he pulled away.

'And we must leave, because I am through with waiting. Leave the bottle and start back. I'll catch up with you.'

'Now?' She reached behind herself to hold the hooks in place.

'Go. Put some distance between us.'

'I may want to stay here longer.'

'Em, do you consent to return to the house with torn clothing?'

She laughed. 'If it were dark, I might aspire to return with no clothing at all.'

'Get your shoes and go. And, when I get there, I would like you in my bed.'

She didn't move.

'Get your slippers.'

'But you like my feet.'

He lifted the bag and swung it in a circle. 'Go. Now.'

She carried her slippers and ran ahead.

Grabbing the bottle, he waited as she outpaced him.

Then he rushed to catch up with her. He was surprised at her speed with no slippers on her feet and her free hand holding up her skirt.

She dropped one slipper along the way and he sped up, and she stopped and he slowed. The other slipper passed by him and she turned to pull up her skirt with both hands, and took off again.

He took another sip of wine and started after her.

He let her stay in front and didn't catch her

until she arrived at the outside of the house, then he pulled her next to his heart.

She could scarcely stand upright and the race had helped tame his desires somewhat.

Her face had a sheen of moisture over it and he gave her a chaste kiss. At the doorway, he caught her arm, stopping her, and he lifted her, carrying her over the threshold, kicking the door shut and taking her up the stairs.

He placed her on her feet so he could open the door and she slipped inside his room.

He shut and locked the door and led her to the side of the bed. His shirt slid away with even more ease than he'd removed it on the night in London and the rest of their clothing followed just as easily, slowing only for kisses that couldn't be denied.

He tossed back the covers and lowered her on to them, following, holding her close to savour all that was Emilie.

He spoke, lips against her skin. 'You maintained that our marriage would allow us to go our separate ways. For you to paint and me to forget about you.'

She moved aside, but remained so close he could only view the outline of her face, and their caresses didn't stop. 'I said nothing about another woman seeing this, or touching you. Ever.

We are married and any ideas I might have had before that vanished when we said the vows.'

'Do you really feel that, Emilie?' Marcus whispered against her neck and her agreement faded away underneath his lips.

He rose on his elbows to study her. 'I made myself a promise. Not anyone else. But myself. That I would be faithful in my marriage, whether anyone else noticed or not.'

'I will notice. And it will mean more than the stars and the earth to me.'

He pressed a gentle kiss of promise against her lips and the kiss deepened into something more.

He backed away, as intent on her whole body as she'd been on his shoulders.

When he felt her skin the length of him, he took his fingertip and began at the hollow of her neck, exploring from the curve of her chin to the hollow below, aware of the skin so much more delicate than his own. Then he traced down, between breasts that peaked for his touch, and continued to the softness of her belly. She interrupted him, pulling him closer, hugging him tight, and he let himself move into her clasp.

But he understood what she waited for and he kissed her as he found the tip of her pleasure, moist from her desire, and he began to work his finger over the tip.

She reached out, fingers gripping him closer.

He pulled her as closely as he could, held her, buried his face in her hair and listened as she gasped and thrust her hips up into his hand. She called out his name and then he let her rest, but not long enough to let her regain her senses completely.

He pushed the sheet away, not wanting any part of her hidden. Resting his lips at her breasts, her heartbeats pounded into him as he scented her skin against his tongue.

He moved over her and held one of her legs as he positioned himself above her. Gazing into eyes flecked with light.

He lowered himself into her.

She was his wife and the love that completed him.

He'd fallen in love with her when he didn't know what love was, and he had *waited*, and *waited* and *waited*.

He released inside her, sealing the memory he would cherish the rest of his life. For a moment the world faded into nothingness and only the two of them remained, embracing, and deep in each other's heart.

Chapter Twenty

'Might we do that again?' she asked.

'Of course,' he said, curling her in an embrace.

He held her on his shoulder and interlaced his fingers in her hair. He kissed her forehead.

'When did you fall in love with me?' he asked.

The Emilie that appraised him was not the girl from the trees, but a woman.

'I didn't love you when I married you,' she said. 'But when you brought me here and gave me the forest, and gave me all that I could ever want, and watched and didn't try to take it from me, but tried to give me more, then I knew that if I loved, it could only be you. And, even then I do not know if I loved you for sure, but I drew you and could barely sleep because I couldn't stop examining the likeness of you... Each night before I fall asleep and each morning, the first and last things I must do is to study the drawing of you. I don't know if I can let you be.'

'I am fine with that, Emilie. I plan to be a man you can't leave alone. But I may have the same problem with you. Show me the sketchbook of drawings.'

'My watercolours?' she asked, hazy, as his arms captured her.

'No,' he whispered, moving closer. 'The portfolio. The other one. The last one you purchased in London.'

'It's for me only.' She tensed. 'No one else. No one.' She curled against him. 'Lying here with you is so peaceful.'

'Go and get me the sketchbook, Em,' he whispered.

She ignored him and he moved and began to gently push her out of bed. 'Book,' he insisted.

Groaning, she pulled herself up, found her chemise, donned it and explained, 'You mustn't be angry. Or sensitive… To natural beauty.'

Then she slipped away.

Marcus accepted that Emilie might bring the wrong portfolio. He pushed himself out of bed with a sigh and followed her, pulling a sheet snug to cover himself. He knew the kitchen woman or the maid would not come upstairs if they had heard him arrive, but he didn't want to be surprised.

She retrieved the portfolio from behind her washstand and he found he had lost interest in it temporarily, and pulled it from her hands to toss it to the floor. He enveloped the sheet around the two of them and eased her, with a slight stumble, back on to the bed.

When she lay beside him, he rolled to the edge of the bed and, while on his stomach, reached to the floor and pulled the sketchbook closer. The pages were sturdy and he had to pull the thing almost against the bed before he could get the cover open.

The first drawing, his face half in shadow, half out. The mischievous face of a rake.

He hesitated. The person he didn't want to be.

Several more sketches followed. Some more like musings on the same page.

Then, one gripped him.

He was perched aloft on the rooftop. Viewing the drawing, if she had captured him accurately, he didn't comprehend how he kept from falling.

'Is this a true representation?'

'My heart was in my throat. I had to turn away. I couldn't bear to watch you so close to the precipice.'

'I remember nothing like that.'

'I gave Mary direction to tell Jonas privately that he was to take greater care because he would receive no payment if you were damaged in any way.'

Marcus remembered the sly laughter of Jonas one day when he'd asked Marcus to leave the edge work to him as he'd not want Lady Grayson to be a widow.

He flipped the page over and felt as she turned to raise above him enough to press her body against his back. He felt her chin between his shoulder blades and her arm at his side.

Another image captured his chest, contoured with muscle.

The next drawing, himself at a distance, jesting with one of the crew members.

One of him shoving a timber into place, finishing the job. The dirt on his trousers had been sketched and the tension in his back.

Then, he opened to the next page and his face stared back at him, life-sized. A man's likeness—not a youth's or a reckless spirit. But a representation of determination and strength. He touched the page, aware of the intensity in the portrait.

This was no rake, but a man he'd hesitate to anger.

The next drawing didn't take the whole of the page, but portrayed him laughing. He'd never seen himself that way.

He leafed forward. His head darted back and he examined the page in front of him. Naked.

One of her fingers trailed along his side. 'I said I wouldn't paint you naked. I didn't say anything about not sketching you. For myself. To calm me. To help me relax at night.'

The next drawing captured him asleep, his torso draped by a sheet. Another one. Without the sheet.

He continued through the book and each page was of him, none alike. One more sketch of his hand holding a glove.

She'd made a drawing of the back of his head, lifted to the sky, his hair curling at his collar. With each flip of paper, he saw a part of himself captured.

These were no drawings of a boy. This was a person who understood the road he travelled. He viewed the countenance of a man following the journey he had planned. A man he would be proud to know and a man who would lead his children into adulthood.

Emilie might some day paint the portraits of their children, but she would not place her own existence on the other side of the room. She would be in the middle, next to him, and surrounded by family.

He closed the book and could not move without dislodging the woman using him as a bed.

'You draw well. Even the naked ones. You've a good memory.'

'I need another portfolio. That one is almost full. You are my muse, Marc.'

'Move, then,' he said, wriggling so that she would, 'and I will try to give you more inspiration.'

When he had her back safely in his arms, he hugged her tight. 'And you are my muse and Stormhaven is my artwork. You inspired me to return to a place of happy childhood memories and live in a way that I had not fully imagined and did not believe possible.'

Chapter Twenty-One

Emilie rushed to greet the carriage bringing Robert. Marcus waited, keeping her in his vision to see what she was about. This enthusiasm for Robert's return shook him.

As Robert carried his portmanteau from the carriage, Emilie's smile turned to a frown.

Robert returned her gaze. 'Lady Grayson,' he said, with a tilt of his head.

'Robert,' she greeted him formally. 'I have a drawing of a gentle flock of brandy bottles to show you later.'

'Spare me the agony.' Robert put a hand to his head. 'I'm sure some day I'll die from a grievous pencil wound, possibly self-inflicted.'

Emilie moved to the other side of the carriage, dismissing Robert. The carriage drivers unloaded the supplies.

Marcus clasped his hand on Robert's shoulder, stopping him.

'And, how was your trip?'

'Wonderful. Not a single walk into the wilderness. I would not have returned except this is where I am needed most.' His lips firmed. 'Even though you try to poison me with tea.'

'I still laugh when I imagine you choking after that first sip from my wine bottle.'

'I nearly expired and have learned my lesson of pouring liquids first into a glass for my own safety. If not for the wine you provided that night to take the taste out of my mouth, I might have died instantly. And then, even that became contaminated.' His lips pinched.

'You should delve into your occupation more than you delve into drink,' Marcus said and he scowled at Robert. 'And do not be telling any limericks to Emilie.'

'Only the ones suitable for youngsters have I shared.' Robert's cheeks brightened. 'Some things are sacred.'

'You'd best not forget that.'

'I won't. Now, I'm ready to get back to my duties,' he admitted. 'I just don't know if I return as your long-suffering uncle who is a guest, or your dedicated valet.' He sniffed in Marcus's direction. 'Your clothes are rumpled.'

'You are no longer needed as a valet. Emilie has taken to awakening me in the morning. I'm promoting you to butler.'

'Save us all.' He stumbled backwards. 'My obligations have multiplied, but I will continue as your butler, your valet and your uncle. And, of course, Lady Grayson forces me into a maid's job.' He rolled his eyes. 'I shall expect an increase in wages for the three jobs and you receive the uncle advice gratis.'

'We'll see.'

Robert groaned and coughed. 'I should have an increase, given all the heart pitter-pats I will likely have to listen to bouncing from the walls. I can't bear to be near either of you when you are together. I will study to be elsewhere.'

'You will keep Emilie safe when she is painting. The men have missed my help. And her landscapes are good. She plans to place some in a shop in London when she finishes a few more.'

'You have walked in the woods with her?'

'The task is not as onerous as you make it out to be.'

Robert sniffed. 'True. The trees are shady. The water is cool. The food is pleasant. The company is annoying, but diverting.' He peered around to make sure no one listened. 'Do not tell her, but I have brought back some watercolours for me.'

Marcus laughed.

'And have you seen the flower book?'

'Certainly. Exceptionally good work there.'

'Even the ones of you naked as the day you were born?' Robert said, eyebrows raised.

'Yes,' Marcus answered smugly. 'She has made a new drawing.' Marcus savoured the words. He exhaled slowly. 'The new sketch is more accurate. Suitably so.'

'I will be sure to never get near that book again,' Robert snarled, as he stalked away.

'Robert,' Marcus insisted, calling after the other man. 'Do not let anything happen to that book. It is one I'll covet in my old age.'

Marcus could not keep the laughter from his lips. And he whistled a tune so that Robert might hear.

Marcus kept whistling as he turned to the barn where Emilie had disappeared.

She had lost some of her interest in water-colours and some of her interest in the forest. She had gained a new way to occupy herself and he didn't mind. She claimed love made painting better and she had not known how she had managed without it.

He could tell that she had been holding something back from him. He had realised he could nearly read her mind. No artifice concealed Emilie.

He recognised she had a plan now and she would tell him. He could have discovered it already, if he had chosen, in their bedchamber, but he hadn't wanted to talk.

He saw her directing the men with one crate. She had her hand inside the box, clucking. More chickens, he supposed. That always pleased her.

A few moments later, the men returned to their tasks and she came running out, holding her skirts with both hands and beaming with happiness.

'I have a surprise for you, Marc.'

All things considered, he would have to learn to be comfortable when he heard those words from her. He stared carefully at her.

She led him to a pen that had been empty.

A small brown puppy bounded inside it and she opened the pen and took the feisty mongrel in her arms and handed it to him.

'This is to replace the one who ran away and upset you.' She held out the dog to him, ignoring the squirming paws and wet nose.

He smiled at her and took the tan little beast. 'Gus was my dog, but he became fonder of Nathaniel. He used to snap at me and follow Nate. I was near twelve and didn't like that.'

He held the dog carefully tucked under one arm and bent to touch the back of his own leg. 'The scar was a present from Gus.'

He straightened and tried to give the dog a genial pat. If it made her happy, he would try to show some friendship for the animal. 'After he bit me for knocking Nathaniel about, I gave Gus to a little boy where Nathaniel would not discover him and my brother decided he'd run away.' He shrugged. 'I've not mentioned that to anyone, although Mother guessed what had happened.'

Emilie snatched the dog back from him with a growl of her own. 'He is mine, then. And he will be very loving.'

'I felt badly afterwards, but it was too late.' He shrugged and gave her a grin. 'And the boy seemed pleased to have a pet. He had no brothers. And I could not buy him back. The lad did not know a pound from a teacake, yet no amount would induce him to return Gus, and he would not trade him for another dog. I wanted...that caring. I'd never seen such devotion before.'

'You are a blackguard.' She hugged the puppy close as if Marcus would steal him.

'I was a lad. His teeth were like knives. He growled each time he saw me. One day he lunged for me, caught my trousers and I'd had enough.'

'You can never touch this darling puppy. You are not to get near him.'

'I will not. I do not mind if I don't have dog hair on my clothes and no teeth marks on my boots. Gus destroyed every boot I had.'

'You will not be treated to that affection.' She cooed at the dog. 'I will guard him closely.'

'I have every confidence in you.' He watched her nuzzle the dog and calm him in her arms.

He clasped her and the puppy both. 'Put the puppy back in the pen and come upstairs as it is getting dark.'

'I cannot leave the little one alone long.'

'Then we will come back later to check on him. But I love you madly and must hold you in my arms.'

'I love you even more.' She put the pup in his cage and took her husband's hand. 'And I can't leave you alone one moment more than is necessary.'

She bit her lip. 'Are you sure there is no other list of qualities you yearn for in a woman?'

He laughed, interlacing his fingers with hers, and caught her in his arms. He kissed her forehead. 'As I've already said, there never was any such document, but if you wish to see one, look in the mirror.'

With Emilie, he had received the desires of his heart that his mind had not known.

He had been organised on a certain night, as the artist Beatrice had pointed out. He'd searched out the archbishop's office in Doctors' Commons for a special licence after he'd left Hatchards, arranged for Lady Semple and her friends to be at his house and instructed Robert to either take Emilie home, or, if she stayed, to bring Semple to discover the two together. He'd pulled some logic from his depths that forced him into a pursuit of a girl he'd never forgotten and a woman he didn't want to lose. And he had found a life-long partner.

Then he stopped, remembering again the moment that had fallen from his memory, until the sight of her at the soirée had reminded him.

When they were youths, she'd ambushed him from behind and thrust the end of a stick into the back of his coat. She'd shouted, running from the trees, 'Halt. Who goes there?'

He'd turned, seeing a waif squinting at him. 'I want your lemonade,' she'd told him and pointed the stick at his glass. 'Your blood is yellow, like a lemon, and I'm a duelling highwayman and I've a thirst for the lemonade of my victims.'

'Here.' He'd given her the drink with his blessing. After all, he'd almost drunk it to the end.

She'd raised the glass to him, and downed it in a gulp, then thrust the glass aside.

Then, she'd stopped and smiled, coaxing him with her eyes. 'Do you want to play highwayman? We could duel at dawn, or steal.'

'No. I don't steal.'

'I did,' she whispered. 'Just this once, I took

a lemon.' She pointed her stick. 'See, it's in the grass. And so bright against the green.'

He'd stared. He would have missed it had she not pointed it out. 'It's not bright.'

She huffed. 'It is.' She threw down her stick and picked up the lemon and a handful of grass. She held them to him. 'See. Yellow. Green.' She waved them about, the scent of the lemon and the grass wafting under his nose.

Then she tucked the lemon close to her body. 'You can't have it. It's so pretty, like the sun in a painting without the reddish tints.'

That was the moment he realised he didn't see the same as other people did.

'I must warn you, if you journey this trail again, I will steal from you.' She held the fruit behind her back and picked up the stick with the other. She scrunched her shoulders, and pranced as a fencer would.

'And what would you steal? I've no more lemonade. No purse. Nothing of value.'

'A kiss?'

'I'm too tall for you to steal a kiss from me,' he said. 'You'd have to steal my heart.'

'I'm not a princess. I'm a highwayman.' She deliberated. 'But I could draw your heart if I knew what it looked like.'

He remembered the child, but saw the woman. He took her cheeks in his hands. 'You once told me you would draw my heart and you have. I saw it in your portfolio. The feelings I have for you.'

'I said no such thing.'

'Remember the duelling highwayman?' he asked. 'The one at Beatrice's wedding.'

She put her hands over his. 'Oh…' Realisation dawned. 'I took your lemonade.'

'And my heart. Shall we celebrate with a glass of lemonade?'

'Always.' She laughed. 'But simply a little. I don't really prefer it.'

'You don't?'

'No. I wanted to show how tough I was. And I love the shade of yellow.'

'When you held the lemon to me, it was the moment I could understand the colours that escaped me. I could smell the grass and the lemon, and my mind told me what I was missing. And your eyes.'

'And now you can have all the kisses from me that you wish. It can never be enough for me.'

He brushed his lips across hers and held her close.

As he glanced around the estate, he still could not see some colours, but he could feel every shade and every hue, and the world had never looked so bright and beautiful.

* * * * *

COMING SOON!

We really hope you enjoyed reading this book. If you're looking for more romance, be sure to head to the shops when new books are available on

Thursday 31st October

To see which titles are coming soon, please visit

millsandboon.co.uk/nextmonth

MILLS & BOON

Coming next month

MISS LOTTIE'S CHRISTMAS PROTECTOR
Sophia James

'Are you married, sir?'

'I am not.' Jasper tried to keep the relief from his words.

'But would you want to be? Married, I mean? One day?'

She was observing him as if she were a scientist and he was an undiscovered species. One which might be the answer to an age-old question. One from whom she could obtain useful information about the state of Holy Matrimony.

'It would depend on the woman.' He couldn't remember in his life a more unusual conversation. Was she in the market for a groom or was it for someone else she asked?

'But you are not averse to the idea of it?' She blurted this out. 'If she was the right one?'

Lord, was she proposing to him? Was this some wild joke that would be exposed in the next moment or two? Had the Fairclough family fallen down on their luck and she saw his fortune as some sort of a solution? Thoughts spun quickly, one on top of another and suddenly he'd had enough. 'Where the hell is your brother, Miss Fairclough?'

She looked at him blankly. 'Pardon?'

'Silas. Why is he not here with you and seeing to your needs?'

'You know my brother?'

Her eyes were not quite focused on him, he thought then, and wondered momentarily if she could be using some drug to alter perception. But surely not. The Faircloughs were known near and far for their godly works and charitable ways. It was his own appalling past that was colouring such thoughts.

'I do know him. I employed him once in my engineering firm.'

'Oh, my goodness.' She fumbled then for the bag on the floor in front of her, a decent-sized reticule full of belongings. Finally, she extracted some spectacles. He saw they'd been broken, one arm tied on firmly with a piece of string. When she had them in place her eyes widened in shock.

'It is you.'

'I am afraid so.'

'Hell.'

That sounded neither godly nor saintly and everything he believed of Miss Charlotte Fairclough was again turned upside down.

Continue reading
MISS LOTTIE'S CHRISTMAS PROTECTOR
Sophia James

Available next month
www.millsandboon.co.uk

LET'S TALK
Romance

For exclusive extracts, competitions
and special offers, find us online:

f facebook.com/millsandboon

🐦 @MillsandBoon

📷 @MillsandBoonUK

Get in touch on 01413 063232

MILLS & BOON

THE HEART OF ROMANCE

A ROMANCE FOR EVERY KIND OF READER

MODERN

Prepare to be swept off your feet by sophisticated, sexy and seductive heroes, in some of the world's most glamourous and romantic locations, where power and passion collide.
8 stories per month.

HISTORICAL

Escape with historical heroes from time gone by. Whether you passion is for wicked Regency Rakes, muscled Vikings or rugg Highlanders, awaken the romance of the past.
6 stories per month.

MEDICAL

Set your pulse racing with dedicated, delectable doctors in the high-pressure world of medicine, where emotions run high a passion, comfort and love are the best medicine.
6 stories per month.

True Love

Celebrate true love with tender stories of heartfelt romance, f the rush of falling in love to the joy a new baby can bring, and focus on the emotional heart of a relationship.
8 stories per month.

Desire

Indulge in secrets and scandal, intense drama and plenty of s hot action with powerful and passionate heroes who have it al wealth, status, good looks…everything but the right woman.
6 stories per month.

HEROES

Experience all the excitement of a gripping thriller, with an ir romance at its heart. Resourceful, true-to-life women and stro fearless men face danger and desire - a killer combination!
8 stories per month.

DARE

Sensual love stories featuring smart, sassy heroines you'd want best friend, and compelling intense heroes who are worthy of
4 stories per month.

To see which titles are coming soon, please visit

millsandboon.co.uk/nextmonth